DARIT

DARIT

PETER GREGORY

Matador
9 Priory Business Park,
Wistow Road, Kibworth Beauchamp,
Leicestershire. LE8 0RX
Tel: 0116 279 2299
Email: books@troubador.co.uk
Web: www.troubador.co.uk/matador
Twitter: @matadorbooks

ISBN 978 1800460 478

British Library Cataloguing in Publication Data.
A catalogue record for this book is available from the British Library.

Printed and bound in Great Britain by 4edge Limited
Typeset in 10.5pt Adobe Garamond Pro by Troubador Publishing Ltd, Leicester, UK

Matador is an imprint of Troubador Publishing Ltd

For my grandson Joshua, my wife Vera,
and my two sons Andrew and Michael

CONTENTS

PART 1
BRITAIN

PART 2
CHINA

PART 3
ARMAGEDDON

PART 4
A NEW BEGINNING

Part 1

. . .

BRITAIN

1

KICK OFF

The fog was alive. There was no other word for it. The fog was definitely... alive.

That's what it felt like to Carly. In the 28 years of her life Carly Jones had witnessed fogs, or smogs, or whatever the correct term was, many times, but not one like this. The cold amorphous grey mist caressed her face like a clammy hand, a hand searching for something within, something invisible. She could feel it on her legs too, the cold icy feel of a bony hand creeping from her ankles to her thighs. She raised her hand to her face, half expecting it to be seized by something wet and foggy, but all she encountered was... droplets of water. Cold droplets that she wiped away.

She did the same with her legs, brushing the cold droplets away and then rubbing them vigorously to restore some semblance of warmth. But she was careful. She didn't want to ladder the new pair of black fishnet stockings, the high quality stockings she'd purchased that very morning. The stockings that were an essential part of her attire.

Carly Jones had been a street walker, a lady of the night, a prostitute, since the age of fourteen. And she had done well. Very well. As an attractive, sexy, young girl, she was in great demand

and men, wealthy men, paid big money for her services. But Father Time had taken its toll. As she grew older, her looks, and her allure, faded. And so did her clientele. Nowadays, she was forced to look for clients in the less salubrious, seedier, red light pockets of London. Pockets of narrow back streets and alleyways that were a million miles away from the wealthy punters. And tonight, a cold, October, Halloween night, she hadn't had a single client. Not one.

'Damn this bloody fog,' she thought. 'It's so thick the punters can't even see me. And it's so cold.' She shivered.

Just as she was beginning to despair, Carly heard a sound. A faint sound. A sound muffled by the dense fog. It was coming closer. It sounded like footsteps. A man's footsteps. Suddenly, right there in front of her, a silhouette appeared. A shadowy silhouette. The silhouette of a man in what looked like a black cape. A man in a black cape wearing a top hat and carrying a black leather bag. A bag that looked remarkably like a doctor's bag. 'This is my lucky night,' she thought, stepping forward to greet the stranger.

2

THE CΛVE

'Oh, Ben,' said Susan, 'we shouldn't be doing this.'

'Why not,' replied Ben, removing his hand from inside her bra, 'it's what we both want.'

'Well, because you're my boss and it… well, doesn't seem right. Not here. Not at work.'

'Don't worry, it's fine,' he said, undoing the buttons on her white blouse. 'It's fine.'

Practised hands quickly exposed Susan's shapely breasts, breasts that he caressed, first with his hands and then with his tongue and lips, focusing on her nipples. She groaned in delight as his expert touch sent shivers through her trembling body. Encouraged, he slid his hand inside her panties, his fingers quickly finding their way to that most intimate part of a woman's anatomy. Susan shuddered. She could feel her desire mounting and responded by caressing the bulge in his trousers.

'Take me now,' she said, letting her skirt and panties fall to the floor. 'Take me now, Ben.'

'Oh Ben,' she gasped, her voice hoarse and breathless. 'It feels so good.'

'It feels good for me too, Susan,' he said with a hint of breathlessness from his exertions. 'It feels good for me too.'

Then, just as he was on the point of climaxing, the room was plunged into darkness. Total darkness. And the alarm went off.

'Shit,' growled Ben. 'Shit, shit, shit.'

'Don't stop now, Ben. I'm so near to coming...'

But Ben had already withdrawn from her and, as the emergency lighting kicked in, began putting on his trousers. Bathed in the blue glow of the emergency lights, their naked bodies shimmered with a blue radiance as the beads of sweat fluoresced from the ultraviolet component of the light. They looked surreal, like two hazy, fluorescent ghosts.

Ben wondered what the hell had happened. There had never been a power failure before. Not here, deep under the mountains of Snowdonia. 'For Christ's sake,' he thought, 'we've got one of the biggest hydroelectric power stations in the country right here on our doorstep. That's one of the reasons the facility was built here.'

Dressed, he grabbed a torch, checked it was working and made his way towards the door. 'Susan, you stay here and keep an eye on the instruments. Call me if the pods start to warm up.'

'Okay Ben,' she replied, putting on her panties and skirt. Although she was a sensible, level-headed young woman, Susan didn't like being left on her own in this vast underground tomb. Alone with the scores of upright, cigar shaped metal pods spread over the vast area outside the small Control Room of the top secret Cryonics Facility buried deep in the bowels of Snowdonia.

Cautiously, Ben stepped out of the warmth and safety of the Control Room into the cold, cavernous space that housed almost a hundred cryogenic pods. It was a foreboding place even when illuminated but now, with just tiny blue spots of emergency lights marking the aisles, it was distinctly eerie. Spooky. What made it even more spooky was the contents of the pods. Dead bodies.

One per pod. One dead human body frozen in liquid nitrogen at a temperature of minus 196 degrees Celsius.

This wasn't one of the private cryogenic facilities like Alcor in Arizona or the Cryonics Institute in Michigan where the wealthy and, in Ben's view, very stupid and very vain, people paid a fortune to have their bodies frozen in the hope of resurrection at some future date. A date when medical science had advanced to the stage that their fatal illness could be cured and they would be brought back to life. Resurrected from the tomb like a modern day Jesus. No, the bodies here weren't for resurrection. They were for medical and military research. Top secret research by the government and the military. As chief custodian of the pods, he wasn't privy to the type of research being done. His job was to ensure the pods remained at the optimum temperature to keep the bodies in pristine condition. Bodies of criminals and donors who'd bequeathed them for medical research. And, to complete the collection, the odd one or two bodies of 'missing persons'. Bodies stored for present, and future, research in the spacious laboratories at the other side of the vast cave. Laboratories which housed that most precious of human organs. The brain. And, more importantly, laboratories which housed tissues from some of the most famous, and infamous, people who'd ever lived.

As he hurried along the aisle towards his main destination, the laboratories, Ben scanned each of the pods with his torch. He also reflected on what he'd learned about life at very low temperatures.

Ben Davies graduated from Bangor University with a degree in biology, but had found work hard to come by. Jobs in North Wales were scarce, especially for a biologist, and he'd had to accept all kinds of jobs just to be employed. None really utilised his knowledge of biology. Then, in 1999, he'd heard rumours that a new facility was under construction, a facility in a cave in Snowdonia. A facility which might require the services of a biologist. Because of the secrecy of the project, he'd had great difficulty locating the right people but, through sheer tenacity and doggedness, eventually he succeeded.

The rumour was that the new facility involved cryonics, the emerging medical technology of cryopreserving humans and animals with the intention of future revival, and to enhance his chances of being offered a job, he avidly read everything he could find on the subject. He'd always been interested in the natural world, in wildlife. That's one of the reasons he'd become a biologist. And he'd seen David Attenborough's programme on frozen frogs. Frogs that freeze solid in winter but thaw out in spring with no harm done. For most organisms, prolonged sub-zero temperatures causes the water in their cells to freeze and produce ice crystals, ice crystals which ravage the cells, causing irreparable damage and death. Wood frogs, which hibernate at minus 3.3°C in winter, avoid this fate by an ingenious mechanism. As their metabolism plummets, the cells release some of their water, replacing it with glucose. The high concentration of glucose in the residual water acts as an antifreeze, preventing the water in the cells from freezing.

Even more surprising is the Woolly Bear caterpillar that lives in the Arctic. During the polar spring and summer, it eats continuously for four months, then crawls under a rock and settles down to await the long polar winter. As the temperature falls rapidly, its heart stops beating, it ceases to breathe and its body starts to freeze. First its gut, then its blood, until its whole body is frozen solid. In spring, it thaws out and, like Jesus, arises miraculously from the dead. This amazing cycle is repeated a further 13 years until the Woolly Bear caterpillar has built up enough food reserves to complete its metamorphosis into a moth.

He'd also discovered that some primitive organisms could survive, indeed flourish, in extremely cold conditions. These extremophiles, organisms that can survive in both extremely hot and extremely cold environments, flourish around the world.

The cold loving extremophiles, the pyschrophiles, have been found living happily in frozen ice in both Alaska and Siberia in temperatures as low as minus 18°C. To his astonishment, pyschrophiles were known that could even survive temperatures of minus 60°C. On 'warming' to minus 18°C, these *Methanogens* (methane producing organisms) happily resumed their little lives.

They survive at such low temperatures for two reasons. One, because their cell membranes are more fluid and less likely to rupture than conventional cell membranes and two, because they produce an antifreeze, glycerol, to drastically lower the freezing point of the water in their cells.

All these thoughts flashed through Ben's head as he made his way along the aisles of pods to the laboratories at the far end of the cave.

In the Control Room Susan scanned the dials on the console. The temperature of some of the pods was increasing, but there was nothing to worry about. Not yet, anyway. They were still within the prescribed range. The emergency generators were obviously struggling to supply sufficient power to maintain the vacuum that held the temperature of the pods at minus 196°C. She switched her gaze to the cavern looking for Ben. Illuminated with blue light, the rows of pods looked distinctly eerie. They reminded Susan of giant vacuum flasks, but vacuum flasks with contents far different to tea or coffee. In the distance, she could see a light sweeping the pods but couldn't see the figure holding the torch. The lighting was too dim.

As she surveyed the scene, Susan thought about the contents of the pods. Dead bodies, many without heads and most without brains. These vital organs were stored separately inside the laboratories, the laboratories that Ben was approaching. And she remembered how, before they were frozen, the bodies were drained of all fluids, natural, aqueous-based fluids that would freeze to ice crystals and destroy the cells. And how synthetic fluids, synthetic blood that didn't freeze, even at minus 196°C, was pumped into the bodies. And how the prepared bodies, the white, unnatural looking bodies, were lowered into the freezing liquid. And how the liquid nitrogen bubbled and evaporated, forming a white cloud, like a halo, above the pods.

Susan knew that in cryonics, liquid nitrogen was the coolant of choice because it caused rapid freezing on contact with dead, and living, tissue. However, its efficiency is limited by the fact that it boils immediately on contact with a warm object, enveloping the object in insulating and asphyxiating nitrogen gas. This *Leidenfrost Effect* applies to any liquid in contact with an object significantly hotter than its boiling point. Susan also knew that if the temperature in the pods rose too high too quickly, it could trigger a catastrophic build up of pressure, causing them to explode and flood the entire cavern with suffocating nitrogen gas and, even worse, with the body parts of frozen humans. It was something she tried not to think about.

At the back of her mind, and sometimes in her dreams, she envisaged the nightmare scenario of a pod warming up, the lid opening and a 'dead' figure slowly hauling itself out of its confined, cold tomb. A dead figure, resurrected. Come back to life. And she wondered what it would be like. Would it be a 'normal' human being, a person with the same emotions and feelings as before? Feelings of love, and hate. Hate at having put itself through this stupid ordeal. Or would it be a soulless monster, a zombie or a Frankenstein? She shuddered.

The flashlight was shining on the entrance to the laboratories. The high security, air locked entrance. Ben had reached the far end of the cave. She returned her gaze to the console. The temperature of the pods was still rising. She thought about ringing Ben, but decided against it. He'd be back soon.

It had been a long night and Susan felt drowsy. She tried to fight it by focusing on the dials, but her eyelids felt heavy and her body craved sleep. A moment later, her eyes closed, succumbing to her tiredness, and Susan slipped into a light slumber.

A sound awoke her. A faint, shuffling sound. Like shuffling feet. Slowly, she turned around. Two large, orange eyes stared straight at her. Two large, unblinking orange eyes. She screamed. But no one heard. The soundproofing saw to that.

3

HALLOWEEN

She stepped forward to greet the man emerging from the fog. The man wearing a long, black cape with a dark red lining. The man with an ashen grey face and two fangs protruding from his mouth.

'Hi, Scott,' Lisa said, flinging her arms around him. 'I'm so glad you could make it. And your Dracula outfit looks so… real, especially in this fog. Come in, the party's in full swing.'

Scott Rikards was popular with the girls. Very popular. Tall and athletic with jet black hair, brown eyes and a dark complexion, his high cheekbones gave him the appearance of a film star, or sportsman. But it wasn't just his good looks that attracted the girls. They found his relaxed, friendly and charming persona irresistible. His winning smile completed his repertoire. The smile he flashed at Lisa as he accepted her invitation and entered the house.

All the girls had wanted Scott at their Halloween parties, and most had tried to lure him. But he could only attend one and he'd chosen Lisa's. Not because it would be the best, but because she was the girl he was fond of. The girl who, unlike most of the other girls, wasn't always trying to curry his favour. She was an independent, confident girl, a free spirit. She reminded Scott of himself.

When they'd found out that Scott would be attending Lisa's Halloween party, many of the girls cancelled their own and decided to go to Lisa's instead, some of them uninvited. Their audacity at turning up as uninvited guests annoyed Lisa but she was too kind to turn them away from one of America's most celebrated traditions. A tradition Americans celebrated in style.

Statistics show that over 90 per cent of Americans celebrate Halloween and that 65 per cent of adults aged between 18-34 attend Halloween parties. Most houses and gardens are decorated with ghosts and ghouls and giant spider's webs, with the odd humorous tombstone added for fun, like the one in Lisa's garden, IMA GON'R, and everyone dresses for the occasion. Each year, on the 31 October, it seems that the whole of the USA is inhabited by monsters, ghosts, skeletons, witches and devils. Households also stock up on treats to appease the groups of 'trick or treaters' asking for a treat, normally candy or cookies, with the (usually idle) threat of performing mischief on the homeowner or their property if no treat was forthcoming. It is an activity in which an astonishing 95 per cent of American children engage in on Halloween.

Screams and shrieks of delight greeted Scott as he entered the crowded room. Many of the witches, ghosts and skeletons surged forward, jostling to grab his attention. Dracula, surrounded by a horde of devoted followers. Lisa smiled at their naiveté. And their foolishness. She had an inkling who it was that Scott liked.

The boys, who were outnumbered by almost two to one by the girls, simply nodded their heads to acknowledge Scott's arrival. They faced a dilemma. They liked Scott, he was a good mate, but, at the same time, they resented him too. Resented his popularity with the girls. Let them all make fools of themselves, they thought, watching the jabbering throng vying for Scott's attention. It'll all end in tears.

As the evening wore on most of the girls realised the futility of their actions and reverted to drinking and dancing with the other boys. But two persisted. Kimberly and Tammy were doing their utmost to outdo each other and make Scott their companion and, hopefully, their lover for the evening. Fuelled by drink, their exchanges were becoming increasingly bitchy. It had reached the point where both of them were trying to tempt him into bed. Partly because that's what they wanted but mainly to humiliate the loser. Bitchiness abounded.

'Oh Scott,' said Kimberly, 'I love your make up. It's so authentic.' Continuing, she looked straight at Tammy and said, 'But can you still kiss with those fangs?'

'Of course he can,' said Tammy, grabbing a surprised Scott around his neck and kissing him passionately on the mouth. As the kiss ended, Tammy looked at Kimberly with a triumphant gleam in her eyes. 'Of course he can kiss, Kimberly. Of course he can,' she repeated. 'If he wants to.'

'You bitch,' thought Kimberly, seething with anger. 'You fucking, scheming bitch. I'll get my revenge.'

Restraining her anger, Kimberly asked Scott if he'd like another drink. 'Thanks, Kimberly. I'd love another Coors please.'

'I'd like a refill too,' said Tammy, proffering her empty glass, but Kimberly totally ignored her and strode purposefully towards the kitchen. 'Let the bitch get her own fucking drink,' she thought, still seething with anger at what Tammy had just done. Tammy, the brazen hussy. Tammy, the 'hussy with the pussy' as she was known. Tammy, the girl who was trying her level best to sleep with every boy at college. But the one she wanted most, wanted more than anything, had eluded her. So far. But she'd get him. Eventually. In the end. She always did.

The doorbell rang for the umpteenth time. 'More "trick or treaters",' thought Lisa, grabbing the tin of candy and cookies she kept near the door. Lisa didn't object to the 'trick or treaters'. On the contrary, she admired them. Admired the amount of time and effort, and money, they'd spent to make themselves look so scary. But most of all she loved the excited expressions on their faces as they scrabbled in the tin searching for their favourite candy, or cookie. Some people gave them money instead. In Lisa's view, this was wrong. It meant they couldn't be bothered to take the time and effort to buy the sweets. It was pure laziness.

The doorbell rang again. This time, the 'trick or treaters' were accompanied by an adult. A stranger wearing a Scream mask. Unlike the children, the stranger politely declined the candy and cookies. He said his treat would be to join the party for the final few hours. Lisa had experienced this before. Strangers asking to be allowed to join the party. In the main they were harmless people, people who liked to flit from one party to another. Or lonely people who hadn't been invited to any party. Occasionally, however, they were people who'd been thrown out of other parties for being either drunk or causing trouble. Or both. The stranger on her doorstep seemed neither drunk nor a troublemaker, so Lisa let him in.

The drinking, dancing and talking continued apace. The room was awash with the sound of music, conversation, laughing and the occasional argument. At 11-00 p.m., Lisa tinkled her glass. The room fell silent. 'I think it's time for a game of apple bobbing,' she said. 'The tub with the apples is in the dining room.'

'What's the prize for the winner?' shouted Brandon.

'And the forfeit for the loser,' said Randy.

'You'll have to wait and see,' replied Lisa.

Some were good at grabbing an apple floating on the water with their teeth whilst others failed miserably. Generally, the boys fared better than the girls. One girl was really struggling. Tammy. Kimberly spied her chance for a little revenge. As she walked past the kneeling Tammy, the girl with her face over the tub of cold water, Kimberly pretended to stumble. She steadied herself by placing her hand on Tammy's head, forcing it under the water. Completely. 'Oh, I'm so sorry, Tammy,' she lied, as the bedraggled and furious Tammy raised her head from the water and glowered at Kimberly, her make up ruined and her expensive hair-do an absolute mess. Her fury was such that she was, quite literally, speechless. A smile of quiet satisfaction spread across the face of Kimberly as she retreated into the kitchen.

As the clock ticked relentlessly towards the bewitching hour, the time had come to turn off the lights and tell scary stories. 'Right, who wants to begin?' asked Lisa. The awkward silence was broken by a voice from the corner of the room. It was the stranger.

'If you don't mind, I'd like to tell a story.'

'Okay,' said Lisa, as everyone turned towards the stranger in the corner of the dark room, the stranger wearing a Scream mask. 'Go ahead.'

Everyone thought he'd tell a story related to the Scream movies, but he didn't. His story took place in a mansion, a haunted mansion in a remote, desolate location. A mansion where an elderly, frail mother lived with her middle-aged daughter and her husband, a husband the mother had never liked. She considered him a lazy man, a man without ambition, a man who wanted to drift through life on the back of other peoples' endeavours.

One cold, bleak winter, the mother began to experience strange happenings. Weird noises in the dead of night, objects that moved mysteriously from one place to another, and ghostly apparitions. But the really strange thing was that only the mother heard, or saw, anything. Her daughter and son-in-law were adamant: she must be imagining it all. She must be going mad. Going insane. Then, one evening at dinner, the room went cold, icy cold, and the candles started to flicker. All of a sudden, a gust of wind blew the window open, causing a candle to topple over and ignite the curtains. Old, dry curtains that blazed like an inferno. Terrified, the mother, daughter and son-in-law dashed for the door, but it wouldn't open. They hadn't locked it but, try as they might, it would just not open. It wouldn't budge an inch.

The flames spread rapidly and the heat became unbearable. In a final, desperate bid to escape, they tried to reach the window but were beaten back by the intense heat and flames. It was like the fire knew what they were trying to do, and drove them back. Defeated, they huddled together on the floor awaiting their fate. Mercifully, the smoke rendered them unconscious before the voracious flames reached their trembling bodies.

The following morning, the mother awoke to find herself lying on the floor of a burnt out dining room next to the charred bodies of her daughter and son-in-law. On the mirror, scrawled in sooty black letters, was a message; THEY GOT WHAT THEY DESERVED.

The police were at a loss to explain what had happened, but the mother knew. She knew that her daughter and son-in-law wanted their inheritance. They were fed up of waiting for her to die. Instead, they'd devised a plan to have her certified insane. But her protector had come to her rescue. The protector she had missed so much for many years. Her protector in life, and now in death. Her late husband. It was, she believed, his ghost that had started the fire, his ghost that had blocked the escape routes and his ghost that had protected her from being burned to death.

'It proves,' the stranger concluded, 'that passion and desire conquers all, even from beyond the grave.'

'Thanks for that,' said Lisa, 'it was a good story.' Secretly, she wondered why he hadn't ended the story with 'love conquers all'. To her, it seemed a more fitting ending.

As midnight approached, people began pairing off. Some just stood in corners chatting quietly and drinking, some smooched, and some sneaked upstairs to the bedrooms. Lisa was pleased that Kimberly and Tammy had seemingly resolved their differences. She'd seen them talking earnestly in the corner. And she was pleased that people had befriended the lonely stranger. He'd been in conversations with several people, especially Kimberly.

As the clock struck midnight, Tammy surreptitiously slipped out of the room and made her way to the door leading down to the basement. She glanced around to make sure that no one was watching before opening the door and descending the steps into the cold, dark void.

At the far end of the basement a figure stood waiting in the gloom, a man with his back to her. Excitedly, she hurried across the stone floor and embraced him eagerly. 'Oh Scott. I've waited so long for this,' she said.

The figure turned around. 'So have I,' it said. 'So have I.'

4

HEADS AND BRAINS

CRYONICS LABORATORIES : LEVEL 2 and 3 STAFF ONLY, the sign on the door proclaimed. 'Curt yet informative,' thought Ben as he fumbled for his ID card. Holding the flashlight in his left hand, he swiped the card in the illuminated slot on the door, a slot like those found on the doors of modern hotels and, when the indicator light flashed green, he tapped in a four digit code. 'Name,' a robotic, metallic voice commanded. As well as the hi-tech ID card and security code, a voice recognition system safeguarded the entrance to the cryonics laboratories.

'Ben Davies,' he said, watching his voice pattern on the small screen. He waited a few seconds whilst the computer searched for a match in its database.

'Enter, Ben Davies' came the metallic voice, as the door opened automatically.

Ben stepped through the door into a room about 18 foot by 12 foot. It smelled of disinfectant. With polished pine benches running along the two longest sides, it reminded him of a changing room in a leisure centre. But only briefly. The white lab coats hanging from the twelve pegs on each wall, together with white 'caps', gave a hint of its true identity. The containers filled with blue overshoes in the corners of the room confirmed it. It was the air lock to the laboratories.

As a staff member with Level 1 and 2 clearance, Ben knew that he had a maximum of five minutes in which to don a lab coat, headgear and overshoes and exit the air lock before it automatically went into 'lockdown' and set off the alarm, an alarm that was linked to the main gate and the police station. It took him three minutes.

He pressed the green button. The door leading into the laboratory opened with a swishing noise, a noise like that made by the doors in the early episodes of *Star Trek*. It closed with the same noise after he stepped out of the air lock into the dark confines of the main laboratory, the laboratory where the bulk of the 'routine' research was done. Almost immediately, harsh white light flooded the darkened room. The abruptness of it startled him. Recovering his composure, he assessed the layout of the main cryonics laboratory. It was oblong in shape, the air lock through which he'd just entered being in the middle of one of the two long walls. In front of him were eight laboratory benches in parallel, each about fifteen foot long and five foot wide. Shelves, stacked with bottles of chemicals and reagents of various kinds, ran along the centre of each bench. Underneath the benches were cupboards, presumably where the apparatus was stored. At each end of the benches was a sink. On the two shorter walls and the one behind him were fume cupboards and storage units, units specially designed to house the collection of heads and brains. Ahead of him on the other long wall were four doors, each leading to a laboratory. Each door had a nameplate. Like the one to the main laboratory, they were curt and simple:-

CRYONICS LABORATORY

1

LEVEL 3 STAFF ONLY

and so on to 'CRYONICS LABORATORY 4'.

Ben knew these were the top secret laboratories where the key research was carried out by a small number of the leading geneticists, molecular biologists and chemists from around the UK. And he also knew that all four laboratories were protected by the latest biometric security system. To gain access, a person had to have both the palm of their right hand and one of their eyes scanned. Only when the computer had verified they matched one of the few people who had Level 3 clearance were they allowed to enter. He wasn't one of them.

Because of the importance of the laboratories, particularly their precious contents, they took priority over the rest of the facility. They had their own generators, powerful generators, for emergencies such as this, to maintain the ideal conditions for weeks, or even months, to ensure the contents, the priceless contents, came to no harm.

As he prepared for his inspection, Ben felt like a glorified 'Night Steward'. That was one of the jobs he'd taken at a chemical company, a 'Night Steward' who ensured that experiments left to run overnight by the day staff were kept at the right conditions throughout the night. The right temperature, the right concentration and the right pH. Because of the relentless march of technology, it was a job that had become redundant. But it was a job that had probably helped him secure his present position.

He began his inspection. Turning to his left, he walked slowly alongside the special storage units, diligently examining each one for temperature, pH and electrolyte concentration. The heads, and brains, were stored in a clear liquid in separate glass-fronted containers positioned at eye level for easy viewing. As he made his way along them, Ben was both fascinated and horrified at their contents. Some contained complete heads, their faces frozen in grotesque grimaces. Or were they sinister smiles? It was hard to tell. Some had two eyes, two unseeing, staring eyes, whilst others had no eyes at all, just two empty, bony sockets. Two dark gateways to a brain long since dead. Others were devoid not just of their eyes, but their noses too. And some faces were shorn of everything. Eyes, nose, lips and cheeks. For some reason, these bony faces reminded Ben of a pirate's *Skull and Crossbones* flag. But the ones that really caught Ben's eye were the heads without tops. The heads which had been sawed neatly above the eyes and the whole top removed. Some still retained the brain, which stuck out like a grey, rumpled ball. Others were just empty. The brain had been removed, leaving an unnatural black hole.

As he passed the four laboratories at the far end of the room, the four top secret laboratories, Ben wondered what type of research was done in such secrecy. He didn't know for sure, but he had an idea. A good idea. And the thought of it made him shiver. He quickened his pace.

Further round the laboratory, the containers housed brains. Whole brains, slices of brains and fragments of brains. Fragments of all shapes and sizes. 'Obviously,' Ben thought, 'they were parts of the brain that controlled specific functions. Functions like speech and memory and movement. And face recognition.' He'd read somewhere about the *fusiform gyrus*, that part of the brain responsible for face recognition. As he stared at the small lumps of grey matter, he wondered if one of them was someone's *fusiform gyrus*. But the *coupe de grace*, the ultimate horror, was reserved for the end of his inspection. As he made his way back toward the air lock on the final section of wall, Ben couldn't believe his eyes. These containers held human heads that had been cleaved in two, cut vertically from the top of the head to the neck, with each half having one eye, half a nose and half a mouth. In some, the brain had been left intact. Half a brain for half a head. Ben guessed it was to do with experiments on the different functions of the left half of the brain and the right half. These were bad enough but the worst sight was the heads where the brain had been removed. Gazing into the gaping hole of half a head made him feel sick. He wondered what the people who'd bequeathed their bodies for medical research would make of all this. 'Not very much,' he thought.

He was relieved to get back to the air lock. He'd completed his inspection and everything was fine. It was approaching 5-00 a.m. He only had one more hour to work before the first of the day staff arrived. As he was taking off his lab clothes, he thought fondly about a hot, refreshing shower followed by a relaxing evening watching football on TV. Watching Manchester United take on Barcelona in the European Champions League with a can of Carlsberg in his hand.

He also thought about Susan, his young assistant, alone in the Control Room. Susan, the woman he'd fancied for a while. The woman who fancied him too. He knew she didn't like being left alone but, as a junior member of staff, she only had Level 1 clearance; access to the Control Room and the cave. And anyway, someone had to stay in the Control Room.

Suddenly, his mobile rang. He checked the caller. It was Susan. She sounded desperate. Scared out of her wits. 'Ben, get back here right…'

The phone went dead.

5

BERLIN, 1 MAY 1945

The mother kissed each one of her six children as she tucked them into bed. She was a good mother. A caring mother. She'd watched as they washed their faces and cleaned their teeth. And she'd given them a sugary drink to help them sleep. A sugary drink containing morphine to sedate them. And then, before leaving the room, she'd crushed a little white tablet in each child's mouth. On reaching the bedroom door she paused and turned around to take a final look at her offspring. Satisfied that her children were asleep, she stepped on to the landing, closing the door quietly behind her. She wept as she walked down the stairs to the dining room. And wept as she got out the deck of cards to play a lonely game of Solitaire.

Later, she was joined by her husband, Josef. Together, they walked up the steps to the bombed out Chancellery Gardens and said their last goodbyes. The cyanide tablets would have done their job and now it was time for her and her husband to join their children. Magda Goebbels smiled as Josef pointed the gun at her head. A few seconds later, on 1 May 1945, Magda and Josef Goebbels lay dead.

A few miles away, on the outskirts of Berlin, four men and a dog hunkered down beside a battered looking jeep. Four men in British army uniforms and a black Labrador. They sat in silence listening to the distant sounds of gunfire and explosions, occasionally peeking out of their camouflaged hideout to catch a glimpse of the red glow on the darkening horizon. The glow from the exploding bombs and burning buildings as the allied bombers pounded German positions, softening the way for the British and Canadian forces, who'd already crossed the Rhine to the north and were now in the industrial heartland of Germany, the Ruhr.

'That was a bloody big one,' said Freddie, as the sound of a massive explosion reached their ears. 'I bet they've hit a Jerry ammo dump.'

'Definitely,' said Ted, 'unless we've developed a bloody super bomb.'

'It probably was a munitions factory,' said Johnnie, the team leader. 'The bombers are targeting German supplies.'

'I bet it's made one hell of a crater,' said Dick, the fourth member of the elite SAS (Special Air Service) team. 'Big enough to hide St Paul's, eh.'

Unlike the other three members of the team, Dick was a cockney. He'd been born and bred in London and, before being called up, had spent all of his 24 years within 20 miles of England's capital city. Why go anywhere else, he'd say. It's the best place in the world. He was a short, swarthy man with a cheeky grin and a wicked sense of humour, good attributes to have in times of war.

'I'm bloody starving,' said Ted. 'Is it time to eat?'

They'd been holed up for three days now, awaiting orders, and they were getting restless and hungry.

'We've got to eke out our rations, Ted,' replied Johnnie. 'We don't know how long we'll be here. I'm afraid you'll have to wait.'

Ted was a Yorkshire man. Standing six foot four inches tall and weighing seventeen stone, he was the biggest member of the team. He was quiet and reserved, some would say dour, but that would be unfair. He laughed if the occasion warranted it and he had a sardonic sense of humour. And he was fiercely loyal to his mates and would run through the proverbial brick wall to help a friend in need.

Johnnie, Freddie, Ted and Dick were one of the first SAS units. Founded four years earlier in 1941 by Captain David Stirling, the SAS and the other Special Forces units arose from the aftermath of the humiliating defeats of the British army in France and North Africa at the start of World War II. Units of elite, highly trained fighting men taken initially from the British Commandos to form the Parachute Regiment, the Special Boat Service (SBS) and the SAS. They had served with distinction in the North African campaign that ended in victory for Montgomery's 'Desert Rats', and then later in Europe. And now, in the final throes of the war, they found themselves in the heart of Germany.

Along with other Special Forces units they'd been assisting the advance of the British and Canadian armies to the north of Berlin. To the south, American forces had captured the Lorraine and were advancing on Mannheim and the Rhine. To the east, the Russian Red Army had advanced rapidly and were already in Berlin. And that was the problem.

At the Yalta meeting held in February, Churchill, Roosevelt and Stalin agreed that the British, American and Russian forces would enter Berlin simultaneously. But it was obvious that wasn't going to happen. Stalin's Bolshevik troops had entered East Berlin on April 22 and were within touching distance of the *Fuhrerbunker* in the Reich Chancellery Gardens where Hitler was holed up with his wife, Eva Braun. Both Churchill and Roosevelt wanted the British and American forces to be present when Hitler was either captured or killed. They didn't trust Stalin.

The radio crackled. A message was coming through. Johnnie listened intently. It was their orders.

'Hitler's dead,' he said. 'According to the Russians, he committed suicide by the "pistol-and-poison" method of combining a dose of cyanide with a gunshot to the head. His wife committed suicide beside him.'

'The bloody coward,' spat Ted. 'But at least it's saved a show trial.'

'When did the bugger do it?' asked Dick.

'Yesterday,' said Johnnie. 'And there's more. The Germans doused both their bodies with petrol and set them alight.'

'What the bloody hell for?' said Freddie, clearly perplexed.

'Because Hitler had received reports that after his close ally, Benito Mussolini, and his wife had been hanged, their bodies were thrown in the gutter and horribly mutilated by Italian partisans. He didn't want the same fate to befall him and his wife.'

The ensuing silence was broken by Ted. 'So what are our orders, Johnnie?'

Johnnie looked each man in the eye before answering. 'To confirm that Hitler really is dead. To find his remains, and to bring a sample of them home.'

'Bloody hell,' said Dick. 'And how do we do that?'

'Well,' replied Johnnie, 'Hitler and his wife committed suicide in the *Fuhrerbunker* and their charred remains are buried in a shallow grave in the Chancellery Gardens, about three miles from here. We need to act fast. We'll eat the rest of the rations and then check our weapons. We depart at midnight.'

On the stroke of midnight, four men slipped silently from the camouflaged bunker into the darkened ruins of Berlin. With blackened faces and hands, they were almost invisible. So was the black Labrador that padded along behind them.

They'd plotted the route beforehand but the ruined buildings offered few landmarks, especially in the dark. Cautiously, they eased their way down the rubble strewn streets, keeping close to what was left of the once proud buildings of Germany's capital city.

Suddenly, Johnnie's upraised hand signalled danger. Instinctively, they crouched low, listening for the slightest sound. Nothing. Just the stillness of the night. Then, just as they were about to proceed, they heard it. Heard the unmistakable sound of German voices. Urgent voices issuing commands. A bullet zipped overhead, ricocheting off the ruined wall behind them. They'd been spotted. A machine gun began to clatter, spraying bullets in their direction. 'Scatter,' shouted Johnnie, as a flare illuminated the night sky.

Johnnie signalled to Dick and Ted to circle towards the flanks of the machine gun nest, one to the left and one to the right, whilst he and Freddie drew their fire from the front. At this range, their sten guns were no match for a machine gun and they were too far away to throw grenades. They had to get closer.

Johnnie estimated the distance to the machine gun at about 100 yards. To lob a grenade accurately, they'd need to get within 30 yards. He nodded to Freddie and they let off a short burst of fire before moving forwards and sideways, Freddie to the left and Johnnie to the right. A hail of bullets peppered the position they'd just vacated, thudding into the wall and smashing the bricks to smithereens. A few seconds later, they repeated the manoeuvre. Seventy yards. A couple more dashes should do it. As they released another burst from their sten guns, two explosions came from the vicinity of the machine gun, two explosions followed by screams and shouts of the wounded and dying. The machine gun was silent. Moments later, two staccato bursts silenced the screams. Dick and Ted had done their job well.

Johnnie guessed they were halfway to the *Fuhrerbunker*. 'Keep alert and stay silent at all times,' he said. 'Ted, you stay at the back with Sally. Watch her closely. She's trained to stop if she hears unfamiliar human voices. Freddie, you lead. Dick and I will stay in the middle. Okay, lets go.'

This time, they were extra careful. Ted kept a watchful eye on Sally as they flitted from one ruined building to the next. They hid when the moon cast its pale glow and moved when it was obscured by a cloud. Progress was slow. So far, they'd been lucky. They'd had good cover from the ruined buildings but their luck had run out. Ahead lay a flat expanse, a major road, about 30 yards wide. A road they had to cross. There was no way round it. Johnnie felt uneasy. A couple of two storey buildings were still standing on the far side. 'Ideal for a sniper,' he thought. They looked at Sally. She hadn't stopped as they approached the road but now they'd stopped she was sitting obediently waiting for their next move.

Freddie broke the silence. 'I'll go first,' he said. 'After all, I'm the shortest and will make the smallest target.' And he was. At just five feet six inches tall, the happy-go-lucky Brummie was easily the shortest member of the team.

'I don't know,' said Johnnie. 'I've got a bad feeling about this.'

'There's been no reaction from Sally,' said Ted. 'And she's got far better hearing than us.'

'Couldn't we send her across first,' said Dick. 'She's by far the quickest and smallest.'

'What good would that do,' retorted Ted, clearly annoyed that Dick wanted to use his beloved Sally as a guinea pig. 'If there is a sniper, he wouldn't reveal his position for a bloody dog!'

'Okay, okay,' said Johnnie. 'Calm down. Freddie, if you're sure you want to go first, that's fine.'

'I'm sure.'

'Right, then move fast and keep low. We'll keep our eyes on the buildings and provide covering fire if needed.'

'Okay,' said Freddie. 'On the count of three. One. Two. Three.' And he was off, keeping low and zig-zagging. Three shots rang out in quick succession. Three shots fired from the second floor of the building on the far side of the road. The first hit his leg, the second his shoulder and the third his head. He crumpled to the ground like a rag doll. As soon as they saw the muzzle flashes, Johnnie, Ted and Dick opened fire. Slowly, like it was happening in slow motion, a figure fell out of the open window, landing on the concrete pavement with a dull thud.

They didn't know if he was a lone sniper or if there were others. About 20 yards ahead of them Freddie lay groaning in the road.

'Cover me,' said Johnnie, and ran towards Freddie. There were no more shots. The sniper must have been alone.

Freddie was in a bad way. He could have survived the leg and shoulder shots, but not the head shot. Johnnie knew his colleague was dying. 'Did… you… get him?' he said with great difficulty.

'Yeah. We got him, Freddie,' replied Johnnie.

'Good… Complete the… mission… for me, Johnnie,' whispered Freddie, his voice barely audible. His body slumped and his eyes glazed over. He was dead.

'We'll do our damn best, Freddie,' he said. 'We'll do our damn best.'

Dick and Ted had gone to where the body of the sniper had fallen. They couldn't believe what they saw. 'Christ Almighty,' uttered Dick, 'he's just a bloody kid.' Crumpled on the floor was the body of a boy, a boy in civilian clothes who was no more than 12 years old.

'They must be getting really desperate if they're using young kids,' said Ted.

'Young or not,' said Johnnie as he walked the short distance from Freddie's body to where they were standing, 'he's just killed Freddie.'

They covered the remaining half mile to the *Fuhrerbunker* without any further incidents. The Russian flag had replaced the Swastika at Hitler's Headquarters and Russian voices filled the night air. Johnnie motioned for them to stop. 'We've got to play this carefully,' he said quietly. 'The Russians will be jittery. We don't want them to mistake us for Germans. I'll go first and shout the pre-arranged password in Russian. Only when I give the signal are you to follow. Understood?' Ted and Dick nodded.

Johnnie approached the perimeter of the Chancellery Gardens cautiously. He could hear dogs barking. 'Hitler's guard dogs,' he thought to himself. He could just make out the dim figures of Russian soldiers guarding the entrance to the gardens. Taking a deep breath, he arose from his crouching position and walked slowly towards them, his arms in the air. He addressed them in Russian. 'I'm a British soldier. I'd like to speak to your Commanding Officer.' He stopped when the guards pointed their rifles at him, but kept his hands in the air.

'Password,' barked one of them in Russian.

Johnnie answered with the password he'd received just a few hours ago in the coded radio message.

The Russians relaxed. The one who'd asked for the password stepped towards him. 'We didn't expect you for another two or three weeks,' he said in Russian. 'How come you're here so soon?'

Johnnie explained that small units of Special Forces soldiers had been sent ahead of the main force, and that he needed to speak to the Commanding Officer. He also asked if his two comrades could join him. Minutes later, all three of them, and Sally, were inside the *Fuhrerbunker*.

Approaching his 32nd year, Johnnie Standish was a fluent speaker of Russian. He'd graduated from Cambridge with a first in Modern Languages and taken a job as a translator in his home town of Chester. But he found it boring and so, with war clouds on the horizon, he'd enlisted in the army. His leadership potential was spotted quickly and he was fast-tracked through Sandhurst. After distinguishing himself in the Commandos, the army had no hesitation in appointing Captain Johnnie Standish to lead one of the first SAS teams.

'The Commanding Officer will see you now,' the orderly said to Johnnie. Johnnie arose from his chair and followed the orderly into the adjacent office.

'Good evening,' the man behind the impressive wooden desk said in faltering English. 'What can I do for you?'

Johnnie explained the reason for his visit, and showed him the authorisation note signed by Churchill.

The Commanding Officer listened politely and then shook his head. 'The only proof we have that Hitler is dead are the photographs left behind by the Germans,' he said, pushing several black-and-white photographs across the table. They showed a man in German uniform with a bullet hole in his temple. It looked like Hitler.

'You can take one to show your superiors,' the Commanding Officer said.

Johnnie nodded as he accepted the photograph.

'Could I also take a sample of his remains?' Johnnie asked.

'I'm afraid that's not possible. I have strict orders that his grave is not to be disturbed until Stalin himself arrives.'

'I understand,' said Johnnie. 'Thank-you for your time. And the photograph. My men and I will leave before daybreak.' After saluting the Russian general, Johnnie turned on his heels and exited the office.

He explained what had happened to Ted and Dick.

'But we can't leave without a sample of Hitler's remains,' said Dick. 'Not after what's happened to Freddie.'

'I know,' replied Johnnie. 'And I think I know how to get them.'

'It's clear,' said Ted. 'As far as I can tell, there's no one about.'

From their position at the corner of the *Fuhrerbunker*, the Reich Chancellery Gardens seemed devoid of life. It was 4-00 a.m. and, apart from the guards at the main gate, most of the Russian soldiers were asleep. Ted patted Sally on the head. 'Go girl. Go and sniff out the grave and bring back a bone.' The black Labrador bounded off into the darkness, eager to please her master. Although they couldn't see her, they could hear her as she searched the gardens, sniffing for the remains in the shallow grave. Suddenly she stopped and they heard the sound of paws digging frantically in the dry earth. Moments later, she sat at their feet with a bone in her mouth. One of Hitler's bones. A bone still covered with partly charred flesh.

'Good girl,' said Ted, taking the bone and stroking her head. 'Good girl, Sally.' He slipped the bone into the special container they'd brought for the purpose and handed it to Johnnie.

'Time for us to leave,' said Johnnie, 'before they discover what we've done.'

They walked quickly towards the main gate, exchanging cursory greetings as they passed the guards, then quickened their pace as they retraced their steps back to their hideout.

It took less than five minutes for the Russians to discover the disturbed grave. And less than a minute for the patrols to give chase.

Johnnie and his two companions could hear the commotion behind them and began to run. They didn't want to fail now.

They could hear the Russians' voices and see their flashlights. They were gaining. It would be touch and go whether they reached the jeep in time. They could also hear the sound of dogs. Baying, barking, growling dogs. Rottweilers, Johnnie guessed. Lots of them. 'Shit,' he thought, 'that's the last thing we need.' He recognised the ruins to his left. They were only 400 yards from the jeep.

The dogs were close. He could hear them snarling as they pursued their quarry. Realising they wouldn't catch them, the Russians had released the pack of Rottweilers and they were catching up. Fast. Still 200 yards to go. They wouldn't make it.

'Go,' shouted Ted. 'You and Dick go on. I'll join you later.' With that, he turned to face the pack of onrushing, snarling Rottweilers. Sally stood beside him, her teeth bared.

When they got within 50 yards, Ted unleashed a withering burst from his sten gun, cutting down the leading dogs. But the rest carried on. They knew no fear. He managed to shoot two more before the first dog launched itself towards his throat. Instinctively, he swung the sten gun round with all his force, hitting the dog a full blow on the side of its head. It fell to the ground, whimpering, its skull crushed. The second one was on him in a flash. He grabbed its front legs and yanked them apart. He heard bones crack. It too fell in a heap. As he prepared for the next assault, a shot rang out, then another. He felt a hot, searing pain in his chest. For the first time in his life he felt weak. He couldn't stand up. Three more bullets thudded into him. He was dead before his body hit the ground.

Johnnie and Dick had reached the jeep, gunned the engine and turned it around to face the oncoming Russians. Dick manned the Vickers K machine gun, released the safety catch and unleashed a deadly hail of fire. The .303 armour piercing rounds, interspersed with the occasional tracer bullet, decimated the advancing Russians. As Dick swept the machine gun from left to right, four bullets cut a swathe across the leading Russian's midriff, severing the top half of his torso from the bottom half. He was, quite literally, cut in half. Blood spurted everywhere. Two bullets smacked into the neck of his comrade on his left, blowing his head clean off. Like a headless chicken, the decapitated body continued to lurch forward, blood spurting from its neck, until it crumpled to the ground in a heap. Another bullet hit a soldier between the eyes, creating a hole big enough to push a fist through.

Stunned by the carnage created by the firepower of Vickers machine gun, the remaining Russians dived for whatever cover they could find. Even the fearless Rottweilers scattered.

In the darkness, Johnnie glimpsed a black shape stood beside her fallen master. 'Here girl,' he called, hoping against hope that she would come. To his immense relief, she did, half running and half limping towards the jeep. She was too badly injured to jump on to the jeep, so Johnnie got down and lifted her up, whilst Dick kept the Russians at bay with the Vickers machine gun. Originally designed as an air-to-air gun, the Vickers K machine gun was an awesome weapon. It was the weapon of choice for the SAS gun jeeps.

Johnnie slammed the jeep into gear, pushed the accelerator to the floor and sped into the night, heading for the safety of the British and Canadian forces with their precious cargo.

6

THE CLIENT

'Good evening, sir,' Carly said to the stranger emerging from the fog. The smartly dressed stranger in a flowing black cape, top hat and carrying a black leather bag. She noticed that he was wearing black leather gloves too. The thought flashed through her mind that he might not be a doctor after all, but an undertaker. She'd never done 'business' with an undertaker. 'Are you looking for business?'

The man nodded his head.

'Follow me,' she said, linking his arm, 'my place isn't very far.'

'Here's fine,' said the stranger, extricating himself from her grip. 'No one will see us in this fog.'

'Okay,' said Carly, wishing he'd accepted her invitation. Her flat would have been warmer and more comfortable than a cold, foggy back street. 'If that's what you want.'

'It is,' said the stranger.

'I charge fifty pounds for full sex and twenty-five pounds for a hand job,' said Carly, as she began to take off her knickers. 'Is that alright?'

The stranger said nothing, but bent down to unzip his leather bag.

'It's okay, I've got some condoms,' she said, thinking that's what he was looking for, and fumbled in her handbag.

Suddenly, without any warning, a black leather hand clamped her mouth. Her eyes bulged in astonishment and fear. The last thing Carly Jones saw on this earth was a large bladed knife slashing her throat.

7

THE CONTROL ROOM

Ben dashed along the aisles of pods towards the dimly lit Control Room. The Control Room where Susan had made the desperate phone call. The insipid blue light seemed to slow him down. Hinder his movements. It gave the whole cavern an icy chill. A coldness that was enveloping. Although it was no more than 100 yards from the air lock to the Control Room, Ben was surprised at how breathless he was as he swiped his card and opened the door.

Breathing heavily, he scanned the dimly lit room with his flashlight. There was no sign of Susan. Warily, he walked towards the console, flashing his torch ahead of him. He braced himself for what he might find.

Susan's body lay on the floor behind the console. A small pool of blood had formed beside her head. Her mobile phone lay near her outstretched hand.

'Oh my God,' he thought. 'Oh my God. What on earth's happened here.' Tenderly, he knelt down beside her, beside the woman he liked. No, not liked, loved. 'Why,' he thought, 'did it take a dramatic event for peoples' true feelings to rise to the surface.'

She couldn't be dead. Not at such a young age. Gently, he felt her carotid artery for a pulse, hoping with all his heart that he'd feel the regular *beat, beat, beat*, of a living person. And he did. She was still alive! Carefully, he examined her head. A cut on her left temple revealed the source of the blood. He glanced up at the console. There, on the sharp, metal corner, was a red stain. She must have banged her head as she fell.

He went to the sink, soaked a towel in cold water and gently wiped away the blood. He placed the cold, wet towel across her forehead and stroked her face. 'Wake up, Susan. It's Ben. Everything's fine now.'

Her eyelids flickered, and then opened. Slowly. A confused expression spread across her face. 'It's okay,' said Ben, placing a rolled up, dry towel under her head, 'just lie here for a while until you regain your senses. You've been knocked unconscious.'

'Where… where am I?' she said, still dazed. 'What happened?'

'I think you fell and banged your head on the corner of the console,' replied Ben. 'Probably after you rang me. You sounded scared and desperate so I got here as fast as I could.'

'I… I remember now,' she said hesitantly. 'Yes, it's coming back.'

'What happened, Susan? What made you so frightened?'

'After I'd checked the dials on the console I heard a noise, a sort of shuffling noise behind me. I turned around and saw two orange eyes staring at me from the corner of the room. I thought… I know it's silly but at that instant I thought they belonged to a 'dead' person from one of the pods. A dead person come back to life to exact revenge. That's when I made the call. Suddenly, they moved. The eyes moved towards me. And that's when I must have slipped and fell.'

'I've checked the room. There's no one here,' he said. 'So it must have been something else. Do you feel well enough to sit on the chair?' Susan nodded. Carefully, he helped her on to her feet and then held her steady as she walked the short distance to the chair. 'Sit here whilst I make us a cup of tea,' he said, as he went to fill the kettle.

As he waited for the kettle to boil, Ben examined the Control Room. Apart from the glass wall with a door that overlooked the cavern, the other three walls were solid brick. The only other opening was a two foot by two foot metal grill in the corner of the opposite wall. It was the cover for the air duct that supplied fresh air to the Control Room. Perhaps she had seen something in the air duct. The kettle boiled.

Ben and Susan sipped their cups of tea in silence, reflecting on what had just happened. Suddenly, Susan froze. 'There, can you hear it?' she whispered. Ben listened intently. It was faint but he could hear it. A sort of shuffling sound. It was coming closer. He turned around to follow Susan's gaze. And then they both saw them. Two orange eyes peering down from the grill. The lighting was too dim to make out what the eyes belonged to so, slowly and silently, Ben reached for his flashlight. He pointed it at the grill and switched it on. There, caught in the glare of the torch beam, was... a large owl. A large owl with a mouse in its talons. Ben switched off the flashlight, looked at Susan and they both burst into fits of laughter.

It explained everything. The ducting system also housed the electricity cables, cables which the mice must have chewed through to cause the power failure. Mice are the favourite prey of owls and at least one intrepid owl had found its way to a plentiful supply of food.

It was 6-00 a.m. Time to go home. The first of the day staff were arriving as Susan and Ben made their way to the main gate. He reported what had happened, including the reason for the power failure, before making his way to the car park. A can of Carlsberg and a football match beckoned.

8

FRIDAY MORNING MEETING

'Good morning ladies and gentlemen. Welcome to the first Friday morning meeting of November,' said Professor Charles DeLacy, 'and a special welcome to our new recruit, Dr Sheila Wetherall.' Every set of eyes in the large conference room behind the four top secret laboratories turned to look at the newcomer. Sheila's young face flushed at the onslaught of staring eyes but she still managed a weak smile and a nod of acknowledgement. Sat in this one room were most of the top brains in the fields of genetics and molecular biology. A mixture of young, and not so young, scientists garnered from every corner of the UK. Top scientists undertaking top secret, cutting edge research. Top scientists sworn to the utmost secrecy. And the manager, or more accurately, leader, of this highly talented group of individuals, was Professor Charles DeLacy.

Charles DeLacy was a tall, well built man. Now, in his mid-fifties, his grey-white hair gave him a distinguished look, like that of a senior politician or diplomat. And, in many respects, that's what his current job entailed. To ensure that these talented, strong-willed individuals worked as a team, smoothing out any disagreements and massaging wounded egos. As a product of Eton and Oxford University, and coming from a wealthy family, Charles DeLacy could be perceived as the epitome of the 'silver spoon' brigade. He wasn't. Yes, he'd had a privileged upbringing. And yes, he spoke with a posh accent. But Charles DeLacy was anything but a snob and an aristocrat. He was fully aware of the advantageous start that life had bestowed upon him, but he'd put it to good use through sheer hard work and endeavour. He believed fervently that people should attain recognition from what they did, not who they were, and he embodied this mantra in bucket loads. After graduating with a first class honours degree in biology, he did his doctorate in the emerging field of genetics and went on to do pioneering research in both genetics and molecular biology. Charles DeLacy was also a fair man. A man of integrity. And these attributes, allied to his 'managerial' skills, had made him the obvious choice to head up the hugely important, high powered research group.

'Before we get down to the business of reviewing the week's results, I'd like Adam to give Sheila a brief overview of what we do here. Adam.'

As Charles DeLacy sat down, Dr Adam Kavanagh arose from his chair and strode to the front of the room. As one of the brightest young molecular biologists the UK had ever produced, Adam had been head-hunted. Although the salary he'd been offered was generous in the extreme, it was the challenge of the research that lured him into his current job. He'd obtained his degree in genetics from Manchester University but opted to do his doctorate at Harvard in the USA. After completing his PhD, he'd stayed in the USA and quickly made a name for himself in molecular biology. And it was from the USA that he'd been recruited.

'Thanks, Charles,' he began. 'I don't know how much you know about cloning,' he said, looking at Sheila, 'but that's what we're about. Cloning of animals and, er, humans.'

'But I thought that was illegal. The cloning of humans, I mean,' said Sheila.

'It is,' replied Adam. 'That's why this research is top secret.'

'Human cloning is the creation of a genetically identical copy of an existing or previously existing human,' continued Adam, 'and, as you are probably aware, there are three kinds of human cloning.

'*Therapeutic cloning* involves the cloning of adult cells for use in medicine. This is where most of the mainstream cloning work is focused: using stem cells to grow human organs such as kidneys and livers to replace diseased ones. It's an area we are active in ourselves, but it's not the main focus of our research.

'*Reproductive cloning* involves making cloned humans. The technique is similar to that used to create *Dolly the sheep*. You remember *Dolly the sheep* don't you?' he asked.

'Of course I do,' replied Sheila, indignant at his patronising question. 'I'm a molecular biologist for Christ's sake.'

Adam continued, either unaware of Sheila's indignation or choosing to ignore it. 'DNA from the human to be cloned is inserted into an egg whose DNA has been removed. The egg may be a human egg, or it may be that of an animal such as a pig or a cow. The technique has been proven many times but most embryos are destroyed within 14 days.'

'Is that because a normal human embryo only implants itself in the womb at 14 days?' asked Sheila.

'That's correct,' replied Adam, impressed by Sheila's perceptiveness. 'It's done to get around the law because the embryo cannot be considered to be a "person" before 14 days.'

Adam took a sip of water before continuing. 'A major drawback for reproductive cloning is the length of time it takes. The cloned embryo has to be implanted in a woman's womb and gestated for nine months, just like that for a normal baby. And then, if what you want is a cloned adult, you have to wait another two decades.'

'And there are other problems too, apart from the long timescale,' interjected Professor Stuart Ramage, an expert molecular biologist and Adam's boss. 'The success rate of reproductive cloning is very poor. About one to two per cent. Furthermore, of those clones that do survive, many die prematurely from infection or other complications. Indeed, *Dolly the sheep* only lived for six years. So, as you can see, reproductive cloning is beset with many disadvantages. However, work on reproductive cloning done here some time ago dramatically improved the success rate, but that was before my time.'

'Perhaps it's just as well the success rate is low,' said Sheila. 'I don't think it's a good thing to do anyway.'

This unexpected remark caused the rest of the people in the room to exchange glances before Charles nodded to Adam to continue.

'The third, and newest method of human cloning, is *replacement cloning*. Replacement cloning is effectively a combination of therapeutic cloning and reproductive cloning. It entails the replacement of an extensively damaged, failing or failed body through cloning followed by whole or partial brain transplants. In theory, it allows the cloning of an *adult* human. That's why it's so attractive to us. And why, therefore, replacement cloning is the focus of our work here.'

'It's very interesting,' said Sheila, 'but I'm not sure it's ethical.'

'We'll leave that debate for the future,' said Charles, perceiving Sheila's antagonism towards human cloning. He'd perhaps been somewhat economical with the truth when recruiting her, but he hadn't lied. To avoid any public arguments on Sheila's first day he decided to end the introduction. 'Thanks, Adam. That was a good introduction. I should add that we also do some work on animals too, but we'll leave that for now. Right, the induction period's over. Let's get down to business. Stuart, can you update us on your work?'

As Professor Stuart Ramage rose to his feet, Sheila shifted uncomfortably in her chair.

9

THE STRANGER

It wasn't Scott! The man she'd flung her arms around so eagerly wasn't Scott, it was the stranger. The stranger in the Scream mask. Damn that bitch Kimberly. She'd tricked her again. 'Still,' thought Tammy, 'at least I'll get some sex.' Recovering her composure, Tammy asked the stranger if he'd mind removing his mask.

'Why? Does it bother you?' he replied.

'Well, no. Not really. But I'd like to see your face if we're going to have sex.'

'In that case, your wish is my command,' said the stranger, removing the mask.

Tammy was shocked. Not by his looks, but by his age. She'd assumed that he was a similar age to the rest of them, not someone in their mid-thirties. Why was someone of his age at a teenagers' Halloween party in Boston? It was weird. 'Well,' she thought, looking on the bright side, 'I've never had sex with an older man. Maybe he can teach me some new tricks.'

Grabbing him around his neck, she pulled his face towards hers and kissed him passionately on the mouth, just as she had with Scott earlier in the evening. The stranger responded by gripping her buttocks and pulling her towards him. Tammy could feel his erect, expectant penis pressing against her groin and instinctively slid her hand to the bulge in his trousers to unzip his flies. 'Here, let me do that,' said the stranger, removing Tammy's hand.

Tammy followed suit by unzipping her skirt and letting it fall to the floor.

The stranger smiled when he saw she was wearing nylon stockings.

10

DISCOVERY

'Come on, Kathy,' Tim said, tightening his grip on his girlfriend's hand. 'Let's go for it. This fog's a *pea-souper* and there's lots of dark alleyways.'

It was 1-00 a.m. in the early hours of 1 November and both Tim and Kathy were in high spirits after leaving the Halloween party. Even at that time, the main road through the Whitechapel district of London's East End was still busy with traffic. Black cabs ferrying party-goers from one location to another and private cars taking people home after their night out at the cinema, theatre or restaurant. And there were still a number of people like themselves using the oldest form of transport, Shank's pony.

'I don't know, Tim,' replied Kathy. 'It's cold and damp and people might see us. And we've never done it outside before.'

Tim's immediate reaction was to say that the fact they might be discovered added to the thrill, but he thought better of it. Instead, he played the sympathy card. Letting her see that he was very disappointed, he said, 'Okay, Kathy. If that's how you feel. But I'd have really liked to give it a try. For both of us.'

The disappointment in his voice plus his dejected demeanour tugged at Kathy's heart strings. They'd been going out together for over two years now and in all that time he'd never made any unreasonable demands. And they'd made love many times, but never *alfresco*.

'Well, Tim, if you really want to…'

'I do, Kathy. I really do want to.'

'Okay, then,' she replied, 'but only if we can find a secluded alleyway.'

They strolled down the busy road checking the suitability of side streets and alleyways. After about 250 yards, Tim tugged Kathy's hand. 'Look, this one seems ideal,' he said, pointing to a narrow alleyway on their left. And it did indeed seem ideal. It was narrow, badly lit and seemed devoid of shops and cafes. In short, it was a place where not many people would venture, especially at night.

'It looks a bit spooky to me,' Kathy said, 'especially in this fog.'

'But it's dark and quiet and nobody will see us,' said Tim, excitedly.

'I suppose so,' said Kathy, somewhat hesitantly.

Tim had already made up his mind and turned towards the dark, foggy alleyway with a reluctant Kathy in tow.

'We won't have to go far before we're out of sight of the main road,' he said, turning round to face Kathy as they walked away from the main road. Suddenly, Kathy stopped dead in her tracks. Her face was a mask of horror. She screamed so loud that Tim almost fell.

'Who found the body?' asked Detective Inspector (DI) George Roberts to the uniformed officer standing at the crime scene.

'A young couple, sir. They rang 999 at…' he checked his notebook, 'at 1-10 a.m.'

'Has anything been disturbed or moved?'

'Not to my knowledge, sir.'

As he approached the body, he caught a glimpse of something in the corner of his eye. Something faint at the foot of the wall. He walked slowly towards what he'd seen. There, by his feet, was… he wasn't sure what it was. The light was too dim.

'Ian, come over here and shine your torch on this… this…' Lost for the right word, he just pointed to the small mound at his feet.

Illuminated in the beam of light was a small pile of vomit. Human vomit by the look of it.

'Is this related to the crime?'

'No, sir,' replied the uniformed officer. 'It's from the girl. She threw up at the sight of the body.'

'I'm not bloody surprised,' growled Detective Sergeant (DS) Ian Ferguson. 'It's bloody gruesome.'

And it was. The young woman's body had been horribly mutilated. She was lying, almost naked, on her back with her head resting against the wall. Her legs were spread apart and bent at the knees in the typical posture of a woman about to have sex in the missionary position. Her throat had been slashed several times, resulting in deep cuts that almost certainly proved fatal. Her abdomen had been cut wide open causing part of her intestines to hang out. And her liver had been removed.

The killer had also mutilated her genitals and inserted a blunt object in what was left of her vagina. And, finally, he had disfigured her face.

'What a bloody mess,' said DS Ian Ferguson. 'What an absolute bloody mess. The killer must be a fucking madman. An insane, depraved fucking lunatic.'

'It's not a pretty sight, is it,' said George Roberts. 'It's not pretty at all.'

'Do we know who she is?' he asked the uniformed officer.

'No, sir. Not yet. We think she might have been a prostitute. We're making enquiries.'

Back at the office, DI George Roberts and his team reviewed the evidence they'd managed to accumulate.

'The woman,' said DS Ian Ferguson, 'has been identified as Carly Jones, a 28-year-old prostitute. According to the local ladies of the night, in her younger days Carly had been in great demand and worked in the higher class areas of London. However, age had taken its toll and she was forced to look for business in the seedier parts of London, her latest haunts being the back streets and alleyways of the East End. Apparently, the alleyway where she was found was her "spot".'

'Is that all we've got to identify her?' said George, looking bewildered. 'The fact that she was found in a particular spot.'

'No, sir. There's more,' continued the DS. 'Carly always liked to wear black fishnet stockings, if she could afford them, and she always carried the same handbag. A black leather Fiorelli. Also, she always used a specific type of condom, Durex extra strong, to minimise the risk of disease, or pregnancy. Two such packets were found in her Fiorelli handbag. And, although her body was badly mutilated, the girls who identified it said it was the right size, and age, for Carly Jones, and that what remained of the face looked like Carly's. But the clincher was the tattoos. She had a butterfly tattooed on each buttock. The other girls said it was so she could pretend the butterflies were fluttering whilst she was having sex.'

'Well,' said George with a wry smile, 'I've heard of butterflies in the stomach but never of butterflies on the buttocks.'

'Sir,' said Detective Constable (DC) Betty Forbes, 'I've been doing some research on the internet and…'

'I know what you're going to say, Betty,' interjected George. 'That the murder bears all the hallmarks of a Jack the Ripper murder, including the location. Am I right?'

'Yes, sir. You are.'

'Don't look so shocked, Betty. The same idea occurred to me. I'm sorry for interrupting. Please continue.'

'Well, sir…'

'You don't have to keep calling me sir, Betty. George will do fine.'

'Well, er, George, Jack the Ripper targeted prostitutes in the slum areas of London's East End, particularly the Whitechapel district, and he had a distinctive *Modus Operandi*. He slit their throats, mutilated their abdomens and genitals, and sometimes their faces, and left them lying on the ground in provocative sexual poses. And that's precisely what happened to Carly Jones.'

George had discovered exactly the same information himself but he commended Betty nonetheless. 'Good work, Betty. Well done.' The look of satisfaction on her face made him glad he'd paid the compliment. He looked around the room before addressing his next remark.

'Do you think this is a one-off copycat murder, or is Carly Jones the first victim of a serial killer? A modern day Jack the Ripper.'

No one uttered a word.

11

LABORATORY 2

Back in Laboratory 2 Adam and Sheila sipped their cups of coffee. They were sat in Adam's office awaiting the arrival of Sheila's boss, Professor Angela Thomson. As the head of Laboratory 1, she, along with the heads of Laboratories 2,3 and 4, had stayed behind after the meeting to discuss future strategy with Charles DeLacy.

Dr Sheila Wetherall had been selected from a shortlist of impressive candidates as the ideal person to bolster the expanding research on replacement cloning, research that was done in Laboratories 1 and 2. The 26-year-old Cumbrian had graduated with a first class honours degree in genetics at St Andrews and then gone on to do a PhD in molecular biology at the same university, a PhD that was widely acclaimed as one of the finest pieces of research to have been done in that subject. Not surprisingly, Sheila had been snapped up by an international pharmaceutical company but, like Adam before her, had succumbed to the lure of the Cryonics Facility. Charles DeLacy was a good persuader. And so, after just two short years at the pharmaceutical company, she found herself under the bowels of Snowdonia in her new job.

Sheila had been recruited because of her up-to-date expertise in molecular biology, particularly the advances she had made in the cloning and growth of human brain tissue. The cloning of a complete human brain from the DNA of other people, including dead people, was a vital part of the Cryonics Facility's work.

'I've not been recruited under false pretences have I, Adam?' she asked the man sat opposite her.

'What do you mean, Sheila?'

'Well, I was given a glowing account of the type of research being done here by Charles and the benefits to the human race if it was successful. But in the meeting this morning I felt distinctly uncomfortable when you talked about the cloning of complete humans. Not only is it illegal, it's also unethical.'

'Ah, that,' said Adam. 'Surely you don't believe all the hype from the media about human cloning, do you?'

'It depends what kind of hype you mean,' responded Sheila warily.

'Well, that cloned humans wouldn't be "real" humans possessing personalities, emotions and feelings, just some kind of evil, soulless monsters. Frankensteins.'

'No. Of course I don't believe that,' retorted Sheila indignantly. 'I'm a scientist not an easily led member of the general public.'

'Good,' said Adam, 'because it's complete and utter rubbish. A cloned human will be exactly the same as any other human. What most people don't realise is that the cloning of humans happens completely naturally about 4,000 times every single day. Each day around the world about 4,000 identical twins are born. Every single day. And each twin is a perfect clone of the other. I don't see any media furore about that,' said Adam. 'All we're trying to do here is replicate nature's own cloning.'

'I have no argument with any of that,' said Sheila calmly.

'Furthermore,' continued Adam, 'a clone who is a copy of someone else will not be exactly the same, a carbon copy of that person. Cloning cannot re-create what we've assimilated from the environment, neither can it re-create memories. Memory is not transferable, even if two people have the same genetic code. Identical twins are a perfect example that people with an identical genetic code are not mentally linked and do not share memories.'

'Adam,' said Sheila somewhat resignedly, 'get off your high horse. I'm fully aware of all that you've just said and I have no objections to any of it.'

'Then what do you object to, Sheila,' said Adam, getting a little irritated.

'My main objection,' said Sheila in a measured way, 'is not cloning itself but the problems in reaching that stage.'

Adam looked puzzled. 'I don't understand. What do you mean?'

'As Professor Ramage said at the meeting, the success rate of reproductive cloning is abysmally low. One or two per cent. And of those few embryos that do survive, many die whilst others suffer from, er, terrible defects. That's bad enough for animals, but for humans, well... it's totally unacceptable.'

'But all new research carries risks, Sheila, we all know that. And you can't make progress without, er...' The word he was searching for eluded him, but what he meant was casualties.

'Factors such as intellect and mood may not be important for a mouse or a sheep, Adam, but they're vitally important for a human, and we have no idea how cloning affects such things. With so many unknowns concerning human cloning, I just think the attempt to clone humans with our current state of knowledge is dangerous and ethically irresponsible.'

'I hear what you're saying, Sheila, but I reiterate what I said before. You can't make an omelette without breaking eggs. Anyway, think of all the positives. The ability to clone eyes to enable the blind to see, the ability to clone a pancreas to cure diabetes, the ability to clone the brain of a person destined to be a "vegetable" for the rest of their lives, the ability to clone new limbs for people born with deformities and new arms and legs for those damaged beyond repair, even the ability to clone a child killed in tragic circumstances.'

The discussion continued for a further 20 minutes and ended with the two protagonists agreeing to disagree.

A knock on the door interrupted proceedings. It was Professor Angela Thomson, the head of Laboratory 1 and Sheila's new boss.

'I'm not interrupting, am I?' said Angela with a beaming smile as she entered the small office.

'No, no,' replied Adam and Sheila simultaneously. 'We've been discussing replacement cloning.'

'Glad to hear it,' said Angela. 'If you'll follow me to Laboratory 1, Sheila, I'll tell you about our work on therapeutic cloning.'

As they closed the door behind them, Adam reflected on the discussion he'd just had with Sheila. 'Thank God she doesn't know about the early work on reproductive cloning,' he thought. She would have hit the ceiling.

12

BOSTON, 1 NOVEMBER

Captain Bud Eichenhoff addressed the small gathering. His face was grim. 'I've invited Nancy to give us a short resume on the Boston Strangler. His choice of victims, his locations and his method of operation. His *Modus Operandi*. For those of you who don't know, Nancy is a professor of Criminology at the Massachusetts Institute of Technology (MIT). Nancy, the floor is all yours.'

'Between 14 June 1962 and 4 January 1964 the Boston Strangler is believed to have murdered 13 women,' said Nancy. 'He committed the murders in two stages. The first stage of murders occurred between June and August 1962. In those three months, he killed six elderly women aged between 55 and 85. The second stage of murders took place over a longer period, from 5 December 1962 to 4 January 1964. This time, his victims were five young women aged between 19 and 23, and two older women aged 58 and 69.

'All the women were single and lived alone, usually in apartments. Most of the women were sexually molested and some were sexually assaulted.'

'Excuse my ignorance,' interrupted Sergeant Larry McVeigh, 'but what exactly is the difference between being sexually molested and sexually assaulted?'

'The difference,' replied Nancy, 'is that sexual assault involves the act of penetration. In other words, sexual intercourse has taken place. In the case of sexual molestation, no penetration of the victim takes place.'

'Thanks,' said Larry.

Continuing, Nancy said, 'Nearly all the women were strangled, most of them with their own nylon stockings. And in every case, there was no sign of any forced entry into their dwellings. This led the police to believe that the women either knew their assailant or that they voluntarily let them into their homes, believing them to be an apartment maintenance man, delivery man or some other service man.

'On 27 October 1964 a stranger entered a young woman's home posing as a detective. After tying his victim to her bed, he proceeded to sexually assault her. Suddenly, without any warning, he left, saying "I'm sorry" as he went. The woman's description led the police to identify the assailant as Albert DeSalvo and when his photograph was published, many other women identified him as the man who had assaulted them. Later, he confessed to the murders. Despite some inconsistencies, he was tried, convicted and sentenced to life imprisonment in 1967.

'And that, in a nutshell,' concluded Nancy, 'is the story of the Boston Strangler.'

'Thanks for that,' said Bud, nodding his approval at Nancy. 'It was a good, concise account.'

'Wow, it's almost a perfect replica,' exclaimed Larry. 'The murder took place in Boston, the murderer was invited into the house and the girl was sexually assaulted,' he said, emphasising the word *assaulted*, 'before being strangled with her own nylon stockings. It's uncanny.'

'Who found the body?' asked Bud.

'Lisa, the girl who lived at the house and who threw the Halloween party,' Larry replied. 'As the party came to a close and the guests began to leave, she became concerned about Tammy. She'd simply disappeared. The stranger in the Scream mask had left, and so had most of the other guests, when Lisa and Scott began a systematic search of the house. They started upstairs and worked their way down, eventually going into the basement, where they found Tammy's body. She'd been strangled with her own nylon stockings.'

'Anything else?' enquired Bud.

'Yeah. She was naked from the waist down and had obviously had sex because of the traces of semen around her vagina. It's been sent off for analysis and we're expecting the results anytime now.'

At that very moment the door burst open and an excited young forensic scientist rushed into the room. He was still wearing his white lab coat.

'You'll never bloody believe this,' he blurted out, 'but the DNA is a perfect match to that of the real Boston Strangler, Albert DeSalvo!'

Everyone in the room fell silent. You could have heard a pin drop.

'It can't be,' said Bud Eichenhoff breaking the silence. 'Albert DeSalvo was stabbed to death in the infirmary of the maximum security Walpole State Prison in 1973.'

13

COBRA

'I apologise for the short notice,' said the Home Secretary, 'but I've convened this meeting of Cobra in response to the latest events; the murder committed by Jack the Ripper and that by the Boston Strangler. Our counterparts in COBRA in the USA are meeting at this very moment on the same topic.'

Sat in the room in Downing Street with the Home Secretary were some of the most powerful and influential people in the UK. The heads of both MI5 and MI6, the Chief of the Defence Staff, the professional head of the British Armed Forces, the Metropolitan Commissioner of Police, the Chief Scientific Advisor to the government and last, but by no means least, Professor Charles DeLacy.

Contrary to popular belief, the acronym Cobra has a mundane and, if the truth be told, disappointing meaning. Quite simply, Cobra stands for *C*abinet *o*ffice *br*iefing *a*rea, the Cabinet office buildings within Downing Street where the meetings are held. The USA equivalent has quite a different meaning. Based at Fort McClellan Army Base in Anniston, Alabama, the American COBRA stands for *C*hemical, *O*rdinance, *B*iological and *RA*diological warfare, an altogether more apt acronym.

'Ladies and gentlemen,' continued the Home Secretary, 'the murder of a British citizen on British soil by one of your, what shall I say, experimental clones, is a most serious matter. I know I gave my permission for the experiment to go ahead, and I know you will say that a positive outcome has been achieved, but nonetheless, an innocent life has been lost. We need to consider our next move in this matter, and quickly. We don't want the media whipping up a Jack the Ripper frenzy.'

She scanned the faces in the room before continuing. 'Charles, the clone was, er, how shall I put it, *assembled* in your Cryonics Facility. What do you think?'

Charles thought carefully before he answered. He didn't want to jeopardise the work being done at the Cryonics Facility. Important work he felt should continue.

'Well,' he began, playing for thinking time, 'it's a delicate situation. As you are all aware, we took the decision to begin our research on replacement cloning with murderers and serial killers. We deemed such people more expendable than scientists and world leaders. Eventually, after several (he didn't want to reveal the true number) failed attempts, our research produced a viable clone. A clone of one of the most infamous serial killers of all time. Jack the Ripper. A clone that we all agreed had to be released into the real world to see if he would replicate Jack the Ripper's traits. We knew the risks and…'

'Pardon me for interrupting, Charles,' said the Chief Scientific Advisor, 'but I missed the last meeting. How can you have cloned Jack the Ripper when, as far as I am aware, his identity was never discovered?'

Charles was taken aback. He knew the answer but he looked around the room to see if someone else would answer the question. There were no volunteers.

'There were four prime suspects for Jack the Ripper,' he continued, reluctantly. 'Kosminski, a poor Polish Jew who lived in

Whitechapel where the murders were committed. Montague John Druitt, a 31-year-old barrister and school teacher who committed suicide in December 1888. Michael Ostrog, a Russian-born thief and confidence trickster, believed to be 55 years old in 1888 and detained in asylums on several occasions. And finally, Dr Francis J Tumblety, a 56-year-old American "quack" doctor, who was arrested in November 1888 for offences of gross indecency. He fled the country later that same month, having obtained bail at a very high price.

'The authorities knew which one was Jack the Ripper because a prostitute witnessed one of the murders and got a good look at the murderer. At Jack the Ripper. She told the police what she'd seen and, after viewing photographs of potential suspects, identified the murderer. Identified Jack the Ripper.'

'Then why wasn't he apprehended and charged?' asked the Chief Scientific Officer, astounded at this new revelation.

'Because at the time it was considered that revealing his identity was not in the public interest.'

'Not in the public interest,' spat the Chief Scientific Officer. 'Not in the bloody public interest! How can it not be in the public interest when he'd butchered several innocent women?'

'I think he had connections to some powerful, and wealthy, individuals,' intervened the Home Secretary, trying to calm the situation, 'and revealing his identity could have created an international incident.'

'There was a cover up, then,' said the Chief of the Defence Staff.

'I suppose you could put it that way,' replied the Home Secretary, looking distinctly uncomfortable at the way the discussion was going.

'Anyway,' said Charles, 'Jack the Ripper was…'

The red emergency phone rang.

'Excuse me,' said the Home Secretary picking up the receiver. 'It must be urgent.'

She listened in silence to the short message, said, 'Thank you,' then put the receiver down. Her face was stern. 'He's killed again. Jack the Ripper has butchered another woman.'

14

LABORATORY 1

In Angela's office in Laboratory 1 Sheila sipped her second cup of coffee of the morning.

Angela Thomson was surprisingly young for a professor. Barely into her thirties, her round, pleasant face, blue eyes and short, blond hair gave her the appearance of a cheeky Tomboy. She'd studied biology for her degree at Nottingham University and did her PhD on the workings of the human brain under the tutelage of Professor Susan Greenfield at Oxford. Her radical ideas impressed many, including Professor Charles DeLacy, who'd managed to tempt her away from academia to the Cryonics Facility.

'May I ask a naïve question?'

'Go ahead,' said Angela. 'I've asked many myself.'

'Why is the therapeutic cloning work done in secret? It's not illegal.'

'Good question,' replied Angela. 'It's one we've agonised over ourselves. You're quite right, therapeutic cloning isn't illegal, but most of our therapeutic cloning work is done to augment the replacement cloning work. And that is illegal. However, we've reached a compromise. We feel it is grossly unfair, indeed unethical, not to share some of our successes with the wider medical community. Therefore, we disseminate some of our findings to the public domain by publishing papers and by giving lectures at conferences. In this way, the general public also benefits from our work. After all, they're the ones who pay for it.'

'Glad to hear it,' said Sheila, feeling she hadn't been recruited under false pretences after all. 'Can you tell me about some of the work you've done on therapeutic cloning, Angela. It's okay if I call you Angela, isn't it?'

'Of course it is, Sheila. There are no airs and graces in Laboratory 1. Anyway, going back to your original question, some of the work on therapeutic cloning was done before I arrived, but I'll do my best to fill you in.

'Research into cloning has been going on for decades. It came to the fore in 1996 with the birth of *Dolly the sheep*. That success started an upsurge in activity, including a decision to begin the construction of this Cryonics Facility. The government realised that other countries, countries which had no compunction about the ethical issues of cloning, including human cloning, were forging ahead and that we, as a country, needed to keep ahead of the game. We couldn't afford to let other countries, potentially hostile countries I might add, to steal a march in such an important field.'

'Excuse me for interrupting,' said Sheila, 'but exactly which countries are we talking about?'

'I should have thought that would have been obvious,' replied Angela, unsure if Sheila was just probing or really didn't know. 'They're the countries with the aspiration, and the ability, to become dominant world leaders, and the countries which show no concern for human rights.'

'Countries like China and North Korea then,' said Sheila, thoughtfully.

'Correct,' said Angela. 'There are others too but they're the main two.'

Carrying on, Angela explained how the early work had focused on those organs that could already be replaced, organs like kidneys, livers, hearts and lungs. They'd also looked at the pancreas and intestines too, since people died from diabetes and bowel cancer. 'And,' she said, with a hint of satisfaction in her voice, 'now, we can reliably clone all these organs on a routine basis with almost a 100 per cent success rate. In fact, it's so routine that most of the work is carried out in the main laboratory.'

'Impressive,' said Sheila. 'What did you do next?'

'Having sorted out the key human organs, the next step was to sort out the human face. To clone eyes, ears, noses, mouths, skin and even hair. And, I'm pleased to say that this work is also nearly complete.

'Now, nearly all our research is focused on cloning that most complex of organs, the human brain.'

'And that's why I've been recruited,' said Sheila. 'For my work on human brains.'

'Got it in one,' replied Angela. 'Charles moved heaven and earth to recruit you.'

'That's been very interesting, Angela,' said Sheila, 'but I have a question. Why are you cloning the human face?'

For the first time Angela looked uneasy. 'As I said before, most of our work is done in conjunction with the replacement cloning work. The majority of bodies stored in the pods are devoid of brains, and some are headless. The heads, and brains, are stored separately. Most of the replacement clones don't need to *look* like the person whose brain has been cloned, just to *behave* like them. However, in some cases, it is essential that the clone is identical in every respect to the original person. In such cases, we have to clone the facial features as well as the brain.'

'Mm,' said Sheila reflectively. 'The more you tell me the more questions I have.'

'Fire away,' said Angela, 'I'll answer what I can.'

'Well,' said Sheila, drawing out the word, 'how do you, er, connect the cloned head with the body?'

'That's been the second most difficult task we've faced,' replied Angela. 'It's taken the finest brains the world's ever produced, plus the skills of top neurosurgeons, to achieve that.'

'You mean… you've already done it?' gasped Sheila, dumbfounded.

'Yes. Several times,' replied Angela.

Recovering her composure, Sheila said, 'Once the heads have been sewn on… I mean connected, is the, er, clone alive?'

'No,' said Angela. 'At that stage, the clone isn't alive. It has to be stimulated with sophisticated electrical impulses and drugs.'

'A bit like the lightning bolt in the old Frankenstein movies,' said Sheila, smiling.

'It's a lot more complicated than that, but the principle's the same.'

'Good God. The advances you've made are unbelievable.'

'We like to think of them as outstanding,' smiled Angela. 'They're not unbelievable, they've been accomplished.'

'You said that bringing the clone to life was the second most difficult thing you've done. What on earth is more difficult than that!'

'The ability to clone a dead person, in some cases a person who's been dead for a long time, just from their DNA.'

Sheila's mouth fell open. She was speechless.

'But,' she said after a pause, 'to clone a dead person you need to take some of their cells before they die, and then keep them alive in a special culture.'

'Not any more. Our scientists have found a way to clone dead people from their DNA.'

'It's… it's incredible,' whispered Sheila, clearly dumbstruck at what she'd just heard. 'It's like science fiction.'

'It's science fact now,' said Angela.

'One final question. You said the success rate of cloning human organs was practically 100 per cent. Is the success rate the same for replacement cloning?'

For the second time that morning, Angela felt distinctly uncomfortable. She hesitated before answering.

'Er, I'm afraid it's not quite that high,' she said.

'How high?' said Sheila, more abruptly than she intended.

'About 25 per cent, I think,' replied Angela, 'but we're close to getting it up to 50 per cent.'

'Just one in four,' said Sheila, almost to herself. 'And what happens to the clones that aren't a success?' she asked.

'I'm afraid you'll have to ask Adam about that,' said Angela, avoiding Sheila's steely glare. 'Or his boss, Professor Stuart Ramage.'

'I will,' said Sheila. 'I most certainly will.'

She didn't ask what went on in Laboratories 3 and 4.

15

TERMINATION

The November rain lashed against the windowpane with such ferocity that he could barely hear what Rebecca was saying. All he could discern was the end of her sentence, '… and it's imperative we don't lose track of him again, especially in this weather.' Alan nodded his assent before taking another sip of coffee. It had gone cold, just like the first cup over an hour ago. Starbucks was never the hottest coffee in town and they'd been sat at the window table for over two hours now. He watched the rivulets of water snake their way down the window, illuminated with red and white light from the passing traffic. And he watched the figure in the café across the road, a cheap 'greasy spoon' café. The figure who was eating a greasy meal of egg and chips. The figure they'd had under surveillance since lunch time. The figure who was their target.

Normally, Alan Standish received his assignments from his Section Head. But not this time. This time, the code red phone call had come from the very top. From the Head of MI5 himself. 'It was,' said the Head, 'a matter of national security.' He'd told him that a target, known only as C41, had to be terminated. Terminated that very evening. It was an assignment of the utmost importance. The termination was to be carried out away from any crowds and it was vital, absolutely vital, there were no witnesses. Not a single person must witness the termination. Once the termination had been completed, a clean-up team would be despatched immediately to remove the body. To make the job easier, the target had been electronically tagged and the Head of MI5 had activated Alan's Global Positioning Satellite (GPS) tracking device with its signal. Since that call, he and Rebecca had been tailing their target for six hours.

Alan Standish had followed in both his father's and grandfather's footsteps by serving in the SAS. The grandson of Captain Johnnie Standish, who'd served with distinction in World War II, Alan Standish had played a key role in Afghanistan, targeting Taliban movements and positions. On his fortieth birthday, he'd retired from the SAS and joined MI5. Joined the Military Intelligence service to protect his homeland. And that's how he found himself in London on a wet and windy November evening carrying out a high priority assignment with his colleague, Rebecca Worthington.

Rebecca Worthington was younger than Alan. Ten years younger to be precise. Ever since childhood Rebecca had yearned to be a 'spook'. To be a field operative for MI5. She'd always been a bit of a Tomboy, a daredevil. It was in her blood and she needed a job to give her the excitement she craved. A job with a sense of danger. A job with intrigue and mystery. A field operative for MI5 fitted the bill perfectly.

The early part of the day had been dry. Dry but overcast. A typical dreary November day. They were having a light lunch of sandwiches and coke by the lake in St James Park when Alan received the code red phone call. It was a lunch they finished on the hoof. His GPS tracking device showed the target was crossing Westminster Bridge, about a quarter-of-a-mile away and they had to get there. Quick. By the time they'd reached the bridge, the target had descended the steps and was walking with the crowd towards the London Eye. There, he bought a hot dog and ate it sat on a bench beside the River Thames in the Jubilee Gardens.

His attire surprised them. Dressed in a long, black cape, top hat and carrying a black leather bag, he looked like a throwback from the Victorian age. A Victorian doctor, or undertaker. Maybe that was why he mingled with the crowds, to remain 'invisible'. Still, mused Alan, London is full of weird and wonderful people. Perhaps he was just a harmless eccentric. He corrected himself immediately. Of course he wasn't harmless, he posed a threat to national security and had to be terminated.

After finishing his hot dog, the target walked across the Millenium Bridge and continued on to Trafalgar Square, where he paused to feed the pigeons. Initially, Alan and Rebecca had kept just out of sight, relying on the tracking device to pinpoint the whereabouts of the target, but it was a ploy that almost backfired. One instant his signal was loud and clear then, in the blink of an eye, it disappeared. Vanished. He must have entered a subway, or underpass. It couldn't have been the underground because, whenever he approached an underground station, they always made sure he was in their sight.

From Trafalgar Square, the target made his way to Covent Garden. He mooched around the stalls and craft shops, stopping for a coffee at a small outside café whilst he watched aspiring artists strut their stuff. Musicians, jugglers, acrobats, singers and dancers all vying for the crowd's attention. His thirst sated, he continued along The Strand, Fleet Street and Ludgate Hill, and then past St Paul's Cathedral into the City of London. As he passed the Mansion House, his pace quickened as he strode purposely along Cornhill and Leadenhall Street to his final destination, Whitechapel.

Nightfall was approaching when the target entered the small café, one of several cheap cafes in the street. The Head of MI5 had informed Alan that the target would make his way to Whitechapel as darkness fell. And it was here, away from the crowds and in the darkness, that the job was to be done.

It was 7-30 p.m. Darkness had descended like a cloak, enveloping the streets with an eerie blackness. It was the target's time. These were his favourite conditions and he was in his favourite location. He got up from the table, paid his bill and walked briskly into the dark street. He had urgent business to attend to.

As he stepped out into the rain from Starbucks, Alan tightened his raincoat and put on his black bob cap. He was sure the rain had increased in intensity. Driven by a gale force wind, it penetrated his coat and hit his face like icy little bullets. He turned around to make sure Rebecca was behind him. It was time to get the job done. To choose the right moment and the right place to terminate the target. He felt the adrenaline course through his body. The excitement of a kill was mounting. He was sure Rebecca felt the same.

As they tailed the target, both he and Rebecca checked their weapons. In the SAS, the handgun of choice was the Browning Parabellum. It was a powerful weapon but too big and heavy for routine use. For jobs like this he used the Swiss made Sig P228, and special bullets. Bullets designed for hostage situations which explode on impact and don't go through the body causing harm to the hostage (or rupturing the fuselage of a plane). He would use the double tap method of the SAS, firing twice in quick succession, and he would aim for the mouth. A shot to the mouth severs the spinal cord and blows away part of the brain, preventing it from sending a 'pull the trigger' signal to the gunman's finger. The technique had served him well in the SAS and he was sure it would serve him well in MI5.

Rebecca had a Smith and Wesson M and P Compact .40. With a barrel length of just 3.5 inches, this American hand gun was light and easy to conceal. It was ideal for jobs such as this.

The streets were deserted. At least the atrocious weather had had one positive effect.

'He's increasing his pace,' said Rebecca, glancing at her tracking device. 'We need to catch up.'

They quickened their pace as they followed their target through the labyrinth of side streets and alleyways of Whitechapel, side streets and alleyways that he seemed to know like the back of his hand. Because the streets were deserted, they'd had to keep well behind their quarry, relying on their tracking device more than they'd intended. Suddenly, the signal disappeared.

'He must have gone in a subway,' said Alan. 'You know the drill. I'll go in from this side while you go around to the far side. That way, we have him covered.'

'Okay,' said Rebecca, sprinting ahead.

Alan descended the steps of the subway cautiously, his Sig P228 held in front of him. At the foot of the steps, the underpass turned sharp right. Slowly, he edged his way to the corner. Taking a deep breath, he leapt into the underpass, adopting the classic stance of a marksman.

Twelve yards ahead of him, the target was bent down, his back towards Alan. He was searching for something in the black leather bag. A woman stood in front of him, blocking Alan's line of sight. The noise of Alan leaping into the subway startled the target. Quick as a flash, he pulled out a large bladed knife from the bag, held it next to the terrified woman's throat and turned around, ensuring he kept the woman between himself and Alan, using her as a human shield.

'No witnesses. There must be no witnesses. Not a single one.' These thoughts flashed into Alan's head in an instant, as did his options. He had three. Let the target kill the woman, then kill him. Kill the target and the woman. Or, disobey orders and kill the target and spare the woman. He squeezed the trigger twice in quick succession.

16

THE NURSERY

As he leafed through the latest research reports from Laboratories 3 and 4, Adam reflected on the phenomenal progress they'd made since the Cryonics Facility opened in 2000. He was one of the select few who'd had the opportunity to work on different topics. And, as a senior member of staff, one of the few who had access to all of the work being done at the Facility.

Research on cloning began in earnest after the success of *Dolly the sheep* in 1996, not just in the UK but around the world. In the early years, the work in the Cryonics Facility focused on reproductive cloning. Countless experiments were performed on cloning embryos of sheep, pigs and cows. Thousands upon thousands. Rethinking, reworking and refining the techniques until the success rate improved from an abysmal 1-2 per cent to a respectable 50 per cent. One in two instead of one in a hundred. Buoyed by such an improvement, a decision was taken. A decision to commence cloning humans. Ideally, they'd have liked a success rate of 100 per cent, but one in two wasn't bad. In fact, it wasn't bad at all considering the starting point. But humans are more complex creatures than sheep, pigs or cows and the success rate plummeted. Plummeted from 50 per cent down to ten per cent.

Just one in ten. It took a further two years of painstakingly hard work and thousands upon thousands of human embryos to get the success rate back up to 50 per cent. Thankfully, most of the embryos were terminated after 14 days. Terminated before they had the chance to resemble anything remotely human. Even so, terminating living, human embryos affected some of the staff, particularly the female staff.

The first humans to be cloned were infamous serial killers such as Jack the Ripper, and fascist dictators such as Hitler. But the research was beset with problems. Although the success rate for the *embryos* was 50 per cent, many of the successful embryos developed into abnormal foetuses; foetuses with physical deformities reminiscent of the thalidomide babies, and foetuses that were just... monstrosities. Many foetuses that appeared normal later developed serious complications. And of the few that survived beyond one year, a large proportion developed fatal illnesses such as cancer and heart failure. But worst of all were those foetuses which survived into childhood and were physically perfect, but developed horrific mental disorders. This proved to be the heart breaker. The straw that broke the camel's back. Terminating embryos or early stage foetuses which bore no resemblance whatsoever to a human being was bearable, but having to terminate the life of a baby, and, even worse, that of a child, was heart rending. A child who could speak and laugh, love and play. A child with which the staff had formed a bond. A child who trusted them. Having to terminate such an innocent life was unbearable. To some, it was like putting down your own child. Having them 'euthanised' and then having their little bodies incinerated in a white hot furnace. Burnt at a temperature that vaporised every bit of their tiny bodies to atoms, leaving nothing at all behind, not even some ashes to remember them by. It was as if they'd never existed.

In the end, terminating tiny children became too much for some of the staff, particularly young mothers. They threatened to resign and blow the whistle on what was happening. This created a dilemma. A serious dilemma. Such a disclosure could not be allowed. The research was too important to be stopped.

After all the pleas and managerial reassurances failed to change their mind and the first woman said she was going to 'spill the beans' to the media, she was mysteriously hit by a car and killed. The rest of the potential whistleblowers weren't sure if it really was an accident, or if she too had been terminated. When a similar fate befell a second woman who threatened to blow the whistle, the message was loud and clear. Threaten to expose the research and you too will be terminated.

Following the second fatal 'accident', those staff unhappy with working on reproductive cloning were transferred to other duties and replaced with staff who had no qualms about what they were expected to do. The message had been rammed home. Rammed home hard.

Although not directly involved in the euthanasia of babies and children, Adam was aware that it went on. And it troubled him. Troubled him deeply. Troubled him that such practices went on in 21st century Britain.

What was so important about reproductive cloning that the State was prepared to murder innocent people to keep it secret?

The reproductive cloning research had four important aims, none of which, except perhaps the first one, were legal under British law.

(i) To improve cloning techniques.
(ii) To clone humans.
(iii) To clone twins of, initially, infamous people, serial killers such as Jack the Ripper and fascist dictators such as Hitler, and then to study the traits of nature versus nurture by raising them under totally different conditions; one in a

normal, loving family environment by sending them to be Fostered, and one raised under similar conditions to those of the real person in The Nursery, the complex located behind the Lecture Theatre that mimicked a small village. Would the ones reared in loving Foster homes be normal human beings or would they too turn out to be the same as the real life person? It would reveal the strength of genetics on the nature versus nurture issue.

In addition to serial killers and fascists, famous scientists, world leaders and military figures had also being cloned. In Britain, these included Isaac Newton, Charles Darwin and Winston Churchill. Their American counterparts had cloned the Boston Strangler, Stalin, Albert Einstein, Thomas Edison and Theodore Roosevelt.

(iv) The fourth and final aim was a military one. In fact, there were two aims. One, to produce superior military leaders, and two, to produce the ultimate soldier. Brave, strong, fearless, resourceful and obedient. At the Cryonics Facility the clones for the first aim included Nelson, Wellington and Montgomery, whilst those for the second were classified but taken from soldiers who had served with distinction in the Commandos, the Parachute Regiment, the SBS and the SAS.

Viable clones of all the above figures were alive. Although cloned several years ago, they were still children with ages ranging from five to seven. In Britain, they were being raised in The Nursery. Most of the young clones were allowed to intermingle. Child clones of famous scientists mixing with child clones of famous world leaders, serial killers and fascist dictators. It was an intriguing experiment.

The military clones were housed in their own secure unit. Not that they were deemed too dangerous to mix with the other clones – they could hardly be more dangerous than Jack the Ripper or Hitler – but because they wanted to 'rear' them in a more controlled military environment. An environment to develop their military prowess.

About five years ago, a snippet of Intelligence changed everything. A piece of information from a CIA (Central Intelligence Agency) agent in China. Information that China and North Korea were actively involved in research on the *replacement cloning* of humans. A new but risky technique which removed the need to wait two decades for a cloned adult. A technique which, in theory, yielded an instant, *adult* clone. It was seen as much better, certainly much faster, than reproductive cloning.

Britain and the US had to respond quickly. And they did. Within a matter of weeks, a decision was taken to refocus the work from reproductive cloning to replacement cloning. In effect, they had no choice. They couldn't allow China and North Korea to forge ahead in such an important field.

The work on reproductive cloning was wound down, although the experiments already started were allowed to continue, and the bulk of the research switched to replacement cloning. However, unlike reproductive cloning, replacement cloning requires a constant supply of fresh, frozen bodies. Bodies in their twenties for scientists, since that's the age when most scientists do their best work: bodies in their forties for military leaders, and bodies in their sixties for world leaders. Maintaining such a collection of bodies in China and North Korea might not be a problem, but in the West, it wasn't so easy.

As he reflected on all these issues, Adam searched his conscience for the work he was doing. He always came to the same conclusion. It might be unpleasant, but it was necessary. Necessary because of the work being done in North Korea and China. Britain, and the USA, could not let such countries forge ahead. It could prove disastrous.

17

CLEAN-UP

Rebecca was descending the steps on the far side of the subway when the shots rang out. Two shots fired in quick succession. With her Smith and Wesson cocked and ready to fire, she raced the short distance to the corner and leapt into the subway.

At the far side, two figures lay on the floor. The target and a woman. Alan was walking towards them, his gun still in his hand.

'It's clear,' he shouted. 'The target's down.'

Rebecca ran to where the bodies lay. The target's face, or what was left of it, was a bloodied pulp. It was clinging to his body by a thread. Alan's first shot had hit him in the mouth and his second in his neck. Death would have been instantaneous. The face of the woman was splattered with blood, fragments of brain and pieces of bone. She was in shock. A large bladed knife lay beside the bodies.

'What happened, Alan?' she asked.

'He was going to slit her throat. I had to act fast.'

'What do we do with the woman? You know our orders. No witnesses.'

'I can't kill an innocent bystander in cold blood, Rebecca. And neither can you. Fuck the orders. We'll have to think of something else. Fast.'

'I don't know, Alan. The Head said terminating the target was a matter of national security and he was adamant there should be no witnesses.'

'Rebecca, we are not killing an innocent woman who just happened to be in the wrong place at the wrong time. That's the end of it.'

Rebecca said nothing but looked uneasy. After an uncomfortable pause, she said, 'Okay Alan, but I'm not sure about this. What shall we do?'

'The first thing we need to do is seal off the subway from the general public. We don't want any more witnesses,' said Alan.

'I've already sealed off the far entrance,' said Rebecca. 'I locked the metal gates after I'd entered.'

'Good thinking,' said Alan, 'but we need to seal off the other entrance.'

'I'll go,' said Rebecca, 'while you, er, attend to the woman.'

'Good. Ring the clean-up squad when you reach the entrance.'

'Will do,' said Rebecca, as she ran to the far end and disappeared around the corner. He heard her footsteps as she ran up the steps to the entrance.

He had to act fast. They had just five minutes before the clean-up squad arrived.

His first task was to clean the blood and gore from the woman's face. For that, he needed a source of water. He'd started to unzip his flies before realising that he didn't need to urinate on the woman's face. The driving rain would do a better job. For the second time that evening, the weather had done them a favour.

He withdrew a tablet from the little pill box he always carried in case of emergencies. It was a benzodiazepine, a drug that induced loss of memory. Not a permanent loss, just a loss of recent events. He placed it in the woman's mouth. 'Take this,' he said, 'it'll make you feel better.' Still in a state of shock, the woman complied with his request without complaint or argument.

'Stay here while I fetch my colleague.'

She nodded weakly.

Alan sprinted the short distance to where Rebecca was standing guard at the entrance to the subway. It was still pouring down. 'Have you rung the clean-up squad?' he asked.

'Yes. They'll be here in five minutes.'

'Good. I've administered the drug. Can you go down and bring her out? She'll feel more comfortable in the presence of a woman.'

'No problem,' replied Rebecca, dashing down the steps. Less than a minute later, she was at the entrance with the woman.

'I'll take her a couple of streets away and leave her near a café. And with the help of the rain, I'll clean her up along the way,' said Rebecca, getting her handkerchief from up her sleeve.

'Great,' said Alan, 'but be back here within four minutes. We both need to be present when the clean-up squad arrive. Otherwise, they'll get suspicious.'

'Understood,' said Rebecca, wiping the woman's face with the rain soaked handkerchief as she led her away from the entrance.

Exactly four minutes later, the clean-up van came screeching to a halt beside the entrance. It bore the markings of a council refuse van, and the five men who sprang from it continued the deception.

'The body is in the subway,' said Alan to the man in charge. 'It's a bit of a mess.'

'Not a problem,' replied the man in charge. 'I'm sure we've seen worse.'

'Is it okay if we go now?' asked Alan. 'We've had a long day.'

'Yes. That's fine. We'll take over now.'

Relieved the job was done, Alan and Rebecca walked away into the night. Alan waited until they were out of earshot before asking Rebecca what she'd done with the woman.

'Oh, we bumped into a group of girls out on a "do" about

two streets away,' she replied. 'Probably a hen night or a birthday party. I said I'd found the woman wandering the streets and that she'd just been dumped by her boyfriend and was upset and in a state of shock. I think they took pity on her. Anyway, they said they'd look after her.'

'Good work again,' said Alan, 'and don't worry. Everything will be fine. We're MI5 operatives, not cold blooded killers.'

'You're wrong,' thought Rebecca, 'that's precisely what we are. Cold blooded killers.'

The Head of MI5 was pleased. His two operatives had done a good job. A clean kill in a deserted subway that muffled the gunshots. And no witnesses. The clean-up squad had removed the body and 'cleansed' the crime scene. It was as if nothing had happened. Nothing at all. It couldn't have gone better. He leaned back in his sumptuous leather chair reflecting on a job well done. He even allowed himself the luxury of a smile.

The body of C41 was on its way back to Snowdonia, not to be 're-used', but incinerated. That was the fate that awaited any failed clone. Incineration.

About five to six hours later on the other side of the 'Pond', a similar scenario would be re-enacted in Boston. Two CIA agents would terminate the life of the man in the Scream mask. The Boston Strangler. His body too would be incinerated.

18

C22D

As she was crossing the cavern, Ruth Cunningham suddenly remembered her notes, important notes she needed for her presentation the following morning. 'I'm sorry, Dom,' she said to Professor Dom Cruickshank, her boss and head of Laboratory 3, 'but I've left my notes in the office. You carry on. I'll see you at the meeting tomorrow morning.'

'I'll come with you if you like,' said Dom. 'It's a bit spooky in here by yourself.'

'I'm fine, Dom, really. It'll only take me five minutes. You go ahead.'

'Okay, Ruth. See you tomorrow,' he said, before striding towards the exit.

Ruth turned around and retraced her steps back to Laboratory 3.

The laboratory seemed uncannily still. And quiet. In the daytime, Laboratory 3 was alive with the sound of dogs. The sound of padded paws as they prowled their metal cages, the sound of barking and, worst of all, the sound of whining as the dogs yearned to be set free from their metal prisons.

The stillness unnerved her. Something was wrong. She could sense it. Feel it in her bones. She scanned the laboratory. Nothing.

Perhaps she was imagining it. Perhaps the dogs were asleep. She walked through the lab towards her office, focusing her mind on retrieving the papers, but the feelings wouldn't go away. She felt like she was being watched. Watched and stalked. Stalked by something silent and invisible. Silent, invisible and cunning. On reaching the office door, she turned around. Nothing. Then, just as she was swiping her ID card, it pounced. An attack dog the like of which the world had never seen. A black-brown streak hurtling silently towards her. Twelve stones of muscle and bone attacking its prey. A killing machine that would make straight for her throat and crush it in its powerful jaws. Crush it like an egg. As it launched itself, Ruth just had time to raise her arm. The impact of C22D knocked her to the floor. The pain as its jaws clenched around her forearm was excruciating. She could see the intent in its eyes: to kill its prey. She could also see the saliva dripping from its yellow fangs as it swung its head from side to side, trying to tear her arm from her body. To free the path to its main target. Her throat. The stench of its foul breath was overwhelming as its jaws inched ever closer towards their goal.

'Stop,' she shouted in a desperate attempt to halt the attack. 'Stop! STOP!! **STOP!!!**' she screamed. It made no difference. The dog continued its ferocious attack.

The pain was becoming unbearable. Blood spurted everywhere, like a red fountain, drenching both herself and the dog. The loss of blood weakened her. She began to lose consciousness. To drift towards a dreamless sleep. To be free from the pain. She closed her eyes and waited for the welcome relief of oblivion.

19

ASPIRATION

'The world is changing, ladies and gentlemen, and, in my opinion, not for the better. We've known for some time that China, in collaboration with North Korea, is seeking world domination. World domination, I might add, in a conventional, peaceful way. They want to replace the USA as the world's most powerful nation. China is already an economic powerhouse and now, it is committing vast resources to become a top military power. They've built their first aircraft carrier and have several more in the pipeline. They're running an ambitious and successful space programme and have already launched a number of powerful space rockets. And our Intelligence suggests they have an intensive nuclear weapons programme too. Taken together, these developments pose a serious threat, not just to the West, but to the world.'

The Cobra team listened in silence to the Home Secretary.

'But the most frightening aspect,' she continued, 'is that they are ruthless. They'll stop at nothing to achieve their goals. Unlike the West, they have no concern whatsoever for human rights. The Beijing Olympic Games shows what they can achieve. In short, these two countries have the aspiration, and the ability, to achieve their objectives.'

She sat down.

'That's all very well Home Secretary,' said the Chief of the Defence Staff, 'but it'll take them at least ten to fifteen years to get anywhere near to the military strength of America.'

'We know that and I'm sure the Chinese and North Koreans know that too,' she replied.

'Then what's all the fuss about,' said the Head of MI6.

'The things I've talked about are the things that we, and everybody else in the world, know about,' said the Home Secretary. 'It's the things we don't know about that concern us.'

'Things like what?' asked the Head of MI5.

'Well, I can't be too specific but our Intelligence indicates that both North Korea and China have committed huge resources in an attempt to become world leaders in science and technology, especially in areas the West see as unethical. For example, they've been cloning humans for decades, with, apparently, horrific results in the early stages.'

'To what end,' said the Chief of the Defence Staff, 'to produce the ultimate soldier?'

'I'm sure that's one of their aims,' replied the Home Secretary, 'but I'll wager there are others too.'

'Well, there'll be no shortage of fresh bodies,' said the Head of MI6. 'In China, people just simply disappear off the street and are never seen again.'

Charles DeLacy spoke for the first time. 'Home Secretary, do we know if the Chinese are further ahead in their cloning work than we are?'

'That's a good question, Charles, but a difficult one to answer. Just like ours, their research on human cloning is top secret, so it's difficult to say. However, what I can say is that China and North Korea have been cloning humans for much longer than we have. Indeed, it's one of the reasons why the Cryonics Facility was built.

'However, the main reason I called this meeting,' the Home Secretary continued, 'is to inform you of the latest developments. Developments that are so serious it's forced the Russians to take action. At first, the Russians were quite happy with China's plans to overtake the West and become the dominant world power. Being a neighbour and an ally, they presumed it would be in their interests too. But things have changed. Taken a dramatic turn for the worse. The Intelligence is sketchy but it appears that the notorious TRIAD gangs have infiltrated both the Chinese government and their research programmes. Infiltrated them at the highest level. Although it's yet to be confirmed, many of the top positions in both the government and the research programmes are now held by TRIAD members. This new development frightened the Russians so much that it was their government who leaked the information to the West. If things turn nasty, they'd be one of the first in the firing line, along with Japan, China's old enemy. And both countries are very nervous about what is happening.'

'Do we know what their plans are?' asked the Chief of the Defence Staff.

'No,' replied the Home Secretary, 'but I can assure you that their objectives will be far more aggressive and ruthless than the previous ones. It's a worrying development and one we need to monitor very closely. I'll do my best to keep you up-to-date as and when we receive more Intelligence.'

'I take it that the work in China puts us under even more pressure to accelerate our own cloning research?' asked a worried looking Charles.

'I'm afraid it does,' replied the Home Secretary. 'We need to achieve our objectives as quickly as possible, ideally before the Chinese achieve theirs.'

'Have we really no idea at all what they're up to?' repeated the Chief of the Defence Staff, clearly frustrated with the Home Secretary's response to his previous question.

The Home Secretary thought long and hard before answering. 'We do have an inkling about one of their research programmes,' she said, 'and, if it's true, it's evil beyond description. Evil and inhuman. If it ever came to fruition, it would unleash Armageddon.'

Charles asked the question they were all thinking. 'What is it?'

'At this point, I'd rather not say,' said the Home Secretary, 'but as soon as I receive more Intelligence, I can assure you all that you'll be the first to know.'

And on that note, she closed the meeting.

20

LABORATORY 3

The high powered TASER hit the dog in the neck. Its body quivered uncontrollably and slumped to the floor, its jaws releasing their grip on what remained of Ruth's bloodied forearm. Adam dashed to her prone body. She was unconscious. Blood still spurted from the severed artery in her mangled forearm. He knew that if the bleeding wasn't stemmed immediately, Ruth Cunningham would die. Die from severe haemorrhaging. Using the handkerchief from his pocket, he tied a makeshift tourniquet on her upper arm, and then rang for the medics. Located in the medical centre in The Nursery village, they were on the scene within minutes.

'She's in a bad way,' said the middle-aged doctor who'd been at The Nursery since its formation. 'It's touch and go whether she'll make it. She's lost a lot of blood. We'll patch her up as best we can but she needs to go to hospital. Her forearm may have to be amputated.'

Like Ruth, Adam had been preparing his presentation for tomorrow's meeting when his panic alarm went off. Someone was in trouble. He glanced at the display. It was Ruth. It was a condition of employment that all Level 3 staff had to carry a panic alarm on their person at all times, a panic alarm that was only to be activated in an emergency. Leaping from his chair, he dashed to the door, grabbed the TASER and sprinted the short distance to Laboratory 3, where he TASERED the dog.

Adam's prompt action had saved Ruth's life. Later, in hospital, she told Adam she had no recollection of pressing the button on the panic alarm and that it must have been activated automatically when she was knocked to the ground.

Both Adam and Ruth were grateful to the planners and designers of the Cryonics Facility. Planners and designers who'd ensured that safety was paramount. Not only had they insisted that each member of staff carry a panic alarm, they'd also ensured that if, for whatever reason, it wasn't possible to activate it manually, then any sudden, unexpected movement, such as being knocked to the ground, activated it automatically. Furthermore, once activated, a panic alarm automatically overrode the security systems, allowing all staff immediate access to all areas. As a further measure, they'd insisted that every office and every lab housed a powerful TASER, a weapon that delivers an instantaneous paralysing and stunning effect. TASERS to protect them against any renegade clones. Their superiors deemed it better to stun them rather than shoot them. It was quieter and less messy.

'I don't know what went wrong,' said Professor Dom Cruickshank. 'I just don't understand it. C22D was our latest hybrid clone. We thought it was the ultimate attack dog. Obviously, we were wrong.'

'Excuse my ignorance, but remind me again what C22D stands for?' asked Sheila, sipping her cup of coffee in Dom's office, the office that she and Adam had been invited to after the Friday morning meeting had ended to discuss the failure of C22D.

'It's simple, really. C stands for clone, 22 means it's the 22nd viable hybrid and D stands for dog.'

'I just don't understand how it could have escaped from its cage,' continued Dom, pointing to the sturdy metal cages running along the foot of three of the walls of Laboratory 3. 'They're checked constantly, especially every morning and evening.'

'Perhaps someone forgot to lock one of the cages,' said Adam. 'It's easily done.'

'I don't think so,' replied Dom. 'We're pretty strict on things like that.'

'Maybe it was a faulty lock,' said Sheila.

'I'd thought of that too, and checked. It's not that either.'

'Then... it's strange,' said Adam, keeping his thoughts to himself.

'Yes, it is,' replied Dom. 'Very strange.'

'Another puzzle is why C22D failed to respond to Ruth's commands. One of the key traits we're trying to clone is obedience. All our dogs should respond immediately to the command STOP. A command that Ruth shouted several times. But it didn't stop. It's puzzling.'

'You said that obedience is one of the key traits being cloned. What are the others?' asked Sheila.

'Forgive me. I sometimes forget that other people aren't as *au fait* with our work as we are. Anyway, to answer your question, the other key traits we've tried to clone are size, we want them to be large and muscular; strength, they need to be strong; bark, deep and ferocious is best; bravery and courage; fearless; and, last but by no means least, colour.'

'Mm,' mused Adam, 'most of them are self-explanatory. But why colour?'

'Well,' replied Dom, 'research shows that most people fear dogs that are black or brown. Or a mixture of black and brown. It comes near the top of a list of features that frighten people.

'One trait we can't clone is reputation,' continued Dom. 'It's the reputation of certain breeds that scares people the most.'

'Like Pit Bull Terriers and Alsatians?' asked Sheila.

'Lots of breeds have been used as fighting dogs and guard dogs,' said Dom, 'most of which you are probably aware of. Alsatians and Pit Bull Terriers are two of them, even large Poodles, but the two most widely used and feared guard dogs are the Rottweiler and the Dobermann. They display most of the traits mentioned above, including colour. And it's these two breeds, plus one other, that we've focused on.'

'And what's the third breed?' queried Adam, curious as to which one it might be.

'It's the Dogo Argentino.'

'The Dogo… what,' said Adam, somewhat perplexed.

'The Dogo Argentino. The fighting dog of Cordoba. It's a breed started from crossing Boxers, Bull Terriers and the English Bulldog. They're about the size of a Boxer with the build of a Bull Terrier. They are so big and powerful that the Argentinians used them to hunt big game such as wild boar and pumas, even jaguars.'

'They sound fearsome. Do you have one in the lab?' asked Adam.

'It's over there,' said Dom, pointing to a cage on the far side.

'But… it's pure white,' said Adam. 'I thought you said black or brown was best.'

'I did,' replied Dom, 'but you can't have everything. Over the years we've identified which genes are responsible for most of the key traits and endeavoured to clone the best features of each breed to produce the ultimate attack dog.'

'And that was C22D, was it?' asked Sheila.

'Yes it was. We like to imagine it's similar to the mythical METZNER in one of Jo Nesbo's novels. Have you read any of his books?'

'No, I'm afraid I haven't,' replied Adam.

'Me neither,' said Sheila.

'You should. They're good.'

'Well,' continued Dom, 'we obviously have more work to do, especially on the obedience trait.'

Adam reflected on their conversation before asking his next question. 'Is the final aim of your work to clone the ultimate attack dog?'

'Not exactly,' replied Dom. 'The genes responsible for the above traits are passed on to our colleagues in Laboratory 4 so they can…'

'So they can clone the same traits into a human to help produce the ultimate soldier,' said Adam, completing the sentence for him.

'Correct,' said Dom.

'And have our colleagues in Lab 4 succeeded?'

'I'm afraid they'll have to answer that,' said Dom, gulping down the last of his coffee. 'It's classified information.'

'But I thought all the information was shared at the Friday morning meetings.'

Dom smiled. 'Yes, that's the theory. Most of the information is shared, but not all of it.'

Adam finished his coffee, thanked Dom for his time and thought about what kind of information wasn't shared as he and Sheila left Laboratory 3 to walk the short distance to their respective offices.

21

THE LOVERS

Ruth's face lit up as he entered the ward. It was the highlight of her long day. Visiting time. Repeating what he'd done the previous two nights, the man walked across to her bed, bent down and kissed her tenderly.

'Oh Adam, I'm so glad to see you,' she said. 'I miss you so much. It's so boring sat here all day.'

'I miss you too, Ruth,' replied Adam. 'I miss you a lot.'

'How's Dylan? Is he okay?'

'He's fine, Ruth. He's fine.'

'Is he… is he missing me?'

'Of course he's missing you. You know he thinks the world of his mum.'

'And I'm missing him too,' said Ruth, with a tear in her eye. 'I'm missing him terribly.'

'Are you sure you don't want him to visit?'

'I'm absolutely sure, Adam. I don't want him to see me in hospital. Not like this. It's too much for a three-year-old boy.'

'I suppose it is,' said Adam. 'Anyway, he thinks you're away at a conference. That's what we've told him. I think he's enjoying his time in The Nursery. Everyone's making a big fuss over him.'

Ruth's initial enthusiasm waned. 'When will I be able to go home, Adam?' she asked, as the tears welled up in her eyes. 'I miss my little boy so much.'

'I don't know, Ruth. I'll ask the doctor later.'

Like Adam, Ruth Cunningham came from a humble background. The family of three, she was the only child, lived in a council house in the poorer suburbs of St Helens. Her father had a hard, manual job in a local glass factory, working long hours for low pay. His meagre wages barely covered the bills, so luxuries were a rarity. He came from the generation where the father was the breadwinner and the mother stayed at home, meaning there was no second wage to bolster the family finances. Often, money was so tight they'd spend an entire evening looking for coins. When Ruth was young, they pretended it was a game, a game of hide-and-seek to find missing pennies by turning the chair and settee upside down, pulling up rugs and carpets, and searching every nook and cranny in the house to find any lost coins. To a child, it was great fun. But as she grew older and realised that it wasn't a game but a last, desperate act to make ends meet, it broke her heart that her beloved parents had to resort to such measures. She vowed there and then to make the most of her life and, in doing so, help her parents.

Ruth was a gifted girl. She excelled at the local comprehensive school, gaining excellent grades in both her GCSEs and 'A' levels, and went on to Manchester University to study genetics. After graduating with a first class honours degree and with a glowing recommendation from her course tutor, she did a PhD in *Animal Genetics* at Cambridge. After spending two years in a small but prestigious genetics laboratory on the Cambridge Science Park, Ruth Cunningham was recruited by Professor Charles DeLacy to work at the Cryonics Facility. And that's where she met Adam.

One of Adam's roles was to mentor recruits new to the

Cryonics Facility. To take them 'under his wing' and 'show them the ropes'. And it was during this process that he and Ruth found they had many things in common. They shared similar interests: a love of sport: a passion for outdoor pursuits, such as fell walking and white water rafting: meals out, especially at local pubs: and a love of movies. Like many scientists, ravers and nightclubbers they were not.

Over time, their friendship turned into something more. Love. They shared values that others might call old fashioned. They shunned the meet, greet and jump-into-bed culture so prevalent in modern society. Instead, they preferred to build a secure, loving relationship and then, and only then, cement it with sex.

'Adam,' said Ruth munching a grape, 'are we any wiser about what went wrong with C22D?'

'No,' replied Adam. 'I've spoken with Dom and he can't understand it either.'

'Did you… was C22D put down?'

'Yes, Ruth, he was. Any renegade clone is destroyed. They're currently doing lots of tests to try and identify the cause of the malfunction. I'll let you know if they find anything.'

'Thanks, Adam. It's weird. We were convinced that C22D was the ultimate attack dog. I can't believe it… failed.'

'Ah, doctor,' said Adam, noticing the doctor doing his rounds. 'May I have a word?'

'… and you're sure there's nothing you can do?' he asked the doctor out of earshot of Ruth.

'Yes. Absolutely sure. The forearm is damaged beyond repair. It'll have to be amputated.'

'Does Ruth know?'

'No. Not yet. We'd rather tell her when a family member or close friend is present. Shall we tell her now?'

'No, thanks,' said Adam. 'I'd like to tell her myself if that's alright?'

'Are you sure?' said the doctor. 'You never know how they'll react.'

'I'm sure,' said Adam.

'Okay, but I'm here if you need me,' said the doctor.

'Ruth, I've been speaking to the doctor and…'

'Adam, I'm not stupid. I know what you're going to say. I can see for myself that my forearm is beyond help. It'll have to be amputated, won't it?'

'I'm afraid so, Ruth. I'm so sorry.'

'I've been thinking of the options for the last two days, Adam. There are only two. Have a prosthetic or clone a new forearm.'

'And what have you decided?'

'To clone a new forearm, stupid. With all the advances we've made, it's a no brainer.'

'But it'll have to be done at the Facility, not the hospital. You know that, don't you?'

'Of course I know that,' said Ruth, indignantly. 'I'll have the amputation done here and the forearm cloned in your laboratory, Adam. Laboratory 2.'

'Great. I was hoping you'd say that,' said Adam. 'but the forearm will be cloned in Angela's lab, not mine. Either way, it shouldn't present any problems.'

Switching the subject, Ruth said, 'I miss Dylan and I miss you, Adam. I miss you both so much. But I also miss my work too. How's Dom? And how's the work progressing without me?'

'Do you mean the work in Laboratory 3 or the work in general?'

'Both, really. I'm concerned about Ewan Grigg and his team in Laboratory 4 using the genes of C22D if they're faulty.'

'I'll find out what I can and let you know on my next visit tomorrow,' said Adam.

The bell signalled the end of visiting time. 'I love you,' he said, kissing her on the cheek.

'I love you too,' she said to the man departing the ward. 'I love you too.'

22

LABORATORY 4

… the laboratory where the most advanced cloning work in the UK, and probably the world, was carried out. The laboratory in which some of the finest brains experimented on hybrid cloning. Hybrid human-human and human-animal cloning.

Professor Ewan Grigg ran Laboratory 4, together with a team of highly talented geneticists and molecular biologists. His 'right hand man', Professor Debbie Farnham, was, arguably, the foremost geneticist in the world. She had done outstanding work on the human genome, identifying sequences of genes linked to specific human traits. Like her boss, Ewan Grigg, Debbie Farnham was now in her mid-fifties. In contrast, Dr Steve Reynolds, probably the brightest and certainly the most radical molecular biologist to have walked planet Earth, was a mere youngster. Still only 29, he'd already revolutionised the field of molecular biology with his fresh insights and radical ideas. And that's why he'd been recruited. To bring a new way of thinking to the project. To bounce revolutionary, out-of-the-box ideas off Ewan and Debbie. Ideas that Ewan and Debbie could modify and fine-tune using their years of experience. Young and old working together. And it worked. Ewan and his team made excellent progress in one of the most difficult areas imaginable.

The initial aims of the hybrid cloning project were twofold. The first involved human-human hybrids and the second human-animal, mainly human-dog, hybrids.

The successful completion of the Human Genome Project in 2003 provided a massive boost to the team. It was a mammoth feat of human ingenuity involving several countries and taking 13 years. It accelerated the team's first task of identifying the genes, or clusters of genes, responsible for specific human traits. Traits important to their research. It wasn't easy. Approximately three billion base pairs of adenine, thymine, cytosine and guanine make up the 20,000-25,000 genes of human DNA, and identifying those sequences responsible for specific traits proved extremely difficult. Even a simple trait involved substantial numbers of seemingly unconnected sequences of genes. However, thanks to a decade of painstaking work by Debbie Farnham and her team, it was a task that was eventually accomplished.

Their next task was to incorporate selected traits into one single individual to see if they were expressed. The experiment with Jack the Ripper had shown that a single trait could most certainly be expressed, in this case the burning desire to murder and mutilate prostitutes. But would a mixture, a hybrid, of traits be expressed? That's what they were trying to find out.

They'd successfully identified the genes, and in many cases, the clusters of genes, responsible for most of the traits they were interested in, such as intelligence, creativity, leadership, aggression, bravery and fear. All that remained was to clone appropriate traits into single individuals to produce, hopefully, the ultimate scientist, soldier and world leader.

For a scientist, traits such as intelligence, creativity, problem-solving and analytical skills are crucial, and it was these traits the team would attempt to clone into a single brain. Whether the resulting clone would be a brilliant scientist, or something entirely different, they didn't know. They didn't know because their first experiments were being done not on a scientist, but on the ultimate soldier.

Traits for the ultimate soldier were different. Here, traits such as bravery, strength, fearlessness, resourcefulness and obedience were paramount. And that's where the genes from clones like C22D, genes for bravery, fearlessness and obedience, were being used, to incorporate them into a human brain. If successful, it could produce the best soldier the world had ever seen. If it wasn't, well… it could be a disaster. They'd made good progress too, until the setback of a few days ago. The failure of the obedience gene in C22D.

The setback with C22D had caused them to change their plans. Instead of taking a chance and making a hybrid of a human and C22D, they were taking a safer option and attempting to clone a human-human hybrid. A human hybrid using DNA from some of the best SAS, SBS and Parachute Regiment soldiers ever to have served their country. To clone a soldier from just tiny fragments of DNA. The precious DNA that was stored in the vault, alongside the DNA of other famous, and infamous, people from the annals of history. To combine the best sequences of DNA from each soldier to produce the ultimate fighting machine.

They'd already cloned a triple hybrid brain from an SAS, SBS and Parachute Regiment soldier, and chosen the ideal body. That of a muscular young man in his late twenties. Now, all that remained was to connect the two together. For this, they needed the Resurrection Chamber. The Resurrection Chamber currently being used by Professor Stuart Ramage and Professor Angela Thomson to resurrect the SAS soldier they were using in their work. If that experiment failed then… well, they'd have to think very carefully about their own experiment.

23

RUTH

Leaving the family home was a wrench, not just for Ruth but for her parents too. Although poor, they were a happy family. A close knit family who did things together. And when the day came for them to take their daughter, their only daughter, to her accommodation in Manchester, it created tensions and tears.

The weather didn't help. Drizzling rain fell from a sombre, grey September sky as her father drove the old family car, the car packed to the roof with Ruth's belongings, into the Owen's Park campus. He tried to remain cheerful, as did her mother. Both were torn between conflicting emotions. They were proud that their daughter had made it to university, a top university, but sad they were losing her, because that's what it felt like. That she was leaving them and the only home she'd ever known for the entire 18 years of her young life.

'We'll come with you whilst you register,' said her father. 'Just to make sure everything's alright.'

'And we'd like to see your room too,' said her mother, 'if you don't mind.'

'No, of course I don't mind,' said Ruth.

'And we'll give you a hand with your luggage afterwards,' her father said, keeping the conversation flowing. He didn't want any awkward pauses.

'This is lovely,' her mother said as she surveyed the room allocated to her daughter. 'It's like being in a three star hotel.' And it was. The room was modern, spacious, well furnished and had an *en suite* bathroom with a bath and a shower. 'It'll be like you're on holiday.'

'I don't think so, mum,' said Ruth with a smile, 'but it's very nice.'

'Are you sure you'll be alright? Remember, if there's anything you need, just give us a call.'

'I will, mum, and… thanks for everything. You too dad,' she said, giving both of them a hug before they departed.

Back at the car, her mother could suppress the tears no longer. She broke down and cried.

'Don't be silly,' snapped her husband, feeling embarrassed by his wife's tears. 'She'll be fine. She's not a baby. She's 18 for Christ's sake.'

'She's still *my* baby,' said her mother, still sobbing, 'and I'll miss her. I'll miss her a lot. It's the first time she's ever left home.'

Seeing his wife's distress, her husband relented, ashamed of his outburst. He was trying to be manly. To be stoic. In fact, he was being the exact opposite.

'You're right, love,' he said, putting his arms around his wife. 'I'm sorry. I'll miss her too.'

Ruth settled in quickly. Many of her fellow undergraduates came from similar working class backgrounds to herself, which helped enormously. And, if she wanted, it was easy for her to travel the short distance home to see her parents, another fact which made her stay at Manchester University a pleasant one. During her three years, she made some good friends, both male and female, and thoroughly enjoyed her studies in genetics. She'd definitely chosen the right subject, and the right university. Cambridge, however, was a different proposition altogether.

Unlike Manchester, the 31 colleges of Cambridge were populated with people from backgrounds far different to her own. Public school people, from Eton and Harrow. People from wealthy parents. Posh people. And some clever people. Very clever people. For Ruth, it was a culture shock.

There were some people from more humble backgrounds like herself, but they were a minority. At first, these were the people she associated with. Knocked around with. Birds of a feather stuff. But, as time progressed, she found, to her surprise and relief, that most of the people from privileged backgrounds were actually okay. One of them was more than okay. One of them became her best friend.

Graham was her mentor. At 25, he was three years older than Ruth. He'd obtained his PhD the previous year and was in the second year of his post doctoral research on animal genetics, the same topic that Ruth was doing for her doctorate. His background couldn't have been more different. He came from a wealthy family in Windsor, a family with connections to the Royal Family. He was educated at Eton, just a stones throw across the Thames from Windsor, and then at Cambridge, following in the footsteps of his father, a senior civil servant at Westminster. It was a path that many of the wealthy and privileged had trodden.

Not only did he come from a privileged background, Graham was also handsome. He was tall, fair-haired and blue-eyed, blue eyes that were accentuated by his fair complexion. And he was suave and charming. A real gentleman. It was little wonder that he swept Ruth off her feet. In her sheltered life, she had never known anyone remotely like Graham. He introduced her to the delights of Cambridge. Punting on the River Cam, picnicking on The Backs, the lovely lawns behind famous colleges such as Kings

College and Christ College, and sipping a glass of Pimms beside the river. It was a different world to what she had known. She loved it. And she loved the day they'd strolled through the American Cemetery, the beautifully maintained cemetery on the outskirts of Cambridge where hundreds of young American servicemen killed in World War II were laid to rest. The place where they stole their first kiss. The place where their romance began.

Life with Graham was wonderful. Like a fairy tale. Gradually, however, things began to change. Imperceptibly at first, but then faster and faster. She was drawn into a lifestyle that was totally alien to her. A lifestyle of drinking and drug-taking. Soft drugs to begin with, but then harder drugs such as cocaine. It was the start of a downward spiral. And, to top it all, she got pregnant. Pregnant at 23. Pregnant at the beginning of her third and final year of her doctorate.

Ruth was devastated. Getting pregnant was a wake up call. She'd let both herself and her parents down. Her parents who'd sacrificed so much so that she could have a better life. And now, here she was, pregnant and dragged into a lifestyle she didn't want. She'd been foolish. Very foolish. But she vowed to get herself out of this mess. Vowed that somehow she'd rebuild her life.

She assessed her situation. And her options. And then she made her decisions. She'd complete her PhD, both for her own sake and especially that of her parents. It was the least she could do. She'd ask Graham to marry her. After all, it wasn't Graham she had a problem with, just the lifestyle he'd led her into. And she'd tell her parents.

Ruth did all three. She obtained her PhD in animal genetics just before the baby was born. A beautiful baby boy they named Dylan. She told her parents, her elderly parents who had her late in life. They were shocked. Not so much at what she'd done, but shocked that she hadn't told them about Graham, and the baby. They let their modest house in St Helens and rented a small flat on the outskirts of Cambridge so they could look after the baby while she and Graham went to work. And she married a reluctant Graham in a quiet ceremony in the local registry office.

After completing his post doctoral studies, her reluctant husband, Graham, got a job as a junior lecturer in Clare College and, to keep them all together, she accepted a job in the nearby Cambridge Science Park. But it didn't work out. Graham could never settle into the role of a domesticated husband and father and the marriage deteriorated. And, when Charles DeLacy offered her a job at the Cryonics Facility in Snowdonia, she grabbed it with both hands. It was the chance to start afresh. To begin a new life in Wales with her son and her parents. It was an opportunity she couldn't refuse.

Part 2

· · ·

CHINA

24

FATHER OF CLONING

It was a bright May morning. The sun shone down from a cloudless blue sky on the crowd of over 300 scholars and politicians at Shandong University in Jinan, about 250 miles south of Beijing, to honour the late embryologist Tong Dizhou. Above a large bust of Tong hung a ceremonial banner: a banner emblazoned with the words: FATHER OF CLONING.

'Not many people know this,' said Professor Skip Meyers to his young colleague in the crowd, 'but *Dolly the sheep* wasn't the first animal to be cloned successfully. Not by a long chalk. In 1963, thirty-three years before *Dolly the sheep* came into the world, Tong took the DNA from a cell in a male Asian carp, implanted it into an egg from a female Asian carp, and produced the world's first cloned fish. The experiment was a complete success. The cloned fish swam around, ate its fill and even sired baby carp.

'Ten years later, Tong inserted the DNA from an Asian carp into an egg from a European crucian carp, creating the first *interspecies clone.*'

'But why weren't scientists in the West aware of his work?' asked his young Chinese colleague, Dr Chang Lee.

'Because Tong published his findings in relatively obscure Chinese journals. For example, *Acta Zoologica Sinica*, in which the interspecies cloning research appeared, didn't even offer the English language abstract common in non-Western scientific journals.'

'It's amazing, truly amazing,' said Chang, obviously impressed.

'What is?' asked Skip.

'That China has been successfully cloning animals for over 50 years.'

'It is,' said Skip, 'but it's not surprising.'

Chang gave him a quizzical look.

'It's not surprising for two reasons. First, China's morals on cloning are totally different to those of the West, particularly those of the USA. In the United States, the Bush administration forbade embryonic human cloning research, including therapeutic cloning, forcing many American embryologists and geneticists to move to countries like China. I was one of them. I moved to China 24 years ago. I was lucky. I was single but some scientists I knew left their spouse and children behind.'

'Wow. That was one hell of a sacrifice to make,' said Chang.

'It was, but it showed how strongly they felt about doing the research. Research that could ease the suffering of millions. Anyway, in complete contrast to the American government, the Chinese government actively encouraged cloning, including human therapeutic cloning. They constructed state-of-the-art laboratory buildings, created university posts with princely salaries and perks, and provided the capital to establish new biotech firms.'

'I know,' said Chang. 'And what's the second reason?'

'The second reason is the ethical argument. In the West, and yet again the USA is the main culprit, cloning is seen as controversial, even downright wrong, because of the destruction of the cloned embryos. In China, because of long held beliefs, this isn't a problem.'

'Ah, the ancient Confucian idea that a person is only truly considered to be a human after birth so that embryos and foetuses are not counted as human,' said Chang. 'This idea has been around for thousands of years. It's embedded in the Chinese psyche. So for the Chinese, having to destroy lots of embryos is not a problem.'

After a momentary pause Chang asked Skip if it was worrying for the West that the Chinese were so far ahead in the work on cloning.

'No. Not at all,' replied Skip. 'Not if cloning is used in the right way. To help cure serious illnesses such as Parkinson's disease and diabetes.'

'Skip?'

'Yes.'

'Don't you feel you've, er, betrayed your country by helping the Chinese?'

'Betrayed my country? And which country might that be?'

'Why, America, of course,' said Chang Lee.

'Absolutely not,' retorted Skip. 'America deserves all it gets.'

'What do you mean, Skip?'

'In America, the religious politicians have too much influence. They're the ones who oppose research on cloning and the others are too weak to confront them. They're obstructing scientific, and especially medical, progress just like they've done over the centuries, denying millions of ordinary people the right to a better life. All because of their outdated religious beliefs.

'Pardon me for digressing, Chang, but did you know that Galileo Galilei, one of the greatest scientists of all time, was tried for heresy by the Catholic Church for daring to challenge the long held belief that the Earth was the centre of the universe, and that it was the sun that went around the Earth, not the Earth that went around the sun. Tried, convicted and placed under house arrest for the rest of his life. That was in 1633. And even though Copernicus had proven that the Earth did indeed move around the sun in his seminal book *On the Revolutions of Celestial Spheres* published just before his death in 1543, it took the Catholic Church until 1979 to admit they had erred in their treatment of Galileo. Three hundred and forty six years to admit they were wrong!

'Even worse was their treatment of the astronomer Giordano Bruno for proposing that *If the Earth was not the centre of the universe, and all the stars in the night sky were suns, then there must exist an infinite number of earths in the universe, inhabited with other beings like ourselves.* This infuriated the Catholic Church. They lured Bruno to Rome with the promise of a job, where he was immediately handed over to the Inquisition and charged with heresy. He spent the next eight years in chains in the Castel Sant'Angelo, where he was routinely tortured and interrogated before his trial. He was found guilty and sentenced to death. Immediately after the death sentence was pronounced, Bruno's jaw was clamped shut with an iron gag, his tongue pierced with an iron spike, and another iron spike driven into his palate. On the 19 February 1600, he was driven through the streets of Rome, stripped of his clothes and burned at the stake.

'Even now, in the 21st century, they're still getting it wrong and blocking progress. So no, I don't feel I've betrayed my country. On the contrary, I feel my country has betrayed me.'

'I gather that you're not a religious man then,' said Chang with a wry smile.

'No. I'm not. Never have been and never will be. Religion has a lot to answer for.'

'Aren't you worried where all this cloning work might lead?' asked Chang Lee.

'What the hell's he on about,' thought Skip. 'He's like a dog with a bone.' He thought carefully before answering.

'No, I'm not. Not if it's used for the benefit of the human race. But I am worried about the latest developments in China.'

'Developments like what?' asked Chang.

'Like the gradual replacement of top government officials with unelected "unknowns": like the changes in personnel at the upper echelons of the universities; and like the "disappearance" of the scientists at our own research centre. I worry about all of those.'

Furrows appeared on Chang's brow as he pondered what Skip had said. 'Where do you think the scientists have gone?' he asked. 'Do you… do you think there is other cloning work being done? Cloning work that's top secret?'

'I don't know,' replied Skip. 'But I suspect there might be. And I don't like it.'

The bell rang to signal the end of the ceremony. As the American professor and his Chinese assistant walked across the square to their coach, the coach that would take them back to their laboratories at the Shandong Stem Cell Research Centre, Skip reflected on the conversation he'd had with Chang. Why had Chang been so inquisitive? And why had he begun to spend so much time away from the Research Centre? Could it be, he wondered, could it possibly be that Chang knew more than he was letting on about the top secret cloning work going on in China? The thought of it made him shiver.

25

RESURRECTION

Adam touched Sheila on her shoulder. Dressed in white overalls, blue headgear, blue overshoes, white face masks and white gloves, they looked like surgeons in a hi-tech operating theatre, or workers in a semiconductor plant. In a way, they were a bit of both.

'Are you nervous?' he asked the new recruit.

'A little,' replied Sheila. 'Nervous yet intrigued. It's my first, er, resurrection.'

'It's perfectly normal,' said Adam. 'I felt just the same at my first resurrection.'

The entire teams of both Professor Stuart Ramage and Professor Angela Thomson were gathered in Laboratory 2 to watch the final act of their endeavours. The resurrection of a cloned human. The bringing together of a cloned brain from a long dead person and a frozen body. Connecting them together and then instilling the breath of life. Raising them from the dead like some modern day Lazarus.

'It should be a routine resurrection,' thought Adam. Angela and her team had cloned the brain of a dead SAS soldier, a soldier who'd served with distinction in World War II. Captain Johnnie Standish. And now, the fully formed brain was to be 'connected' to the body of a strong, young man taken from a pod in the cavern. A body complete in every respect except for the brain. A body which had been carefully transported from its pod to Laboratory 2 in the mobile 'Resurrection Chamber', the most expensive piece of equipment ever built.

As far as they knew, the Resurrection Chamber was one of only two in the whole world, the second one residing in the USA. Costing over £10 billion each, the Resurrection Chambers were by far the most advanced pieces of engineering and science ever constructed. They reminded Adam of a mummies tomb. A white, plastic sarcophagus with a clear, transparent top. To Adam, it was hard to imagine that something so small cost so much.

One of the reasons for the high cost was the millions of ultra sensitive sensors and probes that lined the interior and touched every part of the frozen body. Sensors and probes to first warm, and later stimulate, the body.

The first stage of the resurrection, the warming stage, had been activated almost four hours ago and was nearly complete. Over the past decade, they'd worked out that the frozen body had to be warmed slowly to preserve the integrity of the cells. The ideal rate, obtained by a combination of science and good, old fashioned trial and error, was one degree Celsius per minute. At this rate, it took exactly three hours and fifty three minutes for a body frozen in liquid nitrogen at minus 196°C to reach the human body temperature of 37°C. When the temperature reached 4°C, the temperature at which liquid water displays its maximum density, and the reason why water at the bottom of ponds and rivers never freezes, a fact essential for aquatic life, the synthetic fluid pumped into the body prior to freezing it was replaced with genetically compatible blood. Blood compatible with both the brain and the body. Blood which contained all the anti-bodies to combat infection and disease.

As the temperature of the body approached 37°C, Angela and Stuart placed the cloned brain of Captain Johnnie Standish ever so carefully into the open skull of the body lying in the Resurrection Chamber. Then, as the body and brain reached the final temperature of 37°C, it was time for the critical parts of the process to begin.

Using advanced laser technology, two neurosurgeons performed the intricate task of connecting the major blood vessels, nerve endings and the spinal cord to the implanted brain, before closing up the skull and joining the skin on the head to that on the body.

'How do you think it's going?' whispered Sheila.

'Fine, as far as I can tell,' replied Adam. 'But it's the next stages that are really crucial. That's when we'll be able to tell whether it's a success or not.'

'What stages are those?' asked Sheila.

'The rewiring and stimulation stages. They're absolutely pivotal.'

'The… what?' said Sheila.

'You'll see,' said Adam. 'They're just starting the rewiring stage.'

Sheila watched as Stuart injected a milky looking liquid into the brain of the clone, and then sat by a small console at the head of the Resurrection Chamber and began typing furiously.

'What's he doing?' she asked, clearly confused. 'Has he injected some drugs?'

'No. Not yet. That comes later. What he's injected is far more interesting than drugs. He's just injected millions of nanobots.'

'Nano… what?'

'Nanobots. Atom sized robots. An army of nanobots to explore every one of the 100 billion nerve cells, or neurons, in the brain, with approximately 200 trillion connections between them. To ensure that each one is in perfect working order and that they're all "wired" correctly.'

Sheila was dumbfounded. 'I didn't know we had technology like that,' she gasped. 'I thought such technology was years away.'

'So do a lot of other people, Sheila, but we have it right here and now. And there's more. Have you heard of quantum computers?'

'Yes, vaguely. They're the ultimate supercomputer aren't they?'

'That's one way of describing it,' said Adam, 'but they're more than that. They work by using the quantum states of atoms and, because of the small size and infinite combinations, their computing power and speed are unbelievable. According to Michio Kaku, the American physicist, a quantum computer the size of a sugar lump would be more powerful than all the computers in the world combined!'

'And do you have one of them too?' she asked, with a trace of sarcasm in her voice.

'Not exactly. We have a crude quantum computer, a sort of halfway house between a real one and a conventional computer.'

'Is that the reason why the Resurrection Chamber cost £10 billion?' asked Sheila.

'It is,' replied Adam. 'Because of that and the nanobots.'

'How long does this stage last?'

'It depends,' replied Adam. 'If there are no problems, then about a couple of hours. If there are major problems, then it could take up to four, or even eight, hours.'

'And how do you know? If there are any problems, I mean.'

'That's what Stuart's doing now. Checking on the progress of the rewiring using the feedback from the nanobots.'

'I'm… I'm speechless. I really am. When I asked Angela how the heads were connected to the bodies and she said they were "sewn" on, I thought that it was a simple operation.'

'I know. It's a shock to everyone when they see a resurrection for the first time.'

Two hours later, the 'rewiring' stage was complete. There'd been no problems.

'Adam?'

'Yeah.'

'Is Stuart a molecular biologist or a theoretical physicist?'

'I thought you'd ask that,' said Adam smiling. 'Everyone does after they've witnessed their first resurrection.'

'Well?'

'Actually, he's one of those rare people. A polymath. He's a very good molecular biologist and a brilliant theoretical physicist.'

Sheila was stunned. Stunned that someone could be a leading world expert in two such complex and completely different disciplines.

'I'm amazed, absolutely amazed,' she mumbled.

'Look,' said Adam, 'they're starting the final stage. Stimulation. This is when we'll really know if the resurrection has been successful.'

The stimulation stage was the crux of the whole process. The point at which the clone either came to life or remained dead. In the stimulation stage, the whole of the body, *but not the brain*, was stimulated with sophisticated electrical impulses, with the strongest impulses directed to the heart. *At the same time*, timing was crucial, a cocktail of drugs was injected into the clone's heart. A cocktail of drugs that included stimulants, like adrenaline, and immuno suppressants. And pain killers. Powerful pain killers to numb the effects of the surgery.

'What happens now?' whispered Sheila, after watching Stuart begin the electrical stimulation and Angela inject the drugs.

'We have to wait about four to five minutes for the heart to pump sufficient oxygenated blood around the body, especially to the brain. During this time, they'll make sure the heartbeat is regular and the clone is breathing normally.'

'And if everything's okay?'

'Then the clone is clinically alive,' said Adam.

'The final step,' continued Adam, 'is stimulating the brain

with a complex pattern of brain waves. A flickering of the eyelids signifies that the brain has been successfully stimulated. It's a sign of consciousness. A sign that the brain is alive and functioning.'

As they waited to see the outcome of the final step, Sheila asked what happened after the clone had been resurrected.

'It's transferred to The Nursery and kept in the Resurrection Chamber for about 24 hours to make sure that everything's alright. Then it's kept in The Nursery for a further five to seven days while it learns about the world, much like a new born baby does, only much faster. After all, it's a new, virgin brain. Then, when it's learned the basics, such as recognition, walking and talking, if it's a scientist, it's moved to the lab to learn about genetics and cloning, hands-on work that's supplemented by talks in the lecture theatre. If it's a soldier, it's moved to the secure unit in The Nursery for testing and training.' He didn't tell her about the Infusion Chamber. That could wait.

'And then?'

'In the case of a scientist, hopefully, it contributes to the work.'

As Adam talked, Sheila watched the clone's face intently, focusing on its eyelids. For a few moments, nothing moved. Then she saw it. Just the tiniest of flickers. A moment later, there was no doubt. The eyelids definitely flickered. Angela and Stuart hugged, and everyone in the lab applauded and cheered.

'Welcome to the world of the living, C47SO,' said Stuart triumphantly. 'It's another successful result. Thanks everybody for a job well done.'

Stuart's closing comments sparked a furious response from Sheila. 'Adam,' she said vehemently, 'does C47SO mean what I think it does?'

Adam wished that Stuart had kept his mouth shut.

26

DOMINATION

'And finally, I'd like to say a big thank-you to all of you. My colleagues and, I hope, my friends, who've made my time here such a pleasant and fulfilling one. You can all be very proud of what you've achieved. I know Tong Dizhou would be proud of the progress you've made. Once again, I thank each and every one of you and wish you all a happy and successful life.'

The room erupted into rapturous applause as Professor Wei Zhuang, the retiring head of the Central Research Laboratories, ended his valedictory address. Some even cried. As Professor Zhuang sat down, the man sat on his right arose from his chair. The stern-faced, austere looking man who nobody knew. Xiong Kang. The applause ceased immediately.

'Thank-you, Professor Zhuang,' he said. 'On behalf of myself and the Chinese government, may I extend our sincere thanks for the work you have done and the results you've achieved. May I also, on behalf of everyone, wish you a long and happy retirement.'

It was a scenario enacted the world over. The retirement of a long standing and valued colleague. But it was a retirement with a difference.

Professor Wei Zhuang had held his position as Head of Research at China's Central Research Laboratories for 17 years. Born in 1960, he'd joined the Centre after completing his doctorate in genetics in 1984, a young man eager to build on the ground-breaking work of Tong Dizhou, the Father of Cloning. His enthusiasm and abilities were quickly recognised by his superiors, as was his excellent work on therapeutic cloning, and promotions duly followed. In 1999, Wei Zhuang was awarded the ultimate accolade; he was appointed the Head of China's Central Research Laboratories.

Tucked away in the north west corner of China, this impressive facility was located in the foothills of the Tian Shan mountains, a range of mountains that run from east to west, dividing two of China's greatest basins, the Dzungarian Basin to the north and the massive Tarian Basin to the south. It was an ideal location. Not only was the Tian Shan area rich in coal, oil and metallic ores, essential raw materials for the construction, and running, of a large facility like the Centre, it was also remote. Hidden from the prying, inquisitive eyes of the 1.3 billion Chinese that inhabit the third largest country in the world (only Russia and Canada are bigger). And, perhaps more importantly, hidden away from the rest of the world.

The decision to build a centre for cloning was taken a few years after Tong's landmark work, with the first phase of the vaguely named Central Research Laboratories being completed in the early 1970s. During the following two decades, expansion was minimal, but the successful cloning of *Dolly the sheep* changed everything. It prompted the Chinese government to pour huge resources into both the infrastructure and the personnel, making the Central Research Laboratories the largest centre in the world for cloning research.

In the audience, two young researchers exchanged glances.

'Have you heard of Xiong Kang?' Dr Qian Shen asked her boss, Professor Hui Wang.

'No. I haven't, not until today' he replied, 'and I don't think anyone else has either.'

'And who's the other person with him?'

'I think he's called Meng Huan, Kang's assistant.'

'He's certainly got the right name,' said Qian. 'He looks fierce. I don't particularly like the look of either of them.'

'Neither do I,' said Hui. 'They both look like nasty pieces of work.'

'Don't you think it's strange that Professor Zhuang's retired?' continued Qian.

'I do,' said Hui. 'I spoke to him about six months ago and he had no intention of retiring. On the contrary, he was really looking forward to overseeing the successful completion of the replacement cloning work. And now, just a few months later, he's retiring. It's weird.'

'Do you think it's because he objected to the changes that are taking place?'

'You mean the big influx of geneticists, molecular biologists and cloning experts from all over China?'

'Not so much that but the refocusing of the work,' said Qian.

'I think he was uncomfortable with the amount of effort being taken from therapeutic cloning and redirected to replacement cloning, especially when the work's directed towards military applications.'

'Like the ultimate soldier?'

'Yes,' replied Hui. 'But what worried him most of all was the top secret research being done in the new laboratories, research that most of the new scientists are working on.'

'You're right,' replied Qian. 'Most of us are worried about that.'

'Hui?'

'Yes, Qian?'

'Have you any idea what kind of work's being done in the new laboratories?'

He'd heard rumours, conflicting rumours, about what might be going on, but nothing concrete. 'No, Qian. I don't,' he replied. 'But I'm sure we'll find out soon enough.'

As Hui and Qian made their way back towards their laboratories, Hui peered into the vast cavern. The cavern that housed the frozen bodies for replacement cloning. The cavern that once housed just hundreds of pods now housed thousands. 'Why on earth do you need thousands of bodies,' thought Hui. The failure rate might be high, but not that high. The rows of pods lined up in their hundreds reminded him of battery hens. Thousands of frozen humans lined up for... for what? He didn't really know. But the new rulers did, Xiong Kang and his henchman, er, assistant, Meng Huan. Them and their close circle of comrades in the top secret laboratories.

Rumours were rife that the upsurge in activity was to meet a deadline. An imminent deadline. And that the top secret research was based on information, Intelligence, obtained from a foreign power. Another country that was also involved in the cloning of humans.

He'd also heard a name for the top secret project. DARIT. He didn't know what it meant, but the rumour was the 'D' stood for Domination.

27

C47SO

Sheila followed Adam to his office. She wanted an answer to her question. And she wanted it now.

After stepping inside, she closed the door. Adam sat behind his desk, stern faced. He didn't want to answer her question but he knew she wouldn't relent. Wouldn't give up. She'd ask him over and over again until he answered. 'So,' he thought, 'I might as well get it over with now.'

'Sit down, Sheila. Would you like a cup of coffee? Or tea?'

'No. Thanks. All I want is an answer to my question. Does C47SO mean what I think it means?"

Adam shifted uncomfortably in his chair before answering. 'I don't know what you think it means, Sheila, but C47SO is the 47th attempt to clone a soldier. It's "SO" because "S" is used to denote scientists.'

Adam watched Sheila intently as he answered her question. Watched her face as it displayed a string of emotions. Incredulity, horror, revulsion and finally fury as what he'd said registered in her brain.

'FORTY-SEVEN!!! You mean you've had 46 failures and this is the 47th attempt?' she spat out. 'Forty-six bloody failures!'

'Not 46 failures,' said Adam as calmly as he could, '46 attempts.'

'And what's the fucking difference?' snarled a furious and incensed Sheila.

'Calm down, Sheila,' said Adam. 'There's no need to rant and rave.'

'There's every bloody need, Adam,' retorted Sheila, 'every bloody need if 46 people have had to be… destroyed.'

'It's not like that, Sheila. Forty-six clones, er, people, haven't had to be destroyed.'

'Then what is it like, Adam? What happened to the 46 people,' said Sheila, emphasising the word 'people'.

'Sheila, in most of the early attempts at resurrection, none of the clones were brought to life. The procedures didn't work. They had to be re-thought and modified. Refined and improved. And then improved some more. It was only at the 31st attempt that a clone "came to life". The clone of a serial killer. A murderer. And then it was only for a few minutes. But we learned with each one. Learned how to improve our techniques. Gradually, their "lifespan" increased from minutes to hours to days and eventually to weeks and months. Currently, two clones are alive. C43SO has been alive for over a year and C45SO for about six months. And now we have C47SO.'

Sheila listened in silence, as if she was in a trance, not comprehending what Adam was saying. Tears were in her eyes.

'Are you alright?' asked Adam.

'I… I can't believe what I'm hearing,' she stammered. 'I can't believe this… this kind of thing is going on in Britain.'

'It's a shock to the system,' said Adam, feeling sorry for the young recruit. 'It's a shock to everyone when they hear it for the first time.'

'I'm sorry for shouting at you, Adam. It's not your fault.'

'It's okay, Sheila. It's okay. I understand.'

'Adam. What happened to C43SO and C45SO? Where are they now?'

'Well, they were placed in the secure unit in The Nursery, the unit where all the military clones are raised. I think they were assessed and put through their paces as soldiers.'

'And did they turn out to be the ultimate soldier?'

'I'm afraid not. It appears the main reason Special Forces soldiers are so good is not one of genetics, but of training. Intense military training. They might have a genetic predisposition to become a good soldier, but most of it, unfortunately for us, is down to the training.'

'So the experiments *were* failures,' said Sheila.

Adam felt uncomfortable again. 'They didn't deliver the ultimate soldier, no.'

Sheila didn't want to ask the next question, but she asked it anyway. 'Where are they now, Adam?'

'As far as I know, Sheila, they're both with the SAS at their base in Hereford.' He didn't dare tell her that one of them had been killed in a training exercise. A test to ascertain if they were the ultimate soldier. But the other, C45SO, had indeed joined the SAS.

'And will C47SO be sent to Hereford too?'

'I think that's the plan,' replied Adam.

'Thanks, Adam,' said Sheila getting up from her chair. 'Thanks for being so honest.'

Adam nodded. 'Sheila,' he said as she turned towards the door, 'you won't do anything stupid, will you?'

'Like what, Adam?'

'Like... like trying to sabotage the work or whistle blowing,' he said, thinking of what happened to previous whistleblowers. 'After all, you've signed the Secrecy Act.'

'No. I won't do any of those, Adam.'

'Sheila.'

'Yes, Adam.'

'One final thing. Think positively. It could be worse. You could be working in China.'

28

EXPANSION

Xiong Kang paced up and down the spacious new office overlooking the spacious new laboratories staffed with scores of scientists from every corner of China. Geneticists, molecular biologists, chemists, theoretical physicists and cloning experts, the cream of China's crop all working here in the Central Research Laboratories. Working on the new discovery. Some, like himself and Meng Huan, were committed to the cause. To the New Order. To Project DARIT. They'd willingly agreed to leave their previous positions and relocate to the mountains of Tian Shan to work in the Central Research Laboratories. But others were reluctant to move, indeed even refused to move. That was unacceptable. When threats of reprisals to family and friends failed to change their minds, the threats were executed. Family members disappeared mysteriously and brown paper packages arrived in the post. Packages with macabre contents. Severed fingers, toes and hands of loved ones. Of children. Young children. And wives and mothers. Limbs severed with the unmistakable signature of the TRIADs, a kitchen meat cleaver. The handful of scientists who still refused to relocate quickly changed their minds when the horribly mutilated body of one of them was dragged from the river. And now, here they all were, willing and unwilling scientists working in the Central Research Laboratories.

Xiong Kang was a "438", the 'deputy mountain master' of China's largest and most powerful TRIAD, *Sun Yee On*. Boasting over 40,000 members, it was considerably larger than the second and third largest Triads, *Who Sing Who* and *14K*. His assistant, Meng Huan, was a "426", a 'military commander' or 'Red Pole', whose expertise of overseeing offensive and defensive operations would prove useful at a later date.

Frustrated with the current world order and the slow pace of China to become the world number one, Xiong Kang's boss, the 'Dragon Head' or 'Mountain' of the *Sun Yee On* TRIAD, its "489", formulated a plan. He arranged a summit of the TRIAD gangs, a meeting of their Dragon Heads, to explain his plan. A plan that would see the disparate TRIAD gangs form an alliance and use their power and influence to infiltrate the top positions of industry, the military and the government, and then to steer China in a direction that he, and they, wanted. A plan called project DARIT. The Dragon Heads embraced his plan and put it into action. Phase one was complete. TRIAD members occupied virtually all the key positions in the country. His boss, "489", was now the President of the Chinese government.

Phase two involved cloning the ultimate soldier. Thousands of them. Thousands of fearless warriors to invade and subjugate China's oldest enemy. Japan. At the same time, North Korea would use its clones to invade South Korea. By conquering and controlling these two rivals, China and its ally, North Korea, would not only control the Far East, they would also be the world's dominant superpower. The world number one.

A few months ago, they'd received Intelligence from their spy at the Cryonics Facility in Britain that changed everything. Intelligence so exciting, so earth-shattering, that the original, already ambitious, plans of Project DARIT were expanded beyond recognition. The world changing discovery could, if developed 'properly', produce a super weapon that would decimate the world's population. Decimate it in such a way as to leave China and North Korea as the undisputed world leaders.

'How much shall I tell them, Meng?' he asked his "426". 'There are too many rumours circulating around. We need to act.'

'What kind of rumours?' asked Meng.

'Like why are we "assembling" thousands of clones of the ultimate soldier, and what are they for? And what's the aim of this new research?'

'Is that it?'

'No. They want to know why so much effort has been put on the new research. And why the big rush? What shall I tell them?'

'Tell them nothing,' said Meng Huan. 'The more we tell them the greater the risk of a leak. They'll find out soon enough.'

29

WARRIOR

The cloning of Captain Johnnie Standish, C47SO, confirmed what they already suspected. That cloning Special Forces soldiers wouldn't produce the type of ultimate soldier they were looking for. A natural born soldier endowed with inherent fighting skills. A strong, brave, courageous, fearless and obedient soldier. A warrior.

In Captain Johnnie Standish they'd cloned one of the best soldiers the SAS had ever produced but, just like its predecessors, clone C47SO still suffered from the same deficiency. All its military skills had to be learnt. They weren't innate, hereditary. To be fair, C47SO learned quickly, very quickly, and rapidly became a top notch SAS soldier. Resourceful, adaptable, tough and tactically astute. But they wanted a warrior and for that, an alternative approach was required. They needed a source of DNA from warriors whose fighting skills were predominantly innate. Inbred. DNA from warriors of old.

Over the past few weeks Steve in particular had deliberated at length as to what other approaches they could pursue. And he always came to the same conclusion. It would have to be a warrior from the past. A legendary warrior with renowned fighting skills.

A fabled warrior from long ago. First, he looked at individuals. He researched some of the most famous warriors the world had ever known. Warriors such as Hannibal, Ghengis Khan and Alexander the Great. To his dismay, he discovered they were predominantly leaders, strategists and motivators rather than true warriors. 'Also,' he thought, 'how would you obtain a sample of their DNA?' It would be nigh on impossible to locate the remains of a single individual from thousands of years ago. That particular problem wouldn't arise with more recent individuals such as Geronimo and Sitting Bull, two of the most famous Red Indian warrior chiefs, but he dismissed them too.

Frustrated by his failure to find a suitable individual warrior, Steve switched his attention to races of warriors. Races such as the Romans. The Romans were undoubtedly good soldiers since they'd conquered and ruled most of the world, including Britain, for hundreds of years. But were they warriors? Steve decided they were not. In his opinion, the Romans were successful because they were organised, well trained and well equipped, not because their soldiers were warriors.

He considered other ancient warrior races. He looked at the Japanese Samurai, the African Zulus, the New Zealand Maoris and the Russian Cossacks. None fitted the bill. Like the Special Forces soldiers, their fighting skills had to be learned. From all his research, one set of warriors stood head and shoulders above the rest. The Spartans.

According to history, the Spartans were the finest warriors to have walked on planet Earth. In Sparta, males devoted their entire lives, from the cradle to the grave, to fighting and war. It's all they ever did. Fighting was in their blood. In their genes. And they were fearless. Before a Spartan warrior went to war, his wife, or some other woman of significance, presented him with his shield saying, 'With this, or upon this,' meaning that true Spartans could only return to Sparta either victorious (with their shield) or dead (carried upon it). 'Yes,' thought Steve, 'he'd inform Ewan and Debbie that the warrior would have to be a Spartan.'

'Excuse my ignorance,' said Debbie, 'but where exactly was Sparta?'

'Sparta, or Lacedaemon as it was also called, was situated on the banks of the River Eurotas in the southern part of Ancient Greece. It was a self-governing city state and maintained its position as the dominant land power for hundreds of years, until it became part of the Roman Empire in 146 BC.'

'Ah, Spartacus and all that,' said Debbie. 'I remember the film starring Kirk Douglas where Spartacus and his men won several battles against the Romans. But they were defeated eventually, weren't they?'

'They were,' said Steve. 'Defeated in a bloody battle at Brittium by Cassus' legions of 50,000 men.'

'And Spartacus?'

'It's unclear what happened to him but it's believed he perished in the battle.'

'Then we'll never find his remains,' said Ewan.

'No. And we don't need to,' replied Steve.

'Why's that,' said Ewan and Debbie simultaneously.

'Because, contrary to popular belief, and the name, Spartacus wasn't a Spartan. He was a Thracian.'

'A what?' said Debbie.

'A Thracian. A tribe of the *Maedi* which occupied the south-west region of Thrace (present day Bulgaria). A Thracian who became a famous gladiator, escaped, and led an army of slaves to famous victories against the Romans.'

'Interesting,' mused Ewan, 'so Spartacus had nothing to do with the Spartans?'

'No, he didn't,' replied Steve, 'unless some of the slaves were Spartans.'

'Can we get some remains of a Spartan soldier?' asked Ewan.

'We can and we, er, I have,' replied Steve triumphantly. 'The Romans and their allies defeated the Spartans in a brutal battle at Gythium in 195 BC, a landmark battle which ended the reign of Sparta. The battlefield was littered with bones, some of which are kept in the Museum of Ancient History in Athens. I requested some samples for research purposes, checked they were Spartan bones, not Roman, and managed to obtain traces of DNA from the bone marrow.'

Ewan and Debbie were irritated by his subterfuge but impressed by his initiative. And the result.

'Good work, Steve,' said Ewan, grudgingly, 'but keep us in the loop next time. Okay?'

'Okay,' said Steve, accepting the slight reprimand.

'I think that's the next experiment sorted then,' said Debbie. 'A hybrid of a Spartan and C22D.'

'C22D?' queried Steve. 'I thought its obedience genes failed.'

'So it seemed,' answered Debbie, 'but despite extensive tests, the post-mortem found no evidence of any faulty genes, including the obedience genes, although they did find some unidentified, alien DNA. Alien DNA that was attached to the obedience genes. Perhaps it was that which caused the malfunction. Anyway, the genes themselves seem perfectly normal.'

'Well, that's settled then,' said Ewan. 'We'll clone a hybrid of a Spartan and C22D. Either it'll be the perfect ultimate soldier or...' His voice tailed off.

30

SERENDIPITY

Chance favours the prepared mind, said Einstein. And there was no mind more prepared than Debbie Farnham's. It was razor sharp. In her entire career she had never failed to spot an unexpected discovery. A spurious result. And wonder. Why has this happened? What does it mean? Where does it lead and how can I use it? And that's precisely what happened during her work on identifying the sequences of genes responsible for certain human traits. An unexpected, but intriguing, discovery. A discovery that she, and Steve, followed up. A discovery that astonished and amazed them. A discovery they certainly weren't looking for.

Debbie and Steve had discovered the combinations of genes responsible for race and ethnicity in humans. The ethnicity genes. The sequences of genes that determine which of the three, or four, great races people belong to. The genes that determine whether we are Caucasian, Mongolian or Negroid. Or the fourth race added later, Australoid.

Most white people, including the British and Americans, are Caucasian. Caucasians dominate the Americas, Europe and Russia. The largest group of Negroids are the black Africans, and blacks descended from black Africans, whilst the Chinese, Koreans and Japanese make up the bulk of the Mongolian race.

Initially, Debbie and Steve had delved deeper, identifying the genes that differentiate the main races into smaller ethnic groupings, but stopped when they realised the implications of what they were doing. They knew what would happen if the work fell into the wrong hands. Knew what would happen if the military found out. It would be the atomic bomb scenario all over again.

They took a decision. Not only to stop the work, but to keep what they had found secret. Keep it to themselves. Only three people knew of the discovery. Debbie, Steve and their boss, Ewan Grigg. They deliberated for days whether a fourth person should be told. Charles DeLacy. On the one hand, he was their leader. A man of integrity. An honourable man. It didn't seem right to deceive him. But, on the other hand, he had regular contact with powerful people at the Cobra meetings. Military leaders and top ranking government officials, such as the Home Secretary. It was a risk but, in the end, they decided he should know.

Charles was an astute man and, like Debbie, Ewan and Steve before him, quickly realised the implications of the discovery. He supported fully their decision to keep it secret, despite the risk to his team and particularly himself. He knew full well that if any member of the Cobra team found out, there'd be hell to pay.

31

DARIT

The mist rolled down the mountains like some amorphous grey amoeba, enveloping everything in its path. A grey shroud that covered the entire landscape. Rain was in the air. He could feel it. And it was cold.

Xiong Kang shivered as he stood outside the main reception area of the Central Research Laboratories. He checked his watch. Five minutes. They should be here in five minutes. But would the grey mist have delayed their arrival? He doubted it. Precisely five minutes later, a black limousine emerged out of the mist like an alien machine from another dimension. It stopped in front of him, as did the four escort vehicles, two in front of the limousine, two behind. He wasn't surprised. As the Dragon Head of the *Sun Yee On* TRIAD, "489" had always insisted on punctuality, and tight security.

Xiong Kang waited whilst the bodyguards took up their positions and conducted a search of the area. "489" had always been a careful man, a cautious man, a thorough man. That's why he'd survived for so long as the Dragon Head of the *Sun Yee On* TRIAD. And now, in his new role as President of the Chinese government, he still exercised the same caution.

Satisfied the threat level was zero, one of the bodyguards opened the door. A man in his mid-fifties stepped out of the car. A well groomed, fit looking man dressed in a grey suit.

'Good morning, Xiong,' he said, 'it's good to see you again.'

'Thank-you, sir,' replied Xiong, bowing his head, 'it's good to see you too. Shall we go inside? Everything's ready.'

Flanked by two bodyguards, the most powerful man in China followed Xiong Kang as he made his way up the stairs and along the corridor to the small private meeting room.

Just two people awaited their arrival, Meng Huan and the Chief Scientist, the person with overall responsibility for all the research. The man who'd replaced Professor Wei Zhuang. They stood up as "489" entered the room.

'Relax, gentlemen,' said "489", 'and please be seated. There's no need for formalities.'

Gathered in this small room were four of the most powerful men in China. Men intent on changing the world. The inner sanctum of Chinese power. The two bodyguards remained outside.

'I've come to update you on Project DARIT,' said "489", 'to let you know where we are and where we need to be.'

'As you know, DARIT stands for 'Domination And Realignment of International Territories.' For those of you with an agile mind, you'll also have realised that DARIT is a most apt name. It's an anagram of TRIAD.'

The people in the room nodded. 'Yes. We'd already figured that out,' said the Chief Scientist.

'DARIT is an ambitious and risky project, but one I feel we can achieve. A project that will see us replace the West and the Third World and leave China and Korea as the undisputed new rulers. Our plans are becoming clearer,' continued "489". 'We have a definite timescale and a better idea of the targets you need to meet here at the Central Research Laboratories.' He paused before continuing. 'Instead of 5,000 ultimate soldiers, I'm afraid we need double that number.'

The Chief Scientist gasped. 'Ten thousand! You need 10,000 soldiers?'

'Yes. We do.'

'But how do we get so many bodies? Bodies of fit, young men. With a success rate of just one in four, we'll need 40,000!' said the Chief Scientist.

'Leave that to us,' said "489". 'It's not a problem. The question is, can you clone 10,000 ultimate soldiers?'

The Chief Scientist looked uneasy. He didn't want to refuse a request from "489". He knew what the consequences would be. But he knew that cloning 40,000 brains and attaching them to 40,000 bodies to produce 10,000 clones was a mammoth task. 'How long do we have to complete the work?' he asked.

'I'll come to that later,' replied "489", 'after we've discussed the second task. The most important task, I might add.'

'I take it you mean the development of the new super weapon,' said the Chief Scientist. 'The super weapon we're developing based on the information we received from our spy at the Cryonics Facility in Britain. The super weapon that will unleash Armageddon.'

'I do,' replied "489". 'How's the research progressing?'

'It's…' he almost said slow, but corrected himself. 'It's progressing steadily,' said the Chief Scientist.

'Good,' said "489", 'but it will have to speed up. As I said earlier, our plans have become clearer. We now have a definite timescale. Dates for the implementation of Project DARIT.' He paused before continuing, watching as the other three people exchanged glances.

'We have decided to implement Project DARIT in two stages. Two stages to mark two key Chinese anniversaries. Stage one, the unleashing of the super weapon, will be launched on

4 May 2019, the 100th anniversary of our hallowed 4 May Movement. The Movement which saw the Chinese people rise up against imperialist encroachment from abroad. Stage two, the simultaneous invasion of South Korea and Japan, will be launched on 1 October 2019, the 70th anniversary of the founding of the "Peoples' Republic of China". That leaves you, gentlemen, just over two years to complete the two tasks. I trust you will deliver. And it goes without saying that what I've just told you is highly confidential. It must not leave these four walls. Is that clear?'

Xiong Kang, Meng Huan and the Chief Scientist nodded their assent.

A silence filled the room. Delivering 10,000 clones was bad enough, but to have the super weapon ready in two years too was nigh on impossible.

It was the Chief Scientist who broke the silence. 'That's very interesting "489", but the targets are extremely, er, challenging. I'm not sure…'

'If you feel you can't achieve them,' interjected "489", 'then tell me now and I'll find someone who can.'

The Chief Scientist shut up.

'Right, gentlemen. I've just one more request to make and then I'll be on my way. I want you to ask our spy at the Cryonics Facility in Britain to do everything in their power to sabotage their cloning work. Everything. Understood?'

They nodded.

'Thank-you, gentlemen,' said "489" arising from his chair. 'I look forward to our next meeting.'

32

Cobra/COBRA

The Home Secretary looked angry. Very angry. 'Not a good sign,' thought Charles, as he took his seat at the table.

He had been summoned, along with the other members of the Cobra team, to an extraordinary meeting, a meeting which only happened in times of national emergency. Charles wondered what new developments could have prompted such drastic action.

'I've just finished speaking to my counterpart in COBRA in America,' said the Home Secretary, 'who's received some new Intelligence from China. Because of tighter security, the Intelligence is sketchy, but it appears that the Chinese government is pouring vast amounts of money and resources into producing thousands of cloned, ultimate soldiers at their Central Research Laboratories. Thousands. An army of cloned soldiers.

'That by itself is worrying enough but the Intelligence also suggests that they are committing even bigger amounts of money and resources into developing some sort of super weapon. A biological super weapon based on a discovery made here in Britain. A super weapon based on information from our Cryonics Facility. It appears, gentlemen, that we have a leak. A spy.'

The people in the room exchanged glances. They were shocked.

'To put it mildly, I have been made to look foolish. The Americans have acquired information that I should know about, but don't. And they are incensed. Incensed that someone in Britain has leaked top secret information to China. I want answers and I want them NOW!' she spat, thumping the table with her fist. 'I want to know how a spy has managed to bypass our strict security procedures. I want the spy identified. And I want to know what discovery the Americans are talking about.'

She looked directly at the man sat opposite her. 'Charles. Have you got something to tell me?'

Every set of eyes in the room focused on Charles. Their glares pierced him like red hot daggers. The moment he'd dreaded had arrived. His mind whirled frantically, trying to think of the best course of action, the best form of reply.

'Well?' said the Home Secretary, looking distinctly irritated.

Charles decided that he had no option but to come clean. To tell them about the discovery. The discovery they'd kept secret. Kept secret for good, honourable reasons. Kept secret precisely to prevent it being used to produce a super weapon. But it had backfired. Big time. It was being used to develop a super weapon, but not by Britain or America, but by a country potentially hostile to both Britain and America. He told them all of the above and waited for the repercussions. He feared the worst.

'What the fucking hell do you think you're playing at?' snarled the Home Secretary, furious at what she'd just heard. 'The future of the whole fucking world is at stake and you and your colleagues think you can play God! That you can decide which information to share and which to keep secret? It's not fucking acceptable, Charles. Do you hear! It's just not fucking acceptable!!' Angry and red faced, she glowered at the man who led the cloning research.

'I'm sorry, Home Secretary,' said Charles, 'but we did it for the best of reasons.'

'I don't care about your fucking reasons,' spat the Home Secretary, 'the decision wasn't yours to take. That's why we have these Cobra meetings for Christ's sake. It's for the people here to decide, Charles, not you.'

Charles was hurt, but not surprised, by the Home Secretary's comments. In her position, he'd have done exactly the same.

'If we'd known of the discovery,' said the Chief of the Defence Staff, 'we may well have taken the decision to develop a new super weapon ourselves, but only as a deterrent. A powerful deterrent to stop other countries from using such a weapon. A bit like the nuclear deterrent.'

'But the atomic bomb was used,' said Charles.

'Ah, but only once, er, twice. And having witnessed its awesome power, it has never been used since.'

'Now, because of your fucking…' the Head of MI6 was about to say stupidity, but corrected himself and said, 'secrecy, we've allowed the Chinese to forge ahead in a vitally important area.'

'I just can't believe how fucking lax your security is,' said the Head of MI5. 'How can someone have leaked vital information from the most top secret establishment in the whole bloody country?'

Charles was beginning to feel distinctly uncomfortable at the accusatory remarks and was on the verge of launching a retaliatory attack as the Home Secretary spoke.

'What's done is done,' she said, somewhat resignedly. 'The question is, what shall we do now? What are our options?'

'The first thing we need to do,' said the Head of MI5 still seething with anger, 'is to find the fucking spy and plug the leak. Have you any idea who it might be?'

'No,' replied Charles, 'I haven't. I don't understand how anyone could have got through all the extensive screening protocols to get Level 3 clearance, but I'll make it a top priority to find him.'

'Or her,' said the Home Secretary. 'It might be a woman.'

'The next thing we need to do,' said the Chief of the Defence Staff, 'is to let our biological warfare people at Porton Down take a look at your discovery and see if they can develop a super weapon before the Chinese.'

'And the third thing we need to do is plant a spy of our own in China, a spy in their research laboratories,' said the Head of MI6.

'And how do we do that?' asked the Home Secretary.

'I think I know the answer to that,' said Charles.

The others listened intently as he explained his idea.

33

TANGLED LOVE

Ewan Grigg had a liking for younger women. Young, attractive, dark-haired, shapely women. Women like Ruth.

His liking of young girls began at his local comprehensive school in Glasgow, a rough school where anything went. Like teenagers the world over, the younger girls preferred the older, more mature boys. They believed boys of 17 and 18 to be more experienced, more worldly wise and a little wealthier than boys of 14 and 15 and constantly pestered them for dates. Ewan was flattered by the attention lavished upon him and took great delight in playing the field. He'd take them to the pictures, have a fumble on the back row and, if the girl was willing, have sex with her. He knew it was illegal, but he could never resist the advances of a pretty young girl, even if she was underage. It was this period of his life, he believed, that initiated his passion for young women.

Ewan had fancied Ruth ever since he'd first set eyes on her. From the day she joined Dom Cruickshank's team almost 12 months ago, he knew he had to have her. Had to bed her. And so, like he'd done countless times before, Ewan Grigg made it his business to find out everything he could about Ruth Cunningham. Dig up her past to unearth something to blackmail her with.

Something to make her do exactly as he wanted. And to keep it all quiet.

With Ruth it was easy. He found out about her drinking and drug-taking at university, her disastrous marriage to Graham, and her young child. But, most importantly of all, he found that she was an adulteress. That she was having a relationship with another man whilst still married to Graham: the *decree absolute* of her divorce had yet to be granted. To Ewan, it was manna from heaven.

To strengthen his position even further, Ewan made a deal with her husband. He offered Graham a considerable sum of money to take legal proceedings against Ruth, but only on his say so. Legal proceedings to show that as a drinker, drug-taker and adulteress, Ruth Cunningham was unfit to be a mother. Unfit to look after a three-year-old boy. Armed with such damning information, Ewan Grigg made his move.

The canteen in The Nursery was emptying. It was 1-30 p.m. and most of the diners had returned to their work. Two of the few that remained sat by a window in the corner. They too had finished their lunch and were preparing to leave. Ewan Grigg dabbed his mouth with the napkin, placed it on his empty plate and looked across the table at the young woman sat opposite. The young woman with a new cloned forearm.

'Before we go back to the lab, may I ask you something?'

Ruth gave him a quizzical look. 'Go ahead,' she said. 'Ask away.'

'I'll come straight to the point, Ruth,' said Ewan, placing his hands on top of hers, 'I know you're seeing Adam but... could I take you out to dinner?'

Ruth was taken aback. Shocked. Shocked to the core. She'd accepted Ewan's invitation to meet him for lunch but she hadn't expected this.

'Look, Ewan,' she said sternly, removing her hands from his, 'thanks for the offer but I don't think that's a good idea. I've got to get back to the lab,' she continued, glancing at her watch and getting up from her chair.

Suddenly, Ewan's demeanour and tone of voice changed completely. 'SIT DOWN!' he barked, 'and listen to what I have to say before you go.'

Startled by his sudden change, Ruth sat down.

'Ruth, you're a lovely, attractive young woman and I've fancied you from the moment I first saw you. My invitation still stands, Ruth, but I want more than just dinner. I want to go to bed with you. I want to have sex with you.'

Ruth was shell-shocked. She listened in stunned silence to what Ewan was saying.

'Ewan,' said Ruth, trembling with anger and indignation, 'I'm really flattered that you find me attractive but there's no way I'm going to bed with you. No way at all. It's Adam I love, not you, and I'm not going to betray him.'

Ewan's smiling face unnerved her.

'Fine sentiments, Ruth, and very honourable, but I think you'll accept my, er, invitation,' he said.

'I most certainly will not,' said Ruth vehemently, 'and if you bloody well carry on, I'll report you to Charles!'

'No you won't,' he said, pulling out a sheet of paper from his pocket. 'I've done a little research on your past, Ruth, and do you know what, I've unearthed some very interesting facts.'

'What kind of facts,' she said, feeling distinctly uneasy.

'Oh, facts like drinking, drug-taking and adultery, Ruth.'

'ADULTERY! I haven't committed adultery,' spat Ruth, 'and the drinking and drug-taking was years ago at university.'

'That's as maybe,' said Ewan, 'but you're having a serious relationship with Adam whilst still married to Graham, and that's adultery.'

'But the divorce is through. I've got the *decree nisi* and…'

'A divorce isn't complete until you've got the *decree absolute*,' said Ewan, 'so technically, you're still married.'

Ruth's body sagged. She knew what was coming next.

'I don't want to, Ruth, but I can make things very unpleasant for you. Very unpleasant indeed. I've already contacted your husband, who's agreed to take legal proceedings against you if you don't comply with my wishes. Legal proceedings to show that a drinking, drug-taking adulteress is not fit to be the mother of a three-year-old child. In short, Ruth, your child, your precious child, will be taken away from you if you don't do as I want.'

A maelstrom of emotions whirled around Ruth's head. She wouldn't let anyone take her child away. Not in a million years. Not Dylan, her precious young son. And she didn't want to betray or, even worse, lose Adam either, the man she loved and who loved her. And she certainly didn't want to have sex with a fifty-odd year old professor. But she was trapped. What could she do?

The words that came out of her mouth surprised her. 'What do you want, Ewan?'

'I'm glad you've seen sense, Ruth. You're a nice girl and I didn't want you to lose your little boy.'

'What do you want?' she repeated, quietly.

'I want three things, Ruth. First and foremost, I want to have sex with you. Second, I want you to tell me about Adam's and Angela's work on replacement cloning, to keep me up-to-date with their latest findings. And thirdly, I want you to keep quiet. To tell no one. That's what I want, Ruth.'

Ruth seemed to shrink. She looked forlorn and dejected. Her eyes, normally so sparkling and full of life, were blank and lifeless. Devoid of hope. She looked like a woman resigned to her fate. A woman trapped between two evils with no means of escape. It was with great reluctance that she uttered her next words.

'When? When do you want me?'

'Friday night. At my place. Be there by 7-30.' As he got up to leave, Ewan made one final remark. 'Oh, Ruth, and thanks for being sensible.' Then Ewan Grigg turned and walked away.

Ruth put her head in her hands and sobbed. Sobbed uncontrollably. Damn you, Ewan Grigg. Damn you! DAMN YOU! **DAMN YOU!** She'd have to comply with his demands. She had no choice. But she'd do it on her terms. He wouldn't have it all his own way, the bastard.

34

A SPY IS CLONED

Charles' idea was a good one. He wanted the CIA agent in China to identify a scientist working on the super weapon at the Central Research Laboratories, obtain a sample of their DNA and let the Americans produce a clone. At the same time, his team would clone an 'assassin' to accompany the cloned scientist to China. Once there, the swap would be implemented. The assassin would eliminate the authentic scientist, allowing the clone to take his place.

'It sounds good,' said the Home Secretary, 'but is it feasible?'

'It is if we can identify a suitable scientist,' said the Head of MI6, 'and obtain a sample of their DNA.'

'I agree,' said Charles, 'but we need more than DNA. We need as much information as possible about the target. This is a case where the clone must be identical to the original in every respect. His face, his body and his brain. Every minute detail must be identical. Furthermore, we need personal information about the target. His family life, upbringing, education, girlfriends, or wife, children, social life and politics. Knowledge about China, genetics and replacement cloning will be supplied by us.'

'How is this information, er, imparted to the clone?' asked the Chief of the Defence Staff.

Charles looked at the Home Secretary before he answered. She nodded her approval.

'It's done by placing the clone's head in the "Infusion Chamber". It looks a bit like the hairdryers used in women's hair dressing salons, but it's a very complex, and expensive, piece of equipment.'

'As expensive as the Resurrection Chamber?' asked the Chief Scientific Advisor.

'No, not quite that expensive,' replied Charles, 'but almost. It's run by a quantum computer. The Infusion Chamber is placed over the head of the clone and the quantum computer uses a series of algorithms to infuse the information into the receptive, virgin brain of the clone. The process is very fast. Normally, it's complete within 30 minutes. It's how we impart basic information to all of the clones. For example, it's how we imparted information on London to Jack the Ripper.'

'And do the Americans have one?' asked the Head of MI5.

'Yes,' replied Charles, 'they have exactly the same equipment as we have.'

'Right, gentlemen,' said the Home Secretary, 'I'll convey our idea to the Americans. I'm sure they'll take it on board if they can identify a suitable scientist and obtain the necessary information and DNA. I'll keep you informed.'

The latest message from COBRA was a strange one. They wanted him to identify a scientist working on the super weapon project at the Central Research Laboratories, to obtain a sample of their DNA, and to obtain as much information as possible, including personal information, about them. And they wanted it quickly.

Skip Meyers had played his role of a disaffected American geneticist to perfection. He was indeed a professor of genetics, but he was also one of the CIA's top agents, an agent who'd been operating in China for 24 years. In that time, he'd supplied valuable Intelligence on China's activities on cloning research, Intelligence that ensured America didn't fall too far behind in this important area. But the Chinese authorities were becoming suspicious, particularly the new, hard line rulers.

It was they who'd appointed Chang Lee as his assistant to try and blow his cover. Chang Lee who, he'd found, was fanatical to the cause. Chang Lee who now spent all his time at the Central Research Laboratories working on the new project. Skip had samples of his DNA from the cups he'd drunk from, as well as lots of personal information of the type they required. In short, Chang Lee was the perfect target.

The COBRA team were astounded at the speed of response from Skip Meyers. The personal information and photographs of Chang Lee arrived within one day of their request, and the DNA samples two days later. They were ready to go.

The Home Secretary relayed the findings to the rest of the Cobra team without calling a meeting. It was time for Charles to clone the assassin.

35

THE TRYST

Ewan went to great lengths to make it an evening to remember. He always did. An evening beginning with a romantic, candlelit dinner for two followed by mad, passionate sex. He'd bought two bottles of *Cotes-du-Rhone* red wine, two cuts of the finest fillet steak, and potatoes and vegetables, and he'd cooked the food to perfection. The lights were low and soft music played in the background. Showered, and dressed in smart casual clothes, he was putting the finishing touches to the dining table when the doorbell rang. He checked his watch. 7-25 p.m. He smiled. He liked punctuality. Bursting with the excitement of the night ahead, he strode briskly to the door.

'Go…od ev…ning, Ewun,' slurred Ruth. 'I'm not… late… am I?'

Ewan couldn't believe his eyes. Standing in front of him was a drunken prostitute. A prostitute dressed in a tight red blouse, tight black skirt, black stockings and red, high heeled shoes. A prostitute with her face caked in make-up. Bright red lipstick, black mascara, false eyelashes and tons of foundation. A prostitute as drunk as a monkey and smoking a cigarette.

Ewan was appalled. She stunk of drink and cigarettes. He loathed smokers and wasn't too keen on drunkards either.

Recovering his composure, he said, 'No, Ruth, you're not late. Come in.' Ruth staggered over the threshold, stumbled, and would have fallen if Ewan hadn't grabbed her. He removed the cigarette from her fingers and led her into the lounge, where she collapsed on to the sofa.

She looked up at Ewan and giggled. 'I'm... ready if... you are,' she said, unbuttoning her blouse.

Ewan had never experienced anything like this. The other girls had always arrived sober, smartly dressed and smelling of perfume. None had transformed into a different person. He hardly recognised the woman on the sofa.

'I think you'd better have a shower,' he said brusquely, 'and use the mouthwash to get rid of that disgusting cigarette smell. The bathroom's at the top of the stairs.'

Ruth was so drunk that he had to push her up the stairs to prevent her falling backwards, and then help her undress. Stood there in front of him, naked and available, was the young woman he'd fancied for a year. The woman he'd fantasised about. The woman he wanted to have sex with. But, instead of being turned on, all he felt was revulsion. Revulsion at what she'd done. At the state she'd turned up in. Maybe he'd feel different after she'd showered and washed out her mouth. He certainly hoped so.

Ewan led the showered Ruth into the bedroom – there'd be no romantic dinner tonight – placed her on the bed and got undressed. He lay beside her and began the foreplay, kissing and fondling her. Normally, this produced an erection, but not tonight. Try as he might, he simply couldn't get it up, even when he made Ruth stroke his manhood. 'It must be her,' he thought. Still drunk, her face streaked with mascara and her breath still reeking of cigarettes, she was a total turn-off. The woman lying beside him bore no resemblance whatsoever to the attractive young woman who worked in Laboratory 3.

He was furious. Furious with himself for not being able to get an erection, but more furious with Ruth for what she had done.

'Get dressed,' he barked, 'and go home. I'll speak to you when you're sober.' She'd made a fool of him this time, but she wouldn't do so again, the bitch. He'd make sure of that. And she'd pay. Pay big time.

36

INSERTION

Adam had been wrong. C47SO, the clone of Captain Johnnie Standish, hadn't been sent to the SAS base at Hereford, he'd been chosen by Charles to be the assassin to accompany the clone of Chang Lee to China. The assassin to terminate the life of the real Chang Lee. But Charles had been careful. Following the Home Secretary's disclosure of a spy at the Cryonics Facility, he'd only told the two people he trusted above all others. Adam Kavanagh and Stuart Ramage. And he'd told even these two trusted colleagues just the bare minimum, that they needed to infuse C47SO with information on air travel, China, particularly the Tian Shan region, and Chang Lee. Nothing else. And nothing about the reason why.

He'd decided on C47SO rather than an ultimate warrior cloned from a Spartan, or Spartan-dog hybrid, because of the nature of the mission. The mission didn't require a brave, fearless, strong, obedient warrior, but a resourceful, adaptable, tough and astute soldier. An SAS soldier. A soldier like Johnnie Standish.

The documents were ready. Mr John Standish, a business representative for a company specialising in hi-tech medical equipment, would fly from London's Heathrow airport to Beijing, where he'd be met by one of Skip Meyer's assistants and driven to Skip's house in Shandong. Meanwhile, the clone of Chang Lee would be flying from Los Angeles' LAX airport where he too would be taken to Skip's house. There, the plan for the 'swap' would be finalised.

For the past few weeks Skip's small network of informants in the Tian Shan region had been watching Chang Lee. Keeping him under surveillance. Recording his every move. Where he lived, where he worked, his routines: what time he left for work, what time he returned home, his friends, his girlfriend (he wasn't married and had no children) and his local haunts. Armed with this information, Skip had devised a plan.

'I've considered several options,' he said to the three men in his front room, 'about where, when and how to do the swap. I could invite Chang here for the weekend under some pretext or other, but that would create unnecessary problems. It could compromise my position. The less contact I have with Chang, the better. No, the best plan is to execute the swap at his house.'

'And where's that?' asked John Standish.

'It's in the village built for the workers at the Central Research Laboratories,' replied Li Sun, Skip's most trusted accomplice. 'I'll point it out to you when we arrive at the village's only hotel on Thursday.'

Skip continued. 'The best time for the swap is Friday evening, because that's when Chang chills out after a hard week's work. He has a meal delivered to his door from the local Chinese take-away and stays inside watching TV. He sees no one on a Friday evening.'

'And it gives me the weekend to, er, acclimatise myself in my new role,' said Chang's clone.

'Precisely,' said Skip.

'That's the where and when sorted,' said Li Sun, 'but what about the how? Silenced pistol, knife, poison…'

'None of those,' interjected John Standish, 'they're too messy and leave traces. I'll break his neck. It's quick, clean and silent.'

'Good,' said Skip, 'that's settled then.'

'Not quite,' said Chang's clone. Skip, John Standish and Li Sun looked at him. What had they forgotten. 'How do we get rid of the body?' he said.

'It slipped my mind,' said Li Sun, 'but I'd thought about that. The safest option is to weigh the body down and throw it into the river. The fish will do the rest.'

'I think that's everything,' said Skip, 'let's get some food.'

Following Li Sun's instructions, John Standish and Chang Lee's clone had booked a window table in a restaurant situated approximately in-between the Central Research Laboratories and Chang's house. A restaurant that Chang Lee passed on his way home from work every night. John Standish checked his watch. 7-15 p.m. They'd finished their meal and were sipping the last dregs of their coffees. Outside, it was going dark. Cones of light from the few street lamps struggled to illuminate the roadway. John Standish and 'Chang Lee' watched the passers-by intently. They needed to be vigilant. They couldn't afford to miss their target.

'There! There he is,' said 'Chang Lee' excitedly, pointing to a figure hurrying along the far pavement. 'That's him, I'm sure of it.'

'We'll wait 20 minutes and then we'll go. Okay?' said John Standish.

'Okay,' replied 'Chang Lee'.

The doorbell rang. Wearing his white, towel bathrobe after his refreshing shower, Chang Lee strode to the front door to collect his meal. He'd ordered his favourite, *Char Siu with black bean sauce*. He opened the door, eager to collect his dinner. He was hungry.

The person holding his meal wasn't his regular delivery man. In fact, he wasn't even Chinese. He was... English. 'What...' It was the last word that Chang Lee uttered. Quick as lightning, John Standish dropped the cardboard container, grabbed Chang Lee's head in a vice like grip, and twisted it violently. A faint, almost imperceptible, crack was all that signalled the end of Chang Lee's life.

37

SABOTAGE

Adam was surprised. Why had Charles convened a meeting on pay and conditions for the Level 3 staff from laboratories 1 to 4? The official pay review was six months away. He'd never done it before.

Charles surveyed the expectant faces of the twenty-one top scientists sat in the lecture theatre. The buzz of conversation filled the air. It ceased abruptly as he arose from his chair. 'Good morning, ladies and gentlemen,' he began. 'First of all, I must apologise for dragging you here under false pretences. This meeting has nothing to do with your pay and conditions. It's about something far more serious. A few days ago the Home Secretary informed me that we have a spy amongst us. A spy who is passing top secret information to a foreign power. A spy who is sat in this very room.' He paused as people absorbed what he'd said. They looked at each other with a mixture of bewilderment and disbelief. 'The information,' he continued, 'is very reliable, and MI5 operatives are checking the records and activities of each and every one of you. As your boss, and with the consent of MI5, I've been allowed to inform you what's going on. I don't expect the spy to give themselves up but I can assure them, whether it's a him or her, that you'll be tracked down and caught. It's just a matter of time. One last thing. Could I ask each and every one of you to be extra vigilant. We can't undo what's been done but we don't want any more leaks. And, of course, it goes without saying that this information is highly confidential. It must not go beyond these four walls. Thank-you.'

Charles had thought long and hard about what to do about the spy. After consulting with MI5, he'd decided the best course of action was to let all the Level 3 staff know that he knew one of them was a spy. It might flush them out or make them nervous, but it might go the other way and precipitate whatever action they'd planned. To bring it forward. It was a risk, but a risk worth taking.

As he walked back to the lab, Ewan realised that what Charles had said was right. He'd have to act fast or it would be too late. His plans would have to be brought forward.

The trial with C22D had been a success. The alien DNA he'd injected, alien DNA developed secretly by himself, completely nullified its obedience genes. He hadn't meant for C22D to attack Ruth. Far from it. She was the young woman he fancied. The young woman he'd groomed for sex. Dom had been the intended target. C22D was meant to attack him when he entered the lab the following morning. He was always the first to arrive in Laboratory 3. But it hadn't panned out that way. No matter, the trial proved the alien DNA worked.

After his humiliating tryst with Ruth, Ewan wanted revenge. He'd give her an ultimatum. Either she met him again, this time as the real Ruth Cunningham, a sober, well-dressed, sweet-smelling, non-smoking, sexy Ruth Cunningham, or he'd tell Graham to initiate legal proceedings against her. He'd have his way with her, boy would he, but this time there'd be no romantic dinner, just violent, raw sex. Raw sex in her laboratory office and, after his lust had been sated, there'd be a surprise. A twelve stone surprise. C24D, a twelve stone killing machine of raw muscle and power with its obedience genes inactivated. After he'd finished with her, he'd push her into the lab and unleash C24D from its cage using the remote control. Then, he'd watch as it tore her to shreds. Not only would it avenge his earlier humiliation, it would shut her up. Shut her up for good. She was becoming too suspicious. But he couldn't do that now. Not after Charles' announcement. It would expose him as the spy and he'd only have killed one scientist. He needed to revise his plans.

Ewan's last communication from China was clear. Inflict as much damage as possible on the Cryonics Facility. He couldn't destroy the information; that was stored securely and encrypted, with multiple back-up systems. Instead, he needed to inflict physical damage. To destroy, or at least immobilise, the two most vital pieces of equipment, equipment that would take years to replace. The Resurrection Chamber and the Infusion Chamber. And kill as many of the Level 3 scientists as possible. This would be his new plan. The only questions to be answered were how and when.

How to kill the scientists was easy. He'd inject all the attack dogs with the alien DNA and release them at the most appropriate time. A time when they'd have unrestricted access to all of the Level 3 scientists in Laboratories 1 to 4. He'd have to think when that would be.

Destroying the Resurrection Chamber and Infusion Chamber would be difficult. Being expensive, vital and unique pieces of equipment, they were stored in the heavily guarded vault in The Nursery, alongside the DNA of famous and infamous people.

To inflict the maximum amount of damage, it was imperative that the release of the attack dogs and the destruction of the equipment happened at the same time, but he couldn't be in two places at once. He needed assistance. An accomplice. Someone who'd be willing to help him destroy the equipment. Someone who was unhappy with what was going on at the Cryonics Facility. He knew who to ask.

If she agreed to his request, Sheila Wetherall would gain entry into The Nursery by feigning illness. Like all Level 3 staff who fell ill at work, she'd be taken to the medical centre in The Nursery village. There, she'd use her womanly wiles to get past the guards and enter the vault. Then, she'd use the high powered TASER to destroy not just the Resurrection Chamber and the Infusion Chamber, but also the precious DNA samples too.

Providing he could persuade Sheila Wetherall to help him, the how question was solved. All that remained was the when. He daren't dally. Charles and the MI5 operatives were closing in.

38

EWΛN GRIGG

Ewan Grigg's lineage was working class. Poor working class. Generation after generation of Griggs' had trodden the same path. It was, they believed, their destiny. Their role in life.

Like many other Glaswegians, Ewan's father found work in the shipyards of the Clyde, the mighty river that flows through the heart of Glasgow. It was here, in the 1960s, that he met his future wife, Mei Tseng. As the name implies she wasn't a Scot, but a Chinese immigrant who shared his ideology of left wing politics. After a short courtship, they married and had two sons, Ewan, and his younger brother, Rob.

In common with other poor, working class families, they lived in Govan. After the closure of the major shipbuilders in the late 1970s, his father switched occupations and became a miner. A miner who became an active member of the National Union of Miners. An activist. A union man who rose to become the senior shop steward of the Lanarkshire miners, and a friend of Arthur Scargill. A union man who played a major role in organising the bitter and divisive miners' strikes of 1984/5. Strikes against Thatcherism. It was, his father believed, Margaret Thatcher's Tory government's revenge against the people who toppled Edward

Heath's government by their excessive pay demands in the 1970s. Revenge against the miners for holding the country to ransom. An attack on the working class by the ruling class. A class war. As a staunch anti-capitalist, Ewan's father did everything in his power to help the miners. Being one of the most active and vociferous leaders of strike action and demonstrations in Scotland, he became a target of the establishment. Of the ruling classes. And it was during one of these bitter demonstrations that a tragedy occurred, a tragedy that was to shape his life. His brother Rob, his beloved younger brother, who was also a miner, was trampled by a police horse. Trampled so badly that he was in a coma for six months. It was an injury which left him brain damaged. An injury that condemned him to a care home for the rest of his life. An injury that devastated the Grigg family.

This tragic event galvanised his father into even more extreme actions, actions that attracted the attention not only of the police, but also of MI5. He was targeted as a troublemaker and a suspected communist. The authorities hounded him, waiting their chance. It arrived one Saturday night. A fight broke out at his local pub. Nothing unusual about that for a Saturday night in a Glasgow pub but, unbeknown to them, this fight involved an undercover policeman. An undercover policeman who received a fatal injury.

The authorities spied their chance. Ewan's father was trying to stop the fight, but witnesses were bribed to testify that it was him who delivered the fatal blow. He was arrested and held in custody.

It was the final straw. He'd given everything he had in the struggle against the ruling classes. He was a spent force. A man framed for a murder he didn't commit. A man who had had enough. A few days before his trial, Ewan's father hanged himself.

The double tragedy of losing her youngest son to a care home and the loss of her husband proved too much for Mei Tseng. After watching her eldest son graduate from Strathclyde University, she committed suicide by jumping into the cold, murky waters of the river Clyde.

Ewan was shattered. Devastated. In just a few short years he'd lost his father, his mother and his younger brother. He blamed the state. It was the state who'd caused brain damage to his younger brother, the state who had framed his father for a murder he didn't commit, and the state who'd caused his mother to jump into the river Clyde. And, he vowed, it would be the state who'd be made to pay.

Whilst studying for his PhD, Ewan became a fervent member of the university's communist party. He forged secretive links with the Chinese members and, over time, gained their trust. When the offer came to spy for China, he grasped it with both hands. His Chinese masters rewarded him handsomely for his Intelligence but, after what his family had been through, he'd have done it for nothing. He hated Britain and everything it stood for.

39

PERSUASION

'Hi, Sheila, could I have a word?' asked Ewan as she passed his lab. 'It'll only take a few minutes.'

'Sure,' replied Sheila, turning around and following Ewan into his office.

'Would you like some coffee, or tea?'

'No. Thanks. I've just had some. What is it, Ewan?'

'I'll come straight to the point, Sheila. I've noticed at the weekly meetings that you've been surprised at some of the things that go on here. Things like the cloning of humans, for example. Things you think are unethical.' He paused, waiting for any reaction. She simply nodded her head in agreement, waiting for him to continue. 'Well, I've been here much longer than you and I feel exactly the same way.'

'Do you, Ewan,' she said excitedly. 'Do you really.'

'Yes, I do,' replied Ewan. 'I feel that cloning humans with our present state of knowledge is not only unethical, it's downright wrong. The failure rate is still too high and the long term consequences are unknown. It's totally unfair on the clones.'

'My sentiments precisely,' gasped a surprised Sheila. 'At least there's one person here who shares my views.'

'You'd be surprised. There are more, but they're too scared to admit it,' said Ewan, warming to his task. 'Sheila,' he continued, 'I've asked you in to see if you'd like to do something about it. Something to put a stop to it or, at the very least, delay it.'

'Like what?' she asked, looking both excited and troubled at the same time.

'Well, like damaging the two key pieces of equipment, the Resurrection Chamber and the Infusion Chamber. They'll take years to replace.'

'And how do we do that?' asked Sheila. 'They're kept under heavy guard in The Nursery.'

'I know,' he replied, 'but I've got the bones of a plan. The only problem is, it needs one hell of a commitment from a woman. A woman like you, Sheila.'

'What kind of commitment?' she asked warily.

Ewan explained his plan. How she'd have to feign illness to get into the medical centre in The Nursery. How the timing would have to be right – when both the Resurrection Chamber and the Infusion Chamber would be in the vault. And how she'd get into the vault and damage the equipment.

Sheila was shocked. Not by his plan to damage the equipment and delay the cloning research, that was fine. She was shocked by the commitment he expected from her. From a young woman he hardly knew. It seemed he wanted her to have sex with each one of the four security guards. Inside the vault. One at a time.

'No way,' said Sheila. 'No way at all. That's asking too much. I'd like to help, I really would, but I'm not having sex with four total strangers. Not for anyone. It would be tantamount to being gang raped. No, I'm sorry, Ewan, I won't do it.'

'But it won't be like that,' said Ewan. 'As soon as you enter the vault with the first guard, you'd TASER him – the TASER's located beside the door – and lock the door. Then, you'd TASER the Resurrection Chamber, Infusion Chamber and the DNA samples. Finally, you'd set off your panic alarm and wait for help to arrive.

'When it does, tell them that the guard forced you inside the vault and tried to rape you. Say that you struggled, fought for your life and that you managed to grab the TASER and subdue him. Unfortunately, during the struggle, the TASER caused some collateral damage to the equipment and the DNA samples. It's a plausible story, one I'm sure they'll believe.'

If Ewan was right, she wouldn't need to have sex with any of the guards. But how could she be sure? She was still unconvinced. 'Ewan? How do you know the guards will, er, agree to my offer? After all, this is a high security facility.'

'I know some of the guards personally,' replied Ewan, 'and one or two of them owe me favours. Big Favours. Once we've decided on the date, I can arrange it so that the guards on duty include the ones who owe me a favour. And I'm sure they'll be receptive to an offer of sex in the vault, especially with a young, attractive woman like you.'

Sheila blushed.

'It sounds good, Ewan, but…'

'It's asking a lot of you, Sheila,' Ewan reiterated, 'but I can't think of a better way. I'll understand if you don't want to do it,' he said.

Sheila was torn between conflicting emotions. She'd like nothing better than to stop, or delay, the human cloning research, but Ewan's plan required a massive commitment from her. And it involved a high degree of risk, especially if things went wrong. She thought about the promise she'd made to Adam. That she wouldn't do anything stupid like sabotage the work. A maelstrom of emotions whirled around her head. She was torn between her head and her heart. Eventually, she spoke. 'Okay,' she said softly, 'I'll do it.' Her heart had won the day.

'That's great,' said a jubilant Ewan. 'I'll find out when the

Resurrection Chamber and Infusion Chamber will definitely be in the vault and let you know. I know you won't, but don't breathe a word of this to anyone.'

'I won't,' said Sheila, 'and thanks for… confiding in me.'

'No. It's me who should thank you, Sheila, for being so brave.'

She gave him a smile as she left his office.

'Good,' thought Ewan, 'if I get the timing right, I can have my bit of fun with Ruth too.'

40

RUTH'S REVENGE

A week on Friday. That was the day when both the Resurrection Chamber and the Infusion Chamber would definitely be in the vault. Ten days away. Longer than he'd have liked but it gave him, and especially Sheila, time to execute their plan.

Ewan had given Ruth his final ultimatum at the beginning of the week, an ultimatum that she had no choice but to accept. He'd told her he'd meet her in her office in Laboratory 3 at 12-30 p.m. on Friday. It should be empty apart from Ruth. Dom and the other three scientists wouldn't return from their lunch break until one-o-clock. Thirty minutes was more than sufficient for what he had in mind.

He'd also informed Sheila. She would feign illness on the Wednesday, be admitted to the medical centre in The Nursery, and have two days to inveigle her way into the vault. She was to set off the panic alarm at precisely 1-00 p.m. The time that most of the scientists would be at lunch. The time that he'd unleash all the attack dogs. Everything was in place. His masters in China would be pleased. Extremely pleased.

Ewan checked his watch. 12-29 p.m. Time to go. As he walked the short distance from his office to Ruth's, he allowed himself the luxury of a little smile. In a touch of irony, he would have the woman he'd fancied for a year in her own office bent over her own desk. This time, she'd better be sober or…

Sat at her desk, Ruth Cunningham looked stunning. She was just as he wanted. Sober, smartly dressed, smelling of expensive perfume, sexy and pleasant. The latter surprised him. He hadn't expected that. It was a welcome bonus, but it wouldn't last long. Not after what he had in store for her.

'Hello, Ewan,' she said. 'Come in.' As soon as he entered the office, he locked the door and closed the blinds.

'I'm glad you've followed my instructions, Ruth,' he said. Grabbing her tightly, he kissed her passionately on the mouth. 'I've waited a long time for this.'

'I think you have,' she thought, feeling his hard, erect penis pressing against her groin. 'I think you have.' She was surprised by his impatience.

Without any warning, he pulled out of the embrace, ripped off her blouse and bra, and forced her to bend over the desk. He was rough and aggressive. Like a man starved of sex. A madman. He yanked her jeans and panties down to her knees, exposing her soft, bare bottom, dropped his own pants then rammed his rock hard penis into her. He fucked her like a depraved animal. 'Is it good, you fucking whore?' he gasped. 'Is it fucking good?'

It was anything but. His violent, aggressive thrusting and vice-like grip hurt like hell. She wanted it to stop, but there was nothing she could do. He was too strong. Too powerful. She'd have to wait for it to end.

He fucked her really hard. Eventually, after what seemed like an eternity, she felt his body tense, and then shudder, as he unleashed a torrent of semen. Thick, creamy semen deep within her vagina. He emitted a long groan of satisfaction, satisfaction that, at long last, his animal lust had been sated. She felt his body relax. Moments later, he withdrew his throbbing, glistening penis.

In her entire young life Ruth had only ever had sex with three men. Her lovemaking with Adam, and Graham, had been enjoyable but this… this wasn't sex. It was rape. Brutal, raw, savage rape. Her body felt sore and bruised.

'Did you enjoy that?' sneered Ewan. Ruth said nothing, just glared at him with silent hatred. 'Put your clothes on,' he snapped. 'We're done.'

As she was getting dressed, Ruth glimpsed a movement from the corner of her eye. It was Ewan. He was pressing a button on a remote control handset, a button that opened one of the cages in the lab. She heard it click. 'You bastard,' she thought, 'even having your way with me wasn't enough, was it? You intend to kill me as well.'

Ruth thought quickly. Her life depended on it. Her only hope was to grab the TASER beside the door, the door that Ewan was unlocking, and TASER him. She made a lunge for the TASER but Ewan realised what she was doing and tried to grab her. But Ruth was too quick. She plucked the TASER from its mounting, pointed it directly at Ewan's chest and squeezed the trigger, all in one seamless, swift movement. The powerful electric shock made his body quiver like a jelly. His eyes glazed over and Ewan Grigg fell backwards through the partly open door into the lab. Even though it was a desperate situation, Ruth thought he looked comical. He lay on his back, unconscious, with his trousers round his ankles and his manhood pointing to the skies. Suddenly, a movement at the far side of the lab caught her attention. C24D had seen the commotion and was coming to investigate. Coming fast. Quick as a flash, she closed the door and locked it.

She watched in horror as C24D attacked Ewan. Watched as it ripped open his throat, severing the main arteries and crushing his windpipe. Watched as it began tearing his body to pieces. His arms, his legs and, aagh, his manhood. Pieces of flesh and bones were strewn everywhere, and blood spurted from the severed arteries. It was horrific, yet compelling, viewing. She couldn't take her eyes off it. She was transfixed. She hated Ewan for what he'd done to her, but she didn't wish this on anyone. Not even him.

Ruth was appalled at how events had turned out. It wasn't what she had planned, but it had killed two birds with one stone. Ewan's death not only ended her blackmail nightmare, it had almost certainly eliminated the spy from the Cryonics Facility too.

She checked her watch. It was approaching 1-00 p.m. People would be returning from lunch unaware that a vicious attack dog was on the prowl. She was about to press her panic alarm when someone beat her to it. She checked the display. It was Sheila Wetherall. She pressed hers anyway.

41

AFTERMATH

Sheila's plan had gone awry. Ewan had lied. During her two days in the medical centre, she'd used all her womanly ways to befriend the guards, dropping hints that she could be available for sex, but only at the right time. And place. And that was just before one-o-clock on Friday outside the vault.

As arranged, she met them at 12-55 p.m. So far so good. But then it went wrong. Horribly wrong. Instead of opening the door to the vault, one of the guards seized her whilst the other three formed a protective circle around them. They intended to take up her offer of free sex but there was no way they were going to let her into the vault. No way at all.

She'd been stupid. Why had she believed Ewan? It was obvious with hindsight that only the best, and most trustworthy, guards would be assigned to protect the Facility's most prized possessions. They'd never allow an unauthorised person access to the priceless DNA samples, nor to equipment costing billions of pounds. Equipment that was vital to the Facility's research. Perhaps Ewan had thought they might agree to her offer. She didn't know. And right now, she didn't care. She'd been stupid and naïve. But she wasn't stupid enough to be gang raped for nothing. She pressed her panic alarm.

'Christ almighty,' gasped Dom, dashing into the lab and seeing Ewan's mangled and dismembered body, 'what the hell's happened?'

Ruth told him everything. How Ewan was blackmailing her. How he'd given her an ultimatum. How he'd bent her over her own desk and brutally raped her. How he was going to let C24D kill her. And how, after a brief struggle by the door, she'd managed to TASER him, causing him to fall backwards into the lab. And how she'd locked herself in the office when she saw C24D approaching and pressed the panic alarm, then watched in horror as the dog tore him to pieces.

'And where's the dog now?' asked Dom.

'I don't know,' replied Ruth, 'but he's on the loose somewhere.'

'I'll call security. They'll deal with him,' said Dom.

'Oh, and there's one other thing,' said Ruth. 'I'm certain that Ewan was the spy. He made me tell him everything I knew about Adam and Angela's research on replacement cloning.'

Dom looked stunned. 'Are you sure?'

'I know it's hard to believe,' she said, 'but I'm sure. It's definitely him. I'd stake my life on it.'

During the next few days, evidence uncovered by the MI5 operatives confirmed Ruth's proclamation. Ewan Grigg had indeed been the spy. They discovered his links to communism and China, links he'd meticulously concealed when obtaining his appointment at the Cryonics Facility. And they also discovered his incriminating, encrypted messages to his Chinese masters, messages that were undeleted because of his sudden and untimely death. Ewan Grigg's demise may have been messy and unexpected but it eliminated one threat. The spy at the Cryonics Facility was dead.

42

ETHNICITY

Fourteen people sat in the Cobra meeting room. Fourteen people awaiting the arrival of the Home Secretary. A quiet buzz of conversation filled the air. The Home Secretary had asked Charles to bring his key scientists to the meeting to discuss recent events and to brief them on the work they'd kept secret. The work on the ethnicity genes. Charles had brought the two senior people from each of the four laboratories. Angela and Sheila from laboratory 1, Stuart and Adam from laboratory 2, Dom and Ruth from laboratory 3 and Debbie and Steve from laboratory 4. Suddenly, the door burst open and the Home Secretary rushed into the room. 'Sorry I'm late,' she said, 'but I've been briefing the PM (Prime Minister) on recent events.

'Thanks for coming everyone. I don't know all of you, but I'm sure I will by the end of the meeting. The reason I've called you here is to address recent events. First, let me say that I'm sad about the death of your colleague, Professor Ewan Grigg, but pleased that the spy has been eliminated. That's removed one major threat. Secondly, I'm pleased to report that we now have a spy of our own. Charles' plan to insert a cloned scientist into China's top secret Central Research Laboratories has been implemented successfully. But the main reason I've called you here today is to learn where we are regarding the ethnicity research and, more importantly, where we go from here.

'Charles, can you start us off?'

'Thank-you, Home Secretary,' replied Charles. 'The ethnicity genes were discovered by Debbie, Steve and, er, Ewan, so I've asked Debbie and Steve to prepare a short presentation. Since the topic is new to most of the people in this room, Debbie will begin with a brief history of ethnicity genes, explain how her team found them, and finally tell us how they might be used to develop ethnic specific biological weapons. Debbie.'

Debbie arose from her chair and strode to the front of the room. 'Thanks for the introduction, Charles, and good morning ladies and gentlemen. As Charles said, most of you are unfamiliar with the topic of ethnicity genes and ethnic specific weapons, so I'll begin with a little history.

'Ethnic specific weapons are not new. As long ago as 1970 Carl A Larson, the head of the "Department of Human Genetics" at the Institute of Genetics in Lund, Sweden, wrote an article for the American military entitled "Ethnic Weapons". It was published in the Military Review in November of that year and was the first published article on the subject. Even then, Larson realised the potential of genetically sensitive chemicals "to subdue enemy populations". He explained that many of the bodily functions are dependent on enzymes, including key functions like the contraction and relaxation of muscle tissue. Blocking such enzymes, he argued, would result in paralysis and death.

'But enzyme blockers were known well before 1970. In Germany in the 1930s, the enzyme blocking action of organophosphates was discovered accidentally by scientists working on experimental insecticides. Those unlucky enough to have worked on, or used them, died. They were so potent that just a single drop on the skin killed in ten minutes. This discovery led to the "nerve gas" *Trilon* used by the Nazis in World War II to exterminate millions of Jews.'

She paused. 'Any questions?'

'Yes, I've got one,' said the Chief Scientific Advisor. 'The organophosphates are specific in the sense that they target the central nervous system, but they're not ethnic specific are they?'

'You're right, they aren't ethnic specific. None of the early chemicals were. We had to wait until 1998 for an ethnic specific biological weapon. In the April of that year, the London Sunday Times reported that Israel was developing an "ethnically targeted" biological weapon that would kill or harm Arabs but not Jews. In developing the "ethno bomb", Israeli scientists had identified distinctive genes carried by Arabs but not Jews. They'd pinpointed a characteristic genetic profile of certain Arab communities, particularly the Iraqi people, and were creating a modified bacterium or virus to attack that gene. This top secret research was done at the Institute for Biological Research in Nes Tsiona, a small town south east of Tel Aviv. In trying to develop an "ethnic bullet" against the Arabs, the Israelis were making use of similar biological studies conducted by South African scientists during the Apartheid era.'

'I remember the Israeli ethno bomb,' said the Head of MI6. 'No one was sure if it was real or just propaganda to scare the Arabs.'

'The latter, I suspect,' replied Debbie, 'because in order to develop a true ethnic genetic virus (EGV), the make-up of the human genome has to be known and that wasn't accomplished until 2003.

'The mapping of the human genome and its publication in 2003 provided a massive boost to geneticists and molecular biologists around the world. It was the starting point for our own work on identifying the sequences of genes that determine key human traits. As we identified the genes responsible for specific human traits, it was almost impossible not to extend it to ethnicity traits. But we stopped when we realised the implications of what we were doing. It just needed someone to develop a deadly virus or bacterium designed to attack the ethnicity genes and, well… In the wrong hands, it would have been disastrous.'

'Unfortunately, that's precisely what's happened,' said the Home Secretary.

'I know,' interjected Charles. 'We're sorry about that, but what's done is done,' he said, repeating the Home Secretary's words from a previous meeting.

Debbie continued. 'Many geneticists believe there aren't any ethnicity genes, that genetic diversity *within* a population is greater than that *between* populations.'

'Isn't it true that 99.9 per cent of the genetic sequence of any two human individuals is identical?' asked the Chief Scientific Advisor.

'Yes, it is,' replied Debbie, 'but the remaining 0.1 per cent still accounts for a total of three million "letters" of the human genome. And,' she continued, '99 per cent of our DNA is identical to that of a chimpanzee, so it doesn't take much for there to be tremendous differences.'

'Is a 0.1 per cent difference sufficient to express ethnic specific genes?' asked Professor Stuart Ramage.

'Absolutely,' replied Debbie. 'Genetic sequences which fulfil the requirements for ethnic specific genes not only exist, they do so in unexpectedly high numbers. Indeed, it's been shown that many hundreds, possibly thousands, of gene sequences suitable for ethnic genetic weapons do actually exist. It's been known for many years that single nucleotide polymorphisms (SNPs) are one of the most common forms of genetic variation, and approximately 40 per cent of SNPs are *population* specific.'

'How specific?' asked the Chief of the Defence Staff.

'It varies,' replied Debbie, 'from a few per cent to greater than 25 per cent.'

'But wouldn't we need a figure approaching 100 per cent for it to be effective?' continued the Chief of the Defence Staff.

His use of 'we' troubled Debbie, but she answered anyway. 'Ideally, yes. In practice, no. As little as 10-20 per cent would wreak havoc amongst enemy soldiers on the battlefield, or on an enemy society as a whole. However, some ethnic specific gene sequences have been discovered with a ratio of 0 per cent to 94 per cent. For example, in one study 94 per cent of African-Americans possessed a gene sequence that was completely absent in Asians. In such a case, an EGV targeted at the African-American gene sequence would kill 94 per cent of them whilst being harmless to Asians.'

'Interesting,' said the Home Secretary, 'but isn't that more use to the Chinese than it is to us? What we need is one that targets the Chinese. Is that possible?'

'The Chinese are part of the Mongolian race, along with the Koreans and Japanese, so it would be difficult to target just the Chinese.'

'You mean there'd be some collateral damage,' said the Chief of the Defence Staff.

'I'm afraid so,' answered Debbie. 'It's impossible to design an EGV that's 100 per cent specific for a large ethnic group. The genetic differences are somewhat blurred. Some of them would survive and some of the other races, including Caucasians like ourselves, would die.'

'That's been a very interesting, and very revealing, insight into the world of ethnicity and ethnic specific biological weapons, Debbie. Thank-you.'

The Home Secretary's sentiments were echoed around the room.

'What I need to know now,' continued the Home Secretary, 'is three things. One, where are we up to with the ethnicity genes? Two, what do we do next? And three, what are the Chinese doing?'

After a general discussion around the table, it was agreed that the first task was to complete the work on identifying the gene sequences for the four main races, with the focus on the Mongolian and Caucasian races and, if time permitted, to try and differentiate the Chinese from the Koreans and especially the Japanese.

The second task, it was agreed, was to develop an EGV targeted at Mongolians, either using a natural agent such as anthrax, smallpox, bubonic plague or ebola, or a more virulent, man-made strain.

'We've got plenty of those,' said the Chief of the Defence Staff. 'I'll contact our boys at Porton Down. They'll need to be involved.'

'Regarding what the Chinese are up to, we'll have to await the first report from our spy,' said the Head of MI6.

'Thank-you, ladies and gentlemen, for a most interesting and informative meeting. I'll be in touch.'

With that, the Home Secretary arose from her chair. The meeting was closed.

43

EGV

'Good morning, Chang. Did you have a nice weekend?' asked Dr Qian Shen.

'Same as usual,' replied Chang Lee. 'Chilled out on Friday night and spent Saturday and Sunday with Bao.'

'How is Bao Tsou? Is she well?'

'Yes, she's fine,' replied Chang. Changing the subject, he asked, 'Where's Professor Hui Wang? Hasn't he arrived yet?'

'He's still in the Monday morning meeting with the Chief Scientist. It seems to be taking longer than normal. Would you like a coffee?'

'I'd love one, thanks, Qian,' answered Chang.

'Good. We'll have one in Professor Wang's office. He shouldn't be long.'

It was the start of Chang's third week at the Central Research Laboratories. The information infused into his brain had served him well. Personal information about the real Chang Lee and scientific information about cloning. By keeping his eyes and ears open, in just two short weeks he'd learned a lot.

Because of Ewan Grigg's treachery, the Chinese were well ahead in the race to develop the first ethnic genetic virus. Like

Debbie and her team, they'd started by scouring the literature to discover everything that had been published on the topic, but it was the information provided by Ewan on the gene sequencing work for identifying human traits, plus their preliminary work on ethnicity genes, that really enabled them to forge ahead. It only required a small step to identify the key genetic sequences responsible for the four main ethnic races and from there to design an EGV.

Priorities had been set. The overriding priority was to identify the genetic sequences which characterise the Caucasian race, the race that presented their main threat. The race that included the majority of white Americans, Britons, Europeans and Russians. Fifty per cent of the entire research effort was directed towards this one aim. In contrast, just ten per cent was devoted to the Negroid and Australoid races, and none at all for the Mongoloid race. They deemed it unnecessary. They were so far ahead in their work on developing an EGV that the Caucasians would be wiped out before any retaliation could be launched. For precisely the same reason, they didn't design an antidote either.

The team was following two approaches, an easier but less effective gene inhibition approach and a more difficult, but very deadly, genomic marker approach.

As two of China's leading experts on gene inhibition, Professor Hui Wang and his colleague, Dr Qian Shen, had been switched from working on replacement cloning to work on the vitally important EGV. Chang was the third member of their team.

Not only was gene inhibition an easier route to an EGV, they also had a head start from Ewan's secret work on developing the alien DNA that successfully neutralised the obedience genes in C22D. It was a great platform from which to start. For their work, they'd chosen mRNA (messenger ribonucleic acid), the molecule that transmits information from DNA to the site of protein synthesis in the cell. There are several ways to inhibit this transfer of information but the one they selected was anti-sensing. In this technique, an externally applied, alien DNA molecule inhibits the activity of mRNA by binding to the corresponding DNA sequence on the mRNA. However, to be effective as an EGV, a population specific genetic sequence has to be identified, a genetic sequence that is vital for the body's survival.

This was what Professor Wang's team, along with several others, were working on. After a number of false leads, they'd identified several genetic sequences exclusive to Caucasians that fulfilled the above criteria. Ideally, they'd have liked to attack the brain or the central nervous system, but found no easy ways to do that. Stopping the heart was a possibility. They could build on the work of beta-blockers but in the end decided against it. The wealth of knowledge on the subject meant that an antidote could probably be discovered. That left two options.

They were well on their way to finalising both the gene sequences for muscle contraction and relaxation, and for the production of red blood cells in the bone marrow. An EGV directed at either one would cause a slow, agonising death. The final choice between these two options would be made in a few weeks time.

As they were sipping the last dregs of their coffee, Professor Hui Wang entered the office. He looked angry. 'Bad meeting?' asked Qian.

'You could say that,' growled Hui. 'It looks as though the genomic marker approach has stalled. They've hit serious obstacles, so that approach might not deliver an EGV in time. It means there's more pressure on us.'

'What kind of obstacles?' asked Qian.

'Well, as you know, the development of ethnic weapons with very specific effects use a genomic marker as a trigger for an activity that is unrelated to the location of the marker. For example, the marker could be on any ethnic specific gene, but once it attracts the tailor-made pathogen, the EGV, the result is always the same, irrespective of the gene's function. If that pathogen is an ebola virus, then the victim will die from ebola.'

'So what's the problem?' asked Chang.

'Viral mutation. Having identified the appropriate genomic marker, the team had to design a DNA sequence to recognise and attack that marker, that marker and no others, and then incorporate it on to the pathogen. And they did. The resulting EGV worked. At first. But when it was mass produced, it behaved like a natural virus and began to mutate. It evolved into a different strain, a strain that was no longer ethnic specific. It's a real problem.'

'Is it because it's an artificial ebola virus?' queried Qian.

'They don't know yet,' replied Hui. 'It could be that but it could also be a reaction by the ebola virus to the attached DNA sequence. Whatever it is, it's really slowed down the work. It's a real stumbling block.'

Selecting the right pathogen had been a problem. All the world's most dangerous pathogens, such as smallpox, anthrax, bubonic plague and ebola, were stored in secure locations in the USA and Russia. China had none. So they had no option but to synthesise a pathogen from scratch. Build it from sequences of DNA and then bring it to life.

The Pathogenic Team, which consumed another 30 per cent of the total effort, had built on the work of US researchers at the State University of New York. In 2002, they synthesised the polio virus from scratch. Starting with the genetic sequence of the virus, its genome, the researchers synthesised viral sequences in the lab, ordered other tailor-made DNA sequences from a commercial source, and then combined them to form the full polio genome. In the last step, the complete DNA sequence was brought to life by adding a chemical cocktail, which initiated the production of a living, pathogenic virus.

The Pathogenic Team realised this technique was applicable to other viruses which have similarly short genetic sequences (genomes), and that at least five such viruses were considered to be potential biowarfare agents. They chose the ebola virus.

The final team working on the EGV was the Delivery Team. By listening to snippets of conversation in the canteen, Chang learned that four methods had been considered.

The first method, spreading the EGV by contagion just like a natural virus, was dismissed quickly. It was too slow and unpredictable. It would take years to spread across land masses as large as the USA, Canada, Europe and Russia, giving the Americans and British time to retaliate.

The second method, of using giant planes like B52s fitted with crop spraying equipment, would disperse the EGV quickly and efficiently over large, populated regions such as cities and towns, but they'd be shot down before they got anywhere near their targets.

Infecting the water supplies of such large and disparate geographical areas was also out of the question. The logistics of smuggling vast quantities of an EGV into lots of well protected countries was nigh on impossible.

The best method of delivery, indeed the only option, was to use rockets. Intercontinental ballistic rockets that would release their deadly cargo over densely populated areas. Some of the rockets might be destroyed by the anti-missile defence systems, but enough would get through to fulfil their plan. Enough to wipe out at least 90 per cent of the white populations of Britain, the USA, Canada, Europe and Russia.

All that was required was the pathogen. The EGV.

44

PORTON DOWN

Located north-east of Salisbury, Porton Down has been the centre of Britain's chemical and biological warfare activities since 1940. Following the start of World War II, a secret group was set up at Porton Down by the War Cabinet with a mandate to investigate the reality of biological warfare and, if feasible, to develop a means of retaliation in kind should such weapons be used against Britain and its allies.

Most of the work carried out at Porton Down has remained secret, but it's known that the facility produces a highly effective anthrax vaccine which is sold around the world, and that animals such as mice, pigs and monkeys have been used at various times to test the efficacy of toxic chemicals and lethal nerve agents.

Charles, Debbie and Steve had travelled to Porton Down the previous day, allowing them a full days meeting with scientists from Britain's top research establishment on biological warfare. A meeting to discuss the ethnicity genes and the possibility of designing an EGV. The Chief of the Defence Staff opened the proceedings. 'Right,' he said, 'this isn't a formal meeting. There'll be no minutes taken so you can be as open and frank as you like. I want an informal exchange of ideas to see if an EGV can be developed and, if so, over what timescale. I'm not a scientist and I don't want to, er, inhibit the discussion, so I'll leave you to it. I'll pop back at the end of the meeting to see how you've got on.' He arose from his chair and left the room.

'Okay,' said the senior scientist from Porton Down, 'how do you want to play this, Charles?'

'Well, as a starting point I think it's best if Debbie and Steve give a presentation of their discovery of the ethnicity genes. Then, if your people can give us an overview of biological weapons, we'll see if it's possible to marry the two and design an ethnic specific biological weapon. Is that okay?'

'That's fine,' replied the senior scientist. 'I would have suggested the same myself.'

Over the next two hours Debbie and Steve explained how they'd discovered the genes responsible for the ethnic differences between the four main races, and how they'd began to probe even deeper into the ethnic differences of smaller sub-groups. As they went into the details of particular gene sequences and specificity ratios, Charles' mind began to wander.

'How presentations have changed,' he thought, as he listened to Debbie and Steve. Back in the old days, he used handwritten acetates on an overhead projector. As technology advanced, these progressed to PowerPoint produced acetates and, for really important presentations, good old fashioned 35 mm slides. Nowadays, almost every presentation was done directly from a laptop. The molecular models of the DNA sequences in full, vibrant colour never failed to impress him. He could look at them all day. Steve's concluding remark jolted him from his reverie.

'So those, in a nutshell, are the ethnicity genes that determine whether we are Caucasian, Mongolian, Negroid or Australoid.'

'Thanks for that,' said the senior scientist, 'it was extremely interesting. As Charles requested, Doug will give you an overview of biological warfare agents, and then we'll see if the two can be brought together. Doug.'

Doug Davernport got up from his chair and switched on his laptop. 'As you are aware, there are two types of biological warfare agents,' he said, 'bacteria and viruses. There are thousands of different strains of each. However, only a handful are suitable as biological warfare agents. To make it easier for you, I've summarised the key features of the five most pathogenic agents known,' he said, flashing a table on to the screen. 'Three are bacteria (B) and two are viruses (V).' He paused while they studied the table.

MOST POTENT PATHOGENS

Pathogen	Type	Death	Mortality Rate (per cent)	Contagious
Anthrax (Inhalation)	B (*Bacillus anthracis*)	24-36 hours	75	No
Botulinum toxin	B (*Clostridium botulinum*)	Weeks	Variable	No
Bubonic plague (Lungs)	B (*Yersinia pestis*)	2-6 days	75	Highly
Ebola (ZEBOV)	V (*Ebola*)	1-2 weeks	90	Highly
Smallpox	V (*Variola*)	4-6 weeks	30	Highly

'What do inhalation, lungs and ZEBOV mean?' asked Debbie.

'Good question,' answered Doug. 'It means they're the most potent strains or method of application of that particular pathogen. For example, there are several types of anthrax infection, depending on how it's contracted; cutaneous, through the skin, gastrointestinal, by eating contaminated food, and inhalation, by breathing in the bacterial spores. Inhalation anthrax is by far the most deadly, so for biological warfare, anthrax would be used in this way. Similarly, bubonic plague, which affects the lungs, and ZEBOV, the Zaire ebola virus, are the deadliest forms of those two pathogens.'

'I see,' said Debbie. 'Thanks.'

'What are the symptoms of the various diseases?' asked a curious Steve. 'Are they different or are there some similarities?'

'There are some remarkable similarities,' replied Doug. 'For example, in the early stages of both smallpox and anthrax, the symptoms are exactly like influenza; a mild fever, headache and an aching body.'

'Then how do you know it's smallpox or anthrax and not just the flu?' said Steve.

'If it's anthrax,' replied Doug, 'there's no runny nose, as there would be if it was flu, but a shortness of breath. In the case of smallpox, after two days small red spots develop on the tongue and in the mouth, the smallpox rash, which spreads to all parts of the body within 24 hours. By the third day, the rash becomes raised bumps which, by the fourth day, fill with a thick, opaque fluid and have a depression in the centre that looks like a belly button. This is the major distinguishing feature of smallpox. Finally, they change to pustules, which scab and fall off, leaving scars that disfigure the body for life. The mortality rate may only be 30 per cent, but smallpox is a debilitating, highly contagious disease that lasts for four to six weeks.'

'The botulinum toxin, isn't that what they use in Botox treatments?' asked Debbie.

'Trust a woman to ask that,' replied Doug. 'There are seven types of botulinum toxin and yes, one of them, type A, is used for Botox treatments. One of the seven, I forget which, is the most powerful neurotoxin known. Just 90-270 nanograms is sufficient to kill a person by respiratory failure. Such a microscopic amount is difficult to visualise but it means that just four kilograms of the toxin, if evenly distributed, would be more than enough to kill the entire population of the world. All seven billion of them.'

'Jesus! Isn't that what we're looking for?' gasped Steve. 'It seems ideal.'

'I'm afraid not,' replied the senior scientist. 'The toxin is almost impossible to produce and it would be extremely difficult to convert it into an ethnic specific weapon. Also, the mortality rate from normal botulism is low, about 3-5 per cent. So no, it's not ideal.'

'I suppose another factor,' said Charles, 'is whether we want the agent to be contagious. I see from the table that three of them are whilst two are not.'

'Contagion is a factor,' replied Doug, 'but not a key one. However, other things being equal, a contagious pathogen is preferable to one that isn't.'

'We need to think carefully about that,' said Debbie, as perceptive as ever.

'What do you mean?' asked Doug, looking somewhat perplexed.

'Well,' replied Debbie, 'if the pathogen is contagious, once it has infected the intended victim, a Mongolian say, it will spread to people *of any race*, just like the normal pathogen would, not just Mongolians. In other words, it would no longer be ethnic specific, just a normal pathogen.'

'So,' said Doug thoughtfully, 'it would kill Caucasians unlucky enough to be in the vicinity too, as well as Mongolians. In other words, there would be some collateral damage.'

'Precisely,' replied Debbie.

'Then it's best if the pathogen isn't contagious,' said Charles, 'if we want it to be truly ethnic specific.'

'It seems like it,' said Doug.

'This is all very interesting,' said the senior scientist, changing the subject, 'but I think it's only fair to let you know what we've already found, that bacteria are far too large to tag on to a gene or gene sequence. They are thousands of times bigger, and far more complex, than a virus, so I'm afraid they're out of the question as ethnic specific biological weapons. We included them in the presentation for completeness because they are potential biowarfare agents.'

'In that case,' said Charles, 'it comes down to a choice between the ebola virus and the smallpox virus.'

'Not quite,' replied the senior scientist. 'There are man-made variants.' Seeing the bemused look on the faces of Charles, Debbie and Steve, he continued. 'The structures, and properties, of natural pathogens can be altered to make them more deadly. During the cold war, for instance, scientists in the former Soviet Union did exactly that. They genetically altered bacteria to make them more virulent. They produced "invisible" anthrax, anthrax that was untouched by existing anti-anthrax vaccines, and developed a treatment resistant bubonic plague.'

'Ah, the Black Death that swept Britain and Northern Europe in 1348-50,' said Debbie, 'killing half the population, some 200 million people.'

'The very same,' replied the senior scientist. 'And it reappeared several times at later dates, most famously in the Great Plague of London in 1665-66. It was called the bubonic plague because of the buboes, tender enlarged lymph nodes under the armpits, in the neck or in the groin, ranging in size from 1-10 cm, that were present in 70 per cent of the patients.'

'Do you have any, er, modified pathogens?' queried Steve.

'Yes, we do,' replied the senior scientist.

'Would you care to elaborate?' continued Steve.

'Well,' replied the senior scientist, 'it's top secret and it's not critical to the discussion at this stage, but we've developed a highly contagious genetically modified ebola virus which has a mortality rate of 99.9 per cent.'

'99.9 per cent!' exclaimed an incredulous Steve. '99.9 bloody per cent. That's tantamount to a mass extinction.'

'Yes it is,' replied the senior scientist in a calm voice, 'and that's why it's top secret.'

'In that case,' said a stunned Charles, 'let's keep it that way and never use such an evil, inhumane weapon.' The rest of the people in the room concurred with his statement.

Recovering his composure, Steve asked another, very pertinent, question. 'Do you have any modified ebola and smallpox viruses that aren't contagious?'

'Good question,' replied the senior scientist. 'We don't have any strains that are completely non-contagious – that's almost impossible – but we do have strains that are only mildly contagious.'

'But still as deadly?' asked Steve.

'Not quite as deadly, no, but deadly enough,' replied the senior scientist.

'How deadly,' asked Steve, as persistent as ever.

'The most effective mildly contagious strain has got about a 75 per cent mortality rate,' replied Doug, 'a little lower than the natural ebola virus.'

'But that's a full 25 per cent less than the genetically modified ebola virus,' said an exasperated Steve.

'Yes it is,' interjected Charles, noting the annoyance of the senior scientist with Steve's persistence. Continuing he said, 'I think the mortality rate of both strains are more than sufficient for an EGV. However, the questions we need to answer are these:

which pathogen do we use, the ebola virus or the smallpox virus? And if it's the ebola virus, which one?'

Comparing the properties of the ebola and smallpox viruses from the table on the screen, Debbie said, 'It's got to be the ebola virus, hasn't it? The mildly contagious strain,' she added quickly.

'I agree,' said Steve, 'it's a no-brainer. The mildly contagious ebola virus kills in one to two weeks with a mortality rate of 75 per cent, whereas the smallpox virus takes four to six weeks and only has a mortality rate of 30 per cent. By the way,' he continued, 'I don't think you mentioned the symptoms of ebola and how it kills.'

'No. I don't think I did,' replied Doug. 'The main symptoms are a sore throat, severe headaches and diarrhoea, and death occurs during the second week from a massive blood loss due to internal haemorrhaging.'

'Thanks,' said Steve.

'In answer to your question, Debbie, it's not that clear cut,' said the senior scientist.

'What do you mean?' said Charles, Debbie and Steve in unison.

'It depends on what you want to achieve,' replied the senior scientist. 'If you want to kill 75 per cent of the target population, men, women, children and babies, then the ebola virus is fine. If, however, you want to disrupt and incapacitate the target population, rather than kill the majority of them, then the smallpox virus is the one to go for.'

'I see,' mused Charles. 'It's something the Cobra team will have to think about.'

'It doesn't matter at this stage,' said the senior scientist, 'the principle is exactly the same whichever virus we choose.

'Ah, I think lunch is ready,' he continued, noticing the dinner lady gesticulating frantically at the door. 'When we come back, we'll devise a strategy, a plan of action to develop an EGV. Okay, let's get something to eat.'

'What's your first impression?' Charles asked the Porton Down scientists after they'd returned from lunch. 'Do you think it's possible to develop an EGV?'

The three scientists nodded their heads in agreement, but it was the senior scientist who spoke. 'In theory, yes we do. However, we need more time to discuss the details and work out precisely how it could be done.'

'That's great,' said a delighted Charles. 'While you work out the details, we'll focus all our efforts on selecting the best Mongolian gene sequences for the EGV to attack.'

'What about differentiating the Japanese from the Chinese and Koreans?' asked Debbie. 'We don't want the EGV to kill the Japanese.'

'That's true,' replied Charles, 'but I don't think we'll have time. It's touch and go whether we'll be able to develop a Mongolian EGV by 2019, never mind a highly specific EGV targeted at an ethnic sub-group. Anyway, I don't think many Japanese live in China.'

'Shouldn't we start work on an antidote for Caucasians to protect them against the Chinese EGV?' asked a concerned looking Steve.

'He's got a point,' said the senior scientist. 'After all, we haven't got much time.'

'I agree,' said Debbie. 'We'll start designing a benign DNA sequence to block the ethnicity genes from attack by a hostile EGV.'

'It'll have to be ratified by the Cobra team,' said Charles, 'but go ahead. I'm sure they'll approve it.'

'What about antidotes for the Negroid and Australoid races?' asked Doug. 'Shouldn't we develop them as well?'

'There's no need,' replied Charles. 'The Chinese are only developing an EGV targeted at Caucasians. And anyway, it would divert effort, precious effort, away from the two key tasks. Effort we can't afford to lose.'

'Okay, are we all in agreement?' asked Charles. Everyone nodded their assent. 'Good,' he continued, 'I think that's everything we can do for the time being. Thank-you for a stimulating and enlightening day.'

'There's one more thing,' said the senior scientist. 'At some point, we need to consider issues like mass production and delivery of the EGV. They're not straightforward, and there's the testing too, but we can leave all that for now.'

'When do you want to meet again?' asked Charles.

After a brief discussion with his two colleagues, the senior scientist replied that a meeting in four weeks time would be about right. It would give them time to formulate their ideas. 'We'll hold it up at your place if you like, Charles,' he concluded.

'No problem,' said Charles. 'We look forward to it.'

As the meeting was drawing to a close, there was a knock on the door, the door opened and the Chief of the Defence Staff walked in. 'I'm not interrupting, am I?' he said. 'I just popped in to hear your conclusions.'

The senior scientist looked at Charles before answering. 'We've had a very good exchange of information and, in principle, we think it is possible to design an EGV based on the findings of Charles' team, but we need a few more weeks to be absolutely sure. As for the timescale, it will take years, but until we know more, we can't say how many.'

'Mm,' mused the Chief of the Defence Staff scratching his chin, 'at least it's a start.' He wondered how the Chinese were getting on.

45

INTELLIGENCE

'Ten thousand! They're cloning 10,000 bloody soldiers,' exclaimed an astounded Chief of the Defence Staff.

'That's what our spy in China says,' replied the Home Secretary.

'What the hell for?' said the Head of MI6. 'To start a bloody war.'

'Quite possibly,' said the Home Secretary. 'Our spy has heard rumours, and that's all they are, rumours, that China intends to invade Japan and, at the same time, North Korea will invade South Korea.'

'Bloody hell,' said the Chief of the Defence Staff. 'Do they think the rest of the world will just sit by and watch? They must be mad.'

'As I said, they're just rumours.'

'Did our spy supply any information on their biowarfare research?' asked Charles.

'Yes, he did,' said the Head of America's Central Intelligence Agency (CIA). Everyone turned to look at the large flat screen TV on the wall, the screen that showed their COBRA counterparts in the USA. Charles had never been a fan of videoconferencing, but he could see its advantages. A videoconference could be convened in a matter of minutes. In contrast, face-to-face meetings with their American counterparts would take at least a day to arrange and, in practice, even longer than that. 'Chang is working on one of the teams that's developing the super weapon and he says they're fairly close to having a prototype EGV. An EGV directed at Caucasians.'

'Does he know which pathogen they're using?' asked the senior scientist from Porton Down, the newest member of the Cobra team.

'Yes. It's the ebola virus, but one they've had to synthesise from scratch,' replied the Head of the CIA.

'An artificial ebola virus,' said the senior scientist, as though he was thinking aloud. 'That is interesting.'

'Good God,' remarked the Chief Scientific Advisor, 'if it works, it'll wipe out 90 per cent of the Caucasian race. Ninety per cent of the white populations of Britain, America, Europe and Russia. It would be Armageddon.'

'It certainly would,' said the Head of America's CIA. 'It most certainly would. It's something we can't allow to happen.'

'Do we have any idea of the dates for these attacks?' asked the Home Secretary.

'We don't have any specific dates, no, but our spy seems to think the attacks are planned for 2019,' said the Head of the CIA.

'Jesus Christ, that's only two years away,' said the Chief of the Defence Staff. 'It doesn't give us much time.'

'I'll get our boys to see if there's anything significant about 2019 to the Chinese,' said the Head of the CIA. 'I'll let you know what we find.'

'Thanks, Jim,' the Home Secretary said to the Head of America's CIA. He acknowledged her gratitude with a nod of his head. Turning to face her Cobra colleagues, the Home Secretary continued. 'Right, we need to formulate a response. To consider all our options and devise a plan.'

'The first thing we need to do,' said the Chief of the Defence Staff, 'is to accelerate our own work on an EGV. We need to have one as a deterrent.'

'I agree,' said the senior scientist. 'We'll make that our top priority.'

'The work should proceed faster if there's more collaboration, not just between Porton Down and the Cryonics Facility, but also with our American colleagues too. Do you agree, Jim?' said the Home Secretary looking at the Head of the CIA.

'Absolutely. I'll tell our boys at Anniston to get in touch and do whatever it takes to speed up the research.'

'Another issue we need to discuss,' said the senior scientist, 'is which pathogen to use. We have four choices. The natural ebola virus, the smallpox virus, or one of the two genetically modified ebola viruses.' He explained the differences.

'The thought of killing millions of people, especially children and babies, makes me uncomfortable,' said the Home Secretary. Most, but not all, of the people in the room concurred with her statement. 'Isn't there some other way?'

'Wouldn't the smallpox virus do the job?' asked Charles. 'It would still cause massive disruption but with far fewer casualties.'

'I don't think so,' replied the Chief of the Defence Staff. 'The Chinese have no such compunctions. They're ruthless. They're using the ebola virus and it's imperative we do the same. We have to fight fire with fire.'

'I agree,' said the Chief Scientific Advisor. 'If we let the Chinese know that we have such a devastating weapon, it should act as a powerful deterrent. We shouldn't have to use it. It's a bit like the nuclear deterrent.'

'Even if we did develop such a weapon,' said Charles, 'they'd probably think we were bluffing. After all, we're years behind the Chinese in developing an EGV.'

'We could give them a little demonstration,' said the Chief of the Defence Staff. 'We could drop it on a remote town.'

Charles was appalled. How could any sane person consider such an inhuman act of genocide and, even worse, state it in such a cold-blooded, matter-of-fact way. An act that would condemn hundreds of thousands of innocent victims to a horrible and painful death. Hadn't we learned anything from history? Learned from the horrors of Hiroshima and Nagasaki.

The discussion raged for some time and, although it was far from unanimous, a decision was made. The pathogen for the EGV would be the ebola virus, but not the natural ebola virus nor the mildly contagious one that 'only' killed 75 per cent of the population, but the highly contagious one that killed 99.9 per cent of the population. The scientists argued vehemently against the use of such an evil, inhumane weapon, but to no avail. After all, argued the military faction, if it was the Chinese making the choice, that would be the one they'd choose. Unfortunately, their argument that the most devastating weapon available should be chosen won the day. The hawks had prevailed.

The other key decision taken at the meeting was to approve the development of an antidote for Caucasians against any hostile EGV. It was the start of a race. A race against time. A new arms race. The biowarfare arms race. It was a race they couldn't afford to lose.

46

MODE OF ACTION

The early December snow fell from a leaden sky. Crisp, white snowflakes that covered the mountains of Snowdonia with a fluffy, white carpet. It was picture postcard perfect. 'Isn't it lovely,' said Beatrice Williams to her two colleagues in the car, 'it's just like Switzerland.'

The senior scientist and Doug Davernport nodded their heads in agreement. 'I never knew the scenery up here was so beautiful,' said Doug. 'It's simply stunning, especially with the snow.'

'It is,' said the senior scientist, admiring the view from the car as it sped along the road to the Cryonics Facility. 'It most certainly is.'

Charles and his team sat in the main meeting room awaiting the arrival of the Porton Down scientists. 'They should be here soon,' he said, glancing at his watch. His mobile rang. 'They've arrived and are going through the security checks. Is everything ready?' The people in the room nodded their heads. A few minutes later, the senior scientist, Doug Davernport and Beatrice Williams entered the room. 'Good morning,' said Charles, getting up to greet them, 'we thought the snow might have delayed you.'

'No. The main roads were clear,' said the senior scientist, 'and we set off a little earlier on account of the bad weather.'

'Right,' said Charles, 'you already know Debbie and Steve, but I've invited a few others along today. This is Professor Stuart Ramage, an expert molecular biologist and theoretical physicist, and his colleague, Dr Adam Kavanagh.'

'One of a rare breed,' said the senior scientist to Stuart. 'A polymath. Pleased to meet you. And you too, Adam,' he continued, shaking their hands vigorously.

'This is Professor Dom Cruickshank and his colleague, Dr Ruth Cunningham. Ruth's had a torrid time lately,' continued Charles. He thought about explaining her ordeals but decided against it. Such topics were better discussed informally over lunch.

'I'm sorry to hear that,' said the senior scientist. 'Pleased to meet you.'

'And last, but by no means least, this is Professor Angela Thomson and her colleague, Dr Sheila Wetherall.' The senior scientist shook their hands and then introduced Doug and Beatrice. The formalities over, the people took their seats round the table.

Charles opened the proceedings. 'Have you come to a decision on the feasibility of developing an EGV?' he asked.

'Yes, we have,' replied the senior scientist. 'We've examined a number of ideas and think we've identified how it can be achieved. Beatrice will present our key findings.'

Beatrice Williams got up from her seat, walked to the front of the room with her laptop and switched on the PowerPoint presentation. 'It's very complex,' she began, 'but I'll try to keep it as brief and simple as possible. The first task an EGV has to perform,' she continued, 'is to reach its target. It has to reach the DNA, the human genome, that is located at the centre of each cell in the human body. In order to do that, it first has to enter the body, locate the appropriate cell and then pass through the cell's protective membrane.'

'In other words,' said Angela, 'the dog has to see the rabbit.'

'Precisely,' said Beatrice. 'Not surprisingly,' she continued,

202

'it's something we're quite skilled at. If the lipophilic (fat-liking)/hydrophilic (water-liking) balance is right, and the EGV isn't too big, then it will pass through the cell membrane.'

'Is that why bacteria are no good as EGVs?' queried Ruth. 'Because they're too big to pass through the cell membrane.'

'Yes. Partly that but mainly because they're far too big to tag on to the marker DNA,' replied Beatrice. Continuing, she said, 'That was the easy part. The next task we faced was to design nucleotide sequences to latch on to the ethnic specific gene sequences, on to those sequences and those alone. Again, from the work done here at the Cryonics Facility on identifying the ethnic specific genes, that wasn't too difficult either. The difficult part, and the part that took longest to crack, was this. How do we ensure the EGV is completely harmless to everyone *except* the target population? Remember, it's based on the deadly ebola virus.'

'But you've found a way?' asked Charles.

'Yes, we have,' replied Beatrice. 'We think it's possible to design a nucleotide sequence that not only recognises the ethnic specific genes but also, when it's attached to the ebola virus, neutralises the effects of the pathogen. It renders the ebola virus harmless.'

'In that case,' said Professor Stuart Ramage, 'how does it kill the ethnic specific victims? The ones it's targeted at.'

'Ah, that's the really clever bit,' replied Beatrice. 'Once the EGV binds on to the ethnicity genes, a trigger mechanism built into the EGV is activated, a trigger mechanism which releases the ebola virus. Releases it into the victim's body. And, well, you know what happens then, the victim dies.'

'Very impressive,' said Charles. 'And is all this practical?'

'Most definitely,' said Beatrice, 'but it won't be easy. Designing nucleotide sequences to both recognise the ethnicity genes and neutralise the effects of the pathogen will take time, as will perfecting the trigger mechanism.'

'How much time?' asked Dom.

'It's hard to say,' replied the senior scientist, 'but our best guess is between three to five years.'

'That's too long,' said Charles, 'we need to have it within two years. You heard what the Head of America's CIA said, that China intends to launch its attacks in 2019, just two years away.'

'I know,' replied the senior scientist, 'but three to five years is our most optimistic timescale.'

'It's too long,' reiterated Charles. 'We need to find a way to do it faster.'

Adam Kavanagh spoke for the first time. 'I have an idea.' Everyone in the room turned to look at him. 'I think we should clone some of the finest scientific brains the world has ever known. For example, Einstein, Darwin and Newton, and then educate them with all the latest scientific knowledge and data using lectures, one-to-one tuition and the Infusion Chamber. Hopefully, they'll contribute to the work and help to speed it up.'

'I don't know,' said Charles. 'It's asking one hell of a lot to expect scientists from one and two centuries ago to absorb and understand all the latest scientific knowledge, no matter how great they were in their own era. Modern science will be totally alien to them.'

'I agree,' said Professor Stuart Ramage. 'They may have been three of the greatest scientific minds to have ever lived but I suspect they'll find modern science too overwhelming. It might be beyond them.'

'It's not just the science, either,' chipped in Beatrice. 'It's the modern environment too. Everything will be alien to them; DNA, the human genome, even computers. Newton and Darwin won't even know about electricity and televisions! It'll be a complete culture shock.'

'That's as may be,' said Adam, going on the defensive, 'but they'd still have the same brains. The brains that produced some of the greatest discoveries ever made. Newton's laws of gravity,

Darwin's theory of evolution and Einstein's theory of relativity. Discoveries that revolutionised science. Even if they don't contribute to the minutiae of the work, they might provide that spark of brilliance, that X-factor, to help overcome a seemingly impossible problem. Anyway,' he continued, 'it was just an idea.'

'We can pontificate all day,' said the senior scientist, 'but the fact is we've got nothing to lose. If we do clone them and they contribute to the work, that's great. If they don't, well, we've not lost anything.'

'He's right,' said Charles, 'it's worth a try. After all the early work on murderers, serial killers and more recently soldiers, we've got the success rate of replacement cloning up to 50 per cent, so cloning them shouldn't be a problem.'

The others in the room concurred.

'Okay,' said the senior scientist, 'let's give it a whirl.'

Over the following few weeks, Professor Stuart Ramage and his team in Laboratory 2, in conjunction with Angela Thomson's team in Laboratory 1, wasted no time in cloning three of the best scientists the world had ever known. Using DNA from each of the three dead scientists, Angela Thomson's team cloned their brains. Cloned the complete brains of Isaac Newton, Charles Darwin and Albert Einstein.

In Laboratory 2, Stuart Ramage's team prepared the bodies taken from the pods in the cavern, bodies of young men in their late twenties. Bodies that were in pristine condition. Bodies of people who had died from brain traumas. Bodies that were placed in the Resurrection Chamber and warmed. Bodies in which the synthetic fluids were replaced with genetically compatible blood. Bodies which were connected to the cloned brains by neurosurgeons using techniques developed over two decades. Bodies that were finally brought to life using quantum computers, nanobots, electrical impulses and a cocktail of chemicals.

But the clonings didn't proceed without problems. Cloning works best with fresh DNA, not with DNA that is hundreds of years old. Not surprisingly, the cloning of Isaac Newton, using DNA that was 290 years old, presented the greatest difficulty. It had some flaws because the rewiring stage, which normally took two hours, took 24 hours, and even then wasn't completely successful. Cloning Charles Darwin, who died in 1882, presented fewer problems, but it was the cloning of the most recently deceased scientist, Albert Einstein, that proceeded best. Compared to Newton and Darwin, his 62 year old DNA was positively fresh. Despite these difficulties, after four weeks the team succeeded in producing viable clones of Isaac Newton, Charles Darwin and Albert Einstein or, as they were officially known, C49S, C51S and C53S.

Neither Newton, Darwin nor Einstein made any *direct* earth-shattering contributions to the work, but they did have a massive *indirect* effect. The mere fact of having three of the world's finest ever scientists working alongside them inspired the scientists at both the Cryonics Facility and at Porton Down to attain levels of performance they thought impossible. It was similar to the effect that a famous footballer has on those around him; it lifts their performance. Raises their game. Over time, the enhanced performance of the teams inched the project forward. Together with help from their American counterparts, the timescale was reduced. First by days, then by weeks and later by months. Eventually, the timescale was reduced from the initial three to five years down to an acceptable two to two and a half years, giving them a fighting chance of having an EGV by 2019. The clones of Newton, Darwin and Einstein may not have made the significant breakthroughs, but their presence on the teams had inspired others to make the seemingly impossible possible. So, in an indirect way, Adam's idea proved a masterstroke.

47

RUTH'S RECOVERY

'Ooooh,' shrieked Dylan, jumping up and down in surprise and delight, 'another "ockle bomb".'

'Not "ockle bomb", cockle bomb,' said Ruth, smiling at the excited little boy holding her hand. 'It's a cockle bomb dropped by a seagull. They collect them from the rocks, fly high into the sky and then drop them on to the pavement to crack open their shells so they can eat the cockle that's inside.'

'He won't understand all that,' said Adam as they strolled along Llandudno's wide promenade. 'He's only three.'

'Mummy,' said Dylan with a thoughtful expression on his face, 'do cockles taste nice?'

'The seagulls think they do,' she said with a smile.

'Can I have one, mummy?'

Ruth and Adam looked at each other. 'I don't think you'll like them,' she said.

'Why not? The seagulls do.'

'Tell you what,' said Ruth, spotting a small café across the road, 'let's have an ice cream.'

'Yippee,' shouted Dylan jumping up and down. 'Ice cream. Yummy. Can I have raspberry sauce too?'

'Raspberry sauce and a flake,' replied Ruth. Holding his mummy with one hand and Adam with the other, he skipped across the road eager to claim his treat.

To help Ruth recover from her horrible ordeals, Adam had decided to treat her and Dylan to a weekend by the sea. A weekend at nearby Llandudno. He'd booked the three of them into the Empire Hotel, one of the best hotels in the resort, situated near the tram station. Friday, Saturday and Sunday for them to spend some quality time together.

'I told you he was bright,' said Ruth as they sauntered along the promenade eating their ice creams.

'Bright as a button,' said Adam. 'He obviously takes after his mum.'

Suddenly, out of nowhere, a seagull swooped from the sky and snatched Dylan's ice cream out of his tiny hand. The suddenness of it startled the little boy. Realising his ice cream had gone, Dylan began to cry.

Ruth bent down and embraced him. 'There, there, don't cry,' she said in comforting tones. 'It's alright. We'll buy you another.'

'Nasty seagull,' said Adam, stroking Dylan's hair. 'Nasty, bad seagull.'

'Nasty seagull,' repeated Dylan, stamping his feet. 'Nasty, bad seagull.'

Wiping away his tears, Ruth thought frantically for a treat to cheer him up. 'I know,' she said, stroking his cheeks, 'let's go to the zoo.'

Dylan's little face lit up. 'Zoo, zoo. Yippee. Going to the zoo.'

Located just a few miles away on the hillside overlooking Colwyn Bay, the Welsh Mountain Zoo is one of the major tourist attractions of North Wales. It's beautiful gardens, stunning views and wealth of animals attract huge numbers of visitors. And, being an all year round attraction, it was the ideal place to spend a Saturday afternoon with a three-year-old boy.

After eating a light lunch in the Flagstaff café, they bought Dylan a stick of candy floss. Watching his attempts to eat it was hilarious. More stuck to his face than entered his mouth. They burst into fits of laughter at the little boy with a pink, fluffy beard.

Dylan was entranced. He loved all the animals, especially those he could cuddle and stroke at the Children's Farm, but his favourites were the Californian Sea Lions at Sealions Rock, and especially the Humboldt Penguins. He giggled at the way they waddled about and laughed and cheered at their antics at feeding time. A cheeky seagull tried to muscle in and steal one of the penguins' fish, but the penguins were having none of it. One of them grabbed the seagull's wings with its beak and wouldn't let go. Dylan jumped up and down, shrieking with laughter as the hapless seagull tried frantically to extricate itself from the penguin's grip, its fluttering wings and plaintiff cries a source of huge amusement. Eventually, the penguin relented and released the struggling seagull, but not before Dylan had laughed himself silly. His joy spread to Ruth and Adam. They left the zoo a happy, contented family.

After eating their evening meal in the Empire Hotel, Ruth, Adam and Dylan rounded off a perfect day by watching *Toy Story* at the local cinema.

Sunday was one of those rare December days. Crisp, clear and cold. A day to savour the fantastic views from the top of the Great Orme. To see the craggy white cliffs and the turquoise sea. To marvel at the intricate patterns of red and green woven by the grass and heather. And to see the peace and quiet of St Tudno's church and envy the people who rested forever in its lovely graveyard. After a warm drink in the Captain's Table at the top of the Great Orme, they drove along the scenic coastal road to Conway.

To escape the cold, their first stop was the Butterfly Jungle. To their dismay, it was closed for the winter. Instead, they strolled along the picturesque harbour, passing the world's smallest house, and on to the castle. Sadly, it wasn't to Dylan's liking so they decided to eat early and then return home.

After perusing several cafes, they chose the Galleon Chippy in the centre of town, not because Adam and Ruth wanted fish and chips, but because they served Dylan's favourite meal; sausage, chips and beans.

It may only have been a three day break, but it did them the world of good. A change of scenery, bracing sea air and quality time spent together as a family. All three returned home relaxed and refreshed.

Sheila never told anyone of Ewan's plan to sabotage the equipment, nor of her role as an accomplice, just that the guards took her towards the vault and tried to rape her. When she learned of China's evil intentions to kill billions of innocent people with an EGV, she fully supported the work at the Cryonics Facility, work aimed at averting such a catastrophe. Her naiveté was over.

48

CHINA

'… and you think the 10,000 soldiers will be ready by March 2019?' asked the President.

'That's our latest estimate,' replied the Chief Scientist.

'Impressive,' said the President. 'What's made the difference since our last meeting?'

'Two things,' replied the Chief Scientist. 'One, the extra Resurrection Chambers you've supplied and two, the fact that we've managed to double the success rate of replacement cloning from 25 per cent to 50 per cent. It means we only have to perform 20,000 clonings instead of 40,000.'

'Excellent,' exclaimed the President, looking extremely pleased. 'Excellent news.'

In addition to the President of China and the Chief Scientist, fourteen other people sat in the meeting room; Xiong Kang, Meng Huan and the twelve Team Leaders of the EGV research, including Professor Hui Wang.

'And what's the progress on the super weapon?' asked the President.

The Chief Scientist began the response. 'We are pursuing two approaches. Our favoured approach is to use a genomic marker and an EGV based on the deadly ebola virus.' He looked uncomfortable before continuing. 'However, we're experiencing some difficulties.'

'Can these difficulties be overcome?' asked the President.

'Yes, Mr President, they can,' chipped in one of the senior Team Leaders. 'We think the problem is the interaction of the DNA sequence with the ebola virus. We're evaluating alternative DNA sequences and they're showing some promise.'

'Good,' said the President. 'Keep me informed.'

'There's another problem too,' said the Chief Scientist. 'When we try to mass produce the EGV, it mutates into a strain that isn't ethnic specific. However, our scientists are making good progress on that too. Isn't that right Professor Peng?'

'Yes, it is,' replied Wu Peng 'By lowering the temperature at which the EGV replicates, we've managed to reduce the mutation rate.'

'Doesn't a lower temperature also reduce the replication rate?' asked Hui Wang.

'Yes, it does,' replied Wu Peng. 'We need to strike a balance to get an acceptable rate of replication with minimal mutation.'

'The second approach,' continued the Chief Scientist, 'is gene inhibition. It's a less deadly but still effective way to attack a target population. Really, it's a fall-back option in case the first approach fails.'

'I presume it still uses an EGV?' asked the President.

'Not exactly an EGV but still an ethnic specific biological weapon,' replied the Chief Scientist. 'Hui, would you explain the second approach – in simple terms please?'

Hui Wang explained how they'd designed an ethnic specific nucleotide sequence to neutralise the enzymes necessary for the production of red blood cells in the bone marrow, and how the victims would die a slow, agonising death from acute anaemia. 'Whereas the ebola virus kills in one to two weeks and is highly contagious,' he concluded, 'this approach would take months to kill and isn't contagious.'

'Interesting,' said the President, 'but I prefer option one if possible.'

'I think we all do,' said the Chief Scientist, 'but it's touch and go if option one can deliver on time. Option two almost certainly can.'

'Thanks for that,' said the President. 'Keep up the good work. Before I leave, I've got one or two points to make.

'First, I can tell you that our rocket building programme is on schedule. We'll have more than enough to deliver the EGV, even allowing for some losses.

'My second point concerns spies. Our spy at the Cryonics Facility has been killed. Killed in a horrible manner. And we have a suspicion that there is a spy here at the Central Research Laboratories.' He waited as people exchanged glances and whispered to each other. 'A spy that needs to be rooted out. So I ask each and every one of you to be extra vigilant and to do all in your power to identify them.

'Finally, I want assassination squads sent to Britain and the USA. Use the best of your cloned soldiers. I want one team sent to London to eliminate the Cobra team, and one to the Cryonics Facility to kill the scientists. And I want the same in America.'

'I'll begin preparations immediately,' said Meng Huan.

'Thank-you,' said the President. 'The meeting is closed.'

49

CHANG UNCOVERED

It took a woman. Despite the best efforts of everyone at the Central Research Laboratories, it took the wiles of a woman to unmask the spy.

'Did she? Did she really? You must be joking.' Qian was astounded at Bao's revelation.

'No. I'm not joking. It's true. She slapped him hard across his face, got up from her chair, poured her glass of water over his head and stormed out of the restaurant.'

'Oh my God,' gasped Qian. 'It must have been one hell of an argument.'

'Argument! More like World War III. Everyone in the restaurant stopped what they were doing to watch them,' said Bao.

'And what did the man do?' asked Qian, intrigued by her friend's account of the row.

'Oh, he just dabbed himself with his napkin, took a swig of beer and carried on eating his meal as though nothing had happened.'

'Men!' exclaimed Qian. 'Who'd have them,' she said, bursting into a fit of laughter. Bao laughed too.

'You see,' said Bao, 'being at home isn't boring at all.' They laughed some more. Two friends having a good old fashioned chinwag.

As they did most Friday evenings, Qian and Bao enjoyed a glass or two of wine at their local wine bar. It was the best night for both of them. A relaxing drink at the end of the working week for Qian and a night away from Chang for his girlfriend. Qian Shen and Bao Tsou had been friends since their schooldays, a friendship they cherished and nourished. They loved to chat and gossip. It was in their genes.

'Qian?' said Bao, sipping her wine and looking serious, 'I'm worried about Chang. He, er, hasn't been himself these past few weeks.'

Qian seemed puzzled. 'What do you mean, Bao?'

'Well… Oh, it's nothing. It's probably me. It doesn't matter.'

'Tell me, Bao. What do you mean?'

'He seems… different somehow. Just little things, but his behaviour's not right.'

'Little things like what?' queried Qian.

'It's hard to put your finger on but little nuances, habits. They're different.'

'Such as,' said Qian, becoming more and more intrigued.

'Well, he seems more preoccupied than before, and far away, as though something's troubling him. I know it sounds stupid, but he eats differently. He eats the same food but in a different way. Until a few weeks ago, he was a slow, quiet eater but now, he chomps.'

'Maybe it's the extra pressure we're under at work that's troubling him,' said Qian, 'and making him eat differently.'

'It's not just that,' said Bao. 'Before, Chang always lifted up the seat when he went to the toilet. Now, he doesn't. But the clincher is his lovemaking. The "old" Chang always ensured that I was ''pleasured'', but now, the "new" Chang just wants to satisfy himself. And he doesn't cuddle up to me after we've finished.

'I know they're just little things, but there are too many. He's not the Chang I used to know. The real Chang.'

'Mm,' mused Qian. 'Has he got a twin brother? An identical twin brother?'

'No, not as far as I'm aware,' said Bao.

'Then there's only one explanation,' said Qian triumphantly. 'He must be a clone. A clone of the real Chang Lee.'

'Why do you say that?'

'Because it makes sense. Apparently, there's a spy at the Central Research Laboratories, a spy who's passing vital information to the West. Everyone's racked their brains trying to expose him, but without success. If you're right, that's the answer. The West have replaced the real Chang Lee with a clone. A spy. It's so simple. And brilliant.'

'Bao?'

'Yes.'

'Is it okay if I report our suspicions to Professor Wang?'

'Er, I suppose so,' replied Bao somewhat hesitantly, 'but what if we're wrong. It's a serious accusation to make.'

'You're right,' said Qian. 'I suppose it is. Is there any way to be absolutely sure he's not the real Chang?' asked Qian.

Suddenly, Bao's face lit up. 'Yes! Yes, there is,' she gushed, 'but I won't know for certain until Monday morning.' She explained her idea to Qian.

'Okay,' said Qian, 'I'll arrange to go in work late on Monday morning and meet you in the coffee shop at 9-00 a.m.'

Qian arrived early. Thirty minutes early. She couldn't wait to hear Bao's verdict. Was Chang the spy or wasn't he? She checked her watch. 8-55 a.m. In five minutes time she'd know. Know for sure.

'Good morning, Bao,' she blurted out to the woman entering the coffee shop. 'Well…?'

'It's him! It's definitely him. He's not the real Chang. *My* Chang.'

'Are you sure? Are you absolutely sure?'

'Yes. Definitely. On my birthday, Chang, the real Chang, always does the same thing. He buys me an expensive card, a lovely bunch of fresh flowers and a box of chocolates. Then, we watch a film at the cinema, have a romantic dinner for two in our "special" restaurant, the one we shared our very first meal, and end the night by making love.'

'And?' asked Qian excitedly.

'Well, he bought me a card and some flowers, and a box of chocolates, but they weren't the right ones. He bought me the wrong chocolates. I always have Lindt Selection, not Cadbury's Milk Tray, and my favourite flowers are freesias, but there wasn't a single one in the bunch he bought. The real Chang would never have done that. He took me to the cinema and then to a restaurant for dinner, but it wasn't our special restaurant, and he drank so much that when we got home, he fell asleep. My Chang would never, ever have done that. Never. So yes, I'm absolutely sure he's an impostor.'

Qian couldn't wait to tell her boss. After thanking Bao, she paid the bill and virtually ran all the way to the Central Research Laboratories. She knocked on Professor Wang's door and burst in, breathless. 'The spy. I know who he is,' she gasped. Hui Wang was startled by her entrance and perplexed by her comment. 'It's Chang Lee!'

The thought that a member of his own team was the spy was abhorrent to Hui Wang. 'It can't be,' he said. 'I've known Chang from my university days. He's totally committed to Project DARIT. He's a fanatic.'

'I know,' said Qian, 'but this isn't the real Chang. He's a clone.'

After Qian had explained the events of the past few days, Hui Wang made a decision. 'I'll report what you've found to the Chief Scientist and we'll take it from there. Oh, and good work, Qian,' he said, as he strode out of the office.

The Chief Scientist was relieved the spy had been exposed. It was a weight off his shoulders. 'I'll inform Xiong Kang. He'll probably want to see us all.'

Xiong Kang, Meng Huan, the Chief Scientist, Hui Wang and Qian Shen discussed the various options available to them for several hours before coming to a final decision. For the moment, they'd keep what they'd learned secret. And they would set a trap. A trap to make absolutely sure that Chang Lee was indeed the spy. Then, and only then, would the President be informed. Tomorrow, Hui Wang would leak false information to Chang, important information that the dates for Project DARIT were being brought forward, and then they'd monitor him like a hawk. Monitor him with all the electronic surveillance equipment at their disposal to see if the information was passed on.

They didn't have to wait long. On Tuesday evening a coded call from Chang's house was picked up by their electronic surveillance equipment. It was sent immediately to their headquarters for decoding. It took two days. On Thursday morning, Xiong Kang received a call. Chang Lee had forwarded the false information to both Britain and America. He rang the President.

'Mr President, we've identified the spy. It's Chang Lee. We have two options. One, to kill him. Two, to let him continue feeding false information to our enemies.'

The response was instant. 'Kill him.'

It wasn't only America and Britain who received Chang's message, Skip Meyers received it too. And it troubled him. Troubled him because Chang Lee hardly ever sent mid-week messages, certainly not from his house. But even more troubling was the trace, the faintest hint of a trace, which accompanied the signal. It could only mean one thing. Chang Lee had been rumbled and his last call had been monitored. And probably decoded. It was time to get him out. To extricate him. But they'd have to be quick. The Chinese would waste no time in killing him.

It didn't take Meng Huan long to decide that the best time and place to kill the spy was Friday night at Chang Lee's house. Tomorrow night. He would be all alone in a quiet residential suburb. It would be a quick, clean kill with no witnesses. And, he decided, he'd lead the assassination squad himself. He'd derive great pleasure terminating the life of a traitor.

Refreshed after a hot, invigorating shower, Chang Lee ordered his Chinese take-away and then settled down in front of the TV with a glass of Tsingtao beer. A few minutes later, the doorbell rang. 'That was quick,' he thought, getting up from the sofa and walking to the front door and opening it. 'What the…' Strong, powerful hands clamped his mouth and forced him inside the hallway. A second man slipped out of the shadows, followed them inside and locked the door. Only then did John Standish release his iron grip. 'What the hell are you doing?' shouted a startled Chang Lee, gasping for air.

'We've come to get you out,' said John Standish. 'Now! The assassination squad is on its way. Your cover's been blown. We've no time to lose. Get dressed.'

As Chang Lee discarded his favourite white bathrobe and began dressing, John Standish and Li Sun turned off the TV and all the lights.

'Hurry up,' he barked to Chang. 'We need to go.'

The doorbell rang.

John Standish put his finger to his lips to indicate silence, then motioned for Chang to lie on the floor behind the sofa. He pointed to the far corner of the darkened room. Li Sun nodded and moved as silently as a cat to take up a crouching position. John Standish crouched in the shadows in the opposite corner, ensuring he had a clear line of sight to the front door. His Sig P228 was held in front of him, trained on the front door.

The doorbell rang for a second time.

John knew that in situations such as this, every little advantage, however slight, was vitally important. It gave them that crucial edge. The edge between kill or be killed. Their eyes had had a few minutes to acclimatise to the darkness of the room but, more importantly, they had the element of surprise. The assassins would be expecting an easy kill. An unarmed scientist who wasn't expecting them.

Suddenly, the door crashed open. At the same time, a figure dressed in black combat gear leapt into the room and adopted the unmistakable stance of a marksman. John Standish fired two shots in quick succession at the black figure crouching in the doorway, the classic double tap method of the SAS. The first hit the figure in his mouth, the second between his eyes. He was killed instantly.

Seeing John's muzzle flashes, the second assassin, crouching beside the open doorway, unleashed two rounds in his direction. He felt a searing hot pain in his upper left arm as the second bullet tore through his flesh. 'My God,' he thought, 'they're good. They're bloody good.' A volley of shots from the far corner of the room silenced the second assassin.

Although it seemed to take ages, in reality the firefight was over in seconds. In the blink of an eye. John thought quickly. He knew there'd be more than two. Four was the usual number. He also knew they'd lost the element of surprise. That was gone. The other assassins would have heard the gunshots and they'd be ready. Better prepared. They had to act fast. What would he have done? Sent the other two round to the back of the house or just sent one and kept one in the car? Probably the latter.

'Where's your car?' he shouted to Chang.

'On the drive. We can get to it through the side door.'

'Right. Keep between Li and me. Li, you look out for the assassin in the car. I'll cover our rear. Okay, let's go.'

On reaching the side door, John peered cautiously towards the back of the house. Nothing. Li did the same towards the front. Nothing. 'Okay,' he whispered to Chang, 'you get into the car and start her up. We'll cover you.' Chang did as instructed.

Out of the corner of his eye, John glimpsed the tiniest of movements. Quick as a flash, he spun around and squeezed off four shots in quick succession. There was a groan followed by a dull thud as the assassin from the back of the house crumpled to the floor. 'Three down and one to go,' he thought. 'But where is he?'

As John and Li dashed to the waiting car, a volley of shots rang out from behind a bush in the shadows of the front garden. Li screamed in agony as both he and John returned fire, killing the fourth and final member of the assassination squad. 'Are you hit?' he asked Li.

'It's only a scratch. I'll be fine,' lied Li.

'Good,' said John. 'That's all four accounted for. Let's go.'

As John relaxed and turned his back to get into the car, Li Sun heard a sound behind them. He turned around and saw two shadowy silhouettes emerge from behind the roofline of the house. Caught off guard and illuminated by the street lights, Li and John were sitting ducks.

Meng Huan smiled as he squeezed the trigger.

50

ANTIDOTE

'Do you think it'll make us look different?' Ruth asked her new boss, Professor Debbie Farnham, 'if we block the ethnicity genes, the genes that make us Caucasian.'

'Well, we can't be absolutely sure,' replied Debbie, 'but no, I don't think it will.'

'Good,' said Ruth, who was feeling much better after her short break with Adam and Dylan, 'I like the way I am.'

Following the successful cloning of a Spartan-dog hybrid soldier, an ultimate warrior, and the revelations about China's intentions, the priorities at both the Cryonics Facility and Porton Down had changed. All the effort in Laboratories 3 and 4 on cloning attack dogs and human-dog hybrids was suspended and switched to designing an antidote for Caucasians against an hostile EGV. Being the leading expert on such matters, Debbie Farnham was the obvious choice to lead the new team. They'd had a good start. Because of his untimely and unexpected death, Ewan Grigg hadn't deleted his secret research on the alien DNA he'd designed to neutralise the obedience genes in C22D. Although the obedience genes for a dog are far less complicated than the ethnicity genes for humans, it provided a solid platform from which to begin.

'How long do you think it will take?' Ruth asked her new boss.

'To develop a universal antidote for the Caucasian race?' queried Debbie.

Ruth nodded her head.

'It's certainly not as difficult as designing an EGV,' she said, 'but it's not easy. There are a number of genetic sequences that make us Caucasian and we have to design a benign DNA sequence for each one, a DNA sequence that will prevent any hostile EGV from binding to those sequences. And,' she continued, 'they mustn't cause any ill effects.'

'How long?' reiterated Ruth.

'Well, say it takes 12 months to design the DNA sequences, we still have the problem of testing and then mass producing them for almost two billion people. If we can achieve all that within two years, we'll have done really well.'

Ruth was reassured by Debbie's answer but still felt uneasy about the testing. 'How will the testing be carried out?' she asked. 'Will it have to be done on, er, real people?'

'I'm afraid so,' replied Debbie, 'but if we get it right, it shouldn't cause any harm.'

'But what will we use as the EGV? We don't have access to the one the Chinese are developing.'

'You're right,' said Debbie. 'The best we can do is synthesise our own Caucasian EGV and hope it's similar to the Chinese one. However, that decision will have to be made by the Cobra team. It's out of my hands. Anyway, we're jumping the gun. We need to design the antidote first.'

51

SACRIFICE

'LOOK OUT JOHHNIE!' shouted Li Sun, firing his gun and flinging himself in front of his friend at the same time. 'They're on the roof.' They were the last words he ever uttered. The burst from Meng Huan's gun cut him down. But his warning gave John Standish just enough time to spin around and unleash a deadly hail of fire, a hail of bullets that thudded into the bodies of the two assassins. Meng Huan couldn't believe it. Couldn't believe that his team of ultimate soldiers, and himself, had failed. He thought they were the best, but there was someone better. Disbelief filled his eyes as he, and the other assassin, slumped slowly on to the roof of the house, and then rolled down, landing on the path with a thud.

'Mm,' thought Johnnie, 'a real human sacrificing his life to save two clones. Perhaps we are real humans after all,' he thought, as he and Chang Lee sped off into the blackness of the night.

52

ISSUES

The Christmas and New Year festivities had been and gone. Although they'd provided a welcome respite from the traumatic events of the past two months, the respite was only temporary. Everyone was fully aware that they were involved in the most deadly race the world had ever known. A race to stop China and North Korea from wiping out 90 per cent of the white population of planet Earth. A biological arms race to prevent Armageddon.

As was the norm for modern-day Britain, heavy January snowfalls had paralysed the transport network. Charles, Debbie and Steve had planned to travel to Porton Down by train or, at a pinch, by air, but neither option was available. So, reluctantly, they'd travelled by car. Their worst fears were realised. Although large stretches of the main roads were passable, in the more remote or higher stretches they had to wait in long queues whilst the snowploughs and gritters cleared a path. A journey that should have taken no more than five hours took ten. The red Marriott hotel sign glistening in the snow had never been more welcoming. Tired and exhausted, they ate a late evening dinner and went straight to bed.

The work on both the EGV and the antidote was progressing well. Adam's idea of cloning Isaac Newton, Charles Darwin and Albert Einstein had proved a masterstroke. They inspired the teams working on two very challenging tasks to such an extent that both tasks were ahead of schedule. Because of this, Charles and the senior scientist decided they should get together to begin preliminary discussions on the other issues that lay ahead. Issues like mass production, delivery and testing of the EGV. Issues they had to resolve for the work to be successful. And so, they'd arranged a meeting at Porton Down for the end of January, but forgot about the vagaries of the British winter. Still, Charles and his two colleagues had managed to arrive in one piece and in time for the meeting the following day. Whether they'd be bright-eyed and bushy-tailed was another matter entirely.

'Mass producing a virus under controlled conditions isn't straightforward,' said the senior scientist. 'There are a number of problems. First of all, the production facility has to be completely safe. Safe for the scientists working in it and totally safe for the general public. It's absolutely vital that the viruses are contained. Not a single one must escape. The second problem is mutation. Viruses like to mutate and, if they do, their properties alter. Mutation is a serious problem for natural viruses so what effect the attached nucleotide sequence will have on a genetically altered ebola virus is anyone's guess.'

'Interesting,' mused Debbie. 'Are there any techniques to stop the virus from mutating?' she asked.

'There are one or two, yes,' replied Doug Davernport. 'Temperature control is one, but there are others too.'

'What about delivering the virus?' asked Charles. 'Is that difficult?'

'Yes and no,' replied the senior scientist. 'You could infect the water supplies or rely on natural contagion, but they're unreliable and take time. The best method is to release the virus into the atmosphere. How much and at what altitude depends on the topology of the terrain and the prevailing weather conditions.'

'Have you any experience of, er, delivering biowarfare agents?' asked Charles.

Doug glanced at the senior scientist before answering. He nodded his assent. 'Some very crude experiments were done at the height of the Cold War in the early 1960s when the British government feared that the Soviet Union was planning a chemical and biological attack. They wanted to know how a cloud of germs, or chemicals, would disperse. A Land Rover travelled from Porton Down through Wedmore and around the outskirts of Bristol spraying zinc cadmium sulphide into the air in an attempt to simulate germ warfare. The chemical cloud was tracked by sampling stations in Somerset and Wiltshire, and the results relayed back to Porton Down. The exercise caused great alarm amongst the local population and has never been repeated.

'Nowadays, we use sophisticated computer simulations using a number of factors, such as the size, weight, shape and buoyancy of the virus, and the prevailing weather conditions and topology of the area, information that is available from the satellites that we and America have at our disposal.'

'Is there a best time to deliver an EGV?' asked Steve.

'Yes, there is,' replied Beatrice. 'Many microorganisms are destroyed by the ultraviolet component in bright sunlight, so the best time to deliver a biowarfare agent is either at night, or at dawn when people are getting up and the sun's rays are weak.'

'I didn't know that,' said Charles.

'Not many people do,' continued Beatrice, 'and, not surprisingly, research has been done on incorporating ultraviolet absorbers into the bacteria and viruses to overcome this deficiency.'

'Ah, the active ingredient in suntan lotions which absorb the sun's harmful UVA and UVB rays to prevent our skin from being burnt,' said Debbie.

'The very same,' replied Beatrice.

'Well, I never,' said Charles. 'Whatever next.'

'Does sunlight kill the ebola virus?' asked Steve.

'Yes, it does. The ebola virus is killed rapidly by sunlight. It's one of the reasons why it's been difficult to develop it into an effective bioweapon. That and the fact that it's difficult to aerosolize in a dry form. We've overcome both problems. The attached DNA sequences have rendered the EGV much more resistant to sunlight but, more importantly, they've stabilised the EGV, allowing an airborne delivery of the virus.'

'You've done some excellent work,' Charles said to the Porton Down scientists. 'Well done.'

'So have you,' replied the senior scientist. 'So have you.'

After lunch, they discussed the most controversial topic. Testing.

'Do we have to test the EGV on humans?' asked Debbie, feeling distinctly uneasy that human lives would be sacrificed.

'I'm afraid so,' replied the senior scientist. 'There's no other way. Using animals is no good. They don't possess the ethnic specific human genes. And we need to be absolutely certain that the EGV works.'

'Is there no way to save a person who's been infected?' asked Charles. 'To know that the EGV works by giving them ebola but administering an antidote before it kills them?'

'In theory, it's possible,' replied the senior scientist, 'but in practice I don't think it'll work. There's no really effective antidote for natural ebola, never mind the genetically altered version.'

'So people will have to die then,' said a grim faced Charles.

'I can't see any other alternative,' said the senior scientist.

'Who?' asked Charles.

The silence was deafening.

53

ASSASSINATIONS

'Who found his body?' Xiong Kang asked the nervous young policeman stood beside him.

'My sergeant, sir. He was the first on the scene after the neighbours reported gunshots at Chang Lee's house.'

'And are you sure it's Meng Huan?'

'Yes sir, we are. His ID card identified him as Meng Huan and one of your, er, soldiers who saw the body confirmed it was him.'

'And the whole squad were killed? All six of them?'

'I'm afraid so, sir. They'd all been shot. Shot by professionals I'd say.'

'Were they all killed with the same bullets?'

'No sir. We haven't got the full ballistics report yet but it seems that four were killed with 9 mm bullets, probably fired from a Sig P228, and two with 5.8 mm bullets fired from a QSZ-92 pistol, a Chinese manufactured gun.'

'Thanks,' said Xiong Kang. 'Thanks for letting me know.'

The young policeman nodded, turned around and exited the room.

Xiong Kang stroked his chin. 'Mm,' he thought, 'isn't that what the SAS use? Sig P228 pistols. Whoever it was, he, and his accomplice, must have been good, very good, to kill Meng Huan and five of our best ultimate soldiers.'

The untimely and unexpected death of Meng Huan delayed their plans. Initially, they'd planned to have detailed surveillance data on all of their targets by the end of January, and have completed the assassinations by the end of March. Now, that wasn't going to happen.

Xiong Kang's first task was to bring in a replacement for Meng Huan, another 'Red Pole' or '426' to continue the mission. He interviewed several candidates before choosing Tou Sou, a 'Red Pole' from the *14K* TRIAD. It took several weeks for Tou Sou to familiarise himself with the activities of the Central Research Laboratories, and to find his feet in his new role.

Tou Sou's first decision was to send China's best surveillance experts to London to pinpoint the movements of the key Cobra team members. Preliminary surveillance had already been carried out both by members of the Chinese Embassy and by 'sleeper' cells in London and North Wales. But he wanted more detailed, more accurate, more precise descriptions of the target's every movement. Their routines, their habits, their hobbies, their idiosyncrasies. Everything. He knew that planning was paramount.

His next task was to select the best people, the best assassins, to carry out the assassinations. And for those, he turned to the ultimate soldiers, the thousands of cloned ultimate soldiers, and selected the best of the best.

His final task was to plan the mission itself. Feedback from his surveillance experts in London confirmed what he suspected, that they'd have to assassinate the Cobra team members individually. Downing Street, where the Cobra meetings were held, was too heavily guarded and protected for them to mount an attack.

Having monitored the movements of every member down to the tiniest detail, they'd produced a hit list. They'd kill the 'softest' targets first, those with zero levels of protection. And, as far as possible, they'd make the assassinations look like an accident. That way, it wouldn't arouse suspicion, at least at first.

Four members made up the London assassination squad. Four of the very best ultimate soldiers. More than sufficient to kill an individual civilian but few enough to enter the country without arousing suspicion.

To inflict the maximum amount of damage and casualties at the Cryonics Facility, Tou Sou decided on a team of twelve. They couldn't all travel to Britain together. That would alert the authorities. No, they would have to be sent one by one to different parts of Britain and then meet up in North Wales. It would take longer, but that didn't matter. Not for now, anyway. He'd concentrate on eliminating the Cobra team first. They'd begin with the softest target.

As he did on the last Sunday of every month, the Chief Scientific Advisor caught the tube to visit one of his favourite places, the Natural History Museum. It was something he'd done since he was a child. It was a ritual. The artefacts and fossils fascinated him and he loved the life sized replicas of the dinosaurs. He was also a lifetime friend of the museum's curator, and enjoyed their monthly chats on topics of the day. He never noticed the two burly Chinese gentlemen who'd shadowed his every move, even when they followed him back to the underground station for his journey home.

The platform was busy with tourists and Londoners alike, all eager to get home in time for Sunday tea. A distant rumbling noise signalled the approach of the train. People jostled for position, pushing and shoving to be near the front of the platform. They didn't want to be left behind. A cold wind swept over the platform, the bow wave of the train. Suddenly, he felt a push in his back. He teetered on the edge, trying desperately to stop himself falling on to the track, but to no avail. People screamed in horror as he fell directly in front of the speeding train.

The Cobra team were shocked at his untimely and tragic death. According to eye witnesses, he lost his balance on the crowded platform as people jostled for position as the train arrived. No one noticed the two burly Chinese gentlemen who'd simply melted away into the crowd. It was seen as a tragic accident.

The Metropolitan Commissioner of Police settled down to watch *Match of the Day*. Saturday evenings were his. His to enjoy alone. Alone with a few beers whilst watching the highlights of the day's football matches. And to see how his own team, Arsenal, had got on. He never watched the results beforehand. That spoiled the enjoyment. 'It was more exciting,' he thought, 'watching the highlights without knowing the scores.'

A noise caught his attention. Had his wife returned home early from her sisters? He turned around. No, she hadn't. He returned his gaze to the TV, just in time to see Robin van Persie score a spectacular goal. 'What a goal,' he thought. It was the last thought he ever had. Out of nowhere, powerful hands gripped his head and twisted it violently. His neck snapped like a dry twig.

'Who found the body?' asked DI George Roberts.

'His wife, sir, when she returned from her sisters,' said DC Betty Forbes. 'He was lying at the foot of the stairs. A glass of spilled beer lay nearby. It seems he'd gone to the bathroom and then fell down the stairs and broke his neck.'

'Strange,' said George thoughtfully, 'I didn't think he was a heavy drinker.'

And he was proved right. The autopsy showed that the amount of alcohol in the blood of the Metropolitan Commissioner of Police was well below the legal limit, certainly not high enough to make him drunk and fall down the stairs. Furthermore, the pathologist was convinced that his neck was broken *before* he fell down the stairs, not in the act of falling down the stairs. In other words, the Metropolitan Commissioner of Police had been murdered.

The Cobra team were alarmed. Two deaths in two weeks. The first looked like an accident but the second was definitely a murder dressed up to look like an accident. It was highly likely that both men had been killed. Or assassinated.

The Home Secretary took no chances. She allocated two bodyguards to each Cobra team member, one from MI5 and one from the SAS. She didn't want any more casualties.

It had been a short meeting. The Home Secretary was pleased with the progress at both the Cryonics Facility and Porton Down and ended the meeting early. So, with time on his hands, Charles DeLacy had decided to have a meal before catching the train back to North Wales. He chose an Aberdeen Angus Steak House. Their steaks were pricey but delicious. His two bodyguards joined him. After paying the bill, the three of them stepped out into the warm May evening and began to walk the short distance to Euston station.

'LOOK OUT!' shouted a woman stood in front of them. Johnnie and Alan whirled around. A car had veered off the road on to the pavement and was hurtling straight towards them. Terrified pedestrians scattered in all directions, desperate to avoid the onrushing vehicle. Johnnie and Alan reacted instantly, pushing Charles out of harm's way and diving for cover themselves. The car missed them by inches, screeching to a halt about 30 yards away. Immediately, two assassins in black balaclavas leapt out and began firing in their direction. Pandemonium broke out as passers-by screamed and ran for cover.

Johnnie Standish, C47SO, from the SAS, and Alan Standish from MI5, the grandson of the real Captain Johnnie Standish, ushered a shocked Charles into the nearest doorway, the doorway of a restaurant.

'SAS,' he yelled at the startled customers and staff. 'Get into the kitchen. NOW! You too,' he said to Charles. Then, Johnnie and Alan Standish took up their positions, Alan behind the bar and Johnnie crouched behind an upturned table at the far end of the restaurant, a table with a clear sight of the door. They were ready. Or so they thought.

With a noise like thunder, the assassin's car crashed through the front window, spraying glass in all directions. It ploughed into the empty tables and chairs, scattering unfinished meals and drinks everywhere. Instinctively, Johnnie unleashed two shots at the driver's head, killing him instantly. At the same time, two assassins leapt out from the back of the car, one from each side. Johnnie expected them to use the doors as shields. But they didn't. To his astonishment, one rushed towards him and one towards Alan, unleashing a deadly hail of bullets as they advanced. They were totally fearless. It wasn't what either Johnnie or Alan expected. Bullets thudded into the wooden table, sending splinters of wood flying into the air. One bullet grazed his shoulder. Startled by their adversaries unexpected actions, Johnnie regained his composure just in time to squeeze off two shots in quick succession. Both hit the target. The assassin's mouth. He crumpled to the floor, dead.

Meanwhile, the second assassin had rushed towards Alan, his Kalashnikov spitting a continuous stream of bullets. Alan ducked behind the bar as bottles of whisky and brandy, expensive bottles, exploded behind him, showering him with single malt whisky and cognac.

Memorising the assassin's position, Alan raised his Sig P228 above the bar and fired six shots, one after the other. Two missed completely, two thudded into the bullet proofed torso of the assassin and one hit his arm. But the crucial shot, the one that caused the assassin to sink to his knees, hit him in the throat. Even though he was fatally wounded, the assassin kept on firing. 'Have they no fear,' thought Alan. A single shot ended the firing. It was Johnnie. He'd applied the *coup de grace* with a shot to the head.

Warily, Johnnie and Alan got up from their crouching positions to approach the bodies. To check they were dead. 'Cover me,' Johnnie said to his companion. Alan nodded, his Sig P228 extended in front of him. As Johnnie bent down to examine the first body, a figure sprung up from the passenger seat of the car, a figure who'd been crouched down, waiting for the right moment. His gun was trained on Johnnie.

'JOHNNIE!!!' shouted Alan, firing his gun at the same time. His warning gave Johnnie just enough time to roll out of the way of the bullets. One of Alan's shots hit the assassin's gun arm, causing him to drop the gun. Quick as lightning, Alan and Johnnie pounced before he could retrieve it. They dragged him out of the car and tried to overpower him. Take him prisoner. It was a mistake. Even though he was badly wounded, he fought like a tiger. It took a full five minutes of vicious hand-to-hand fighting and the combined skills of two of the best SAS soldiers to subdue him. For the second time, Johnnie Standish thought how bloody good the assassins were.

The sound of sirens signalled the approach of the security forces, armed police and an SAS unit. An SAS unit that had been kept on standby in Downing Street following the assassinations of two of the Cobra team.

'What the fucking hell's happened here?' said the leader of the SAS unit as he surveyed the carnage inside the restaurant.

Johnnie gave him a quick debrief of the events then, after beckoning Charles to join him and Alan, the three of them departed, leaving the police and the SAS unit to clean up the carnage and attend to the wounded assassin.

A crowd had gathered outside the restaurant. A crowd of curious onlookers hoping to catch a glimpse of the carnage inside.

As Charles, Johnnie and Alan began pushing their way through the crowd, Alan recognised the face of the woman who'd shouted the warning. She looked familiar. He walked over to where she was standing. 'You saved our lives,' he said. 'Thank-you.'

'You saved mine,' she replied. 'In the subway. It's me who should thank you.'

Alan was confused. He was relieved, mightily relieved, that she'd shouted the warning – it had saved their lives – but surprised. Surprised that she'd remembered. The drug he'd given her in the subway to induce temporary memory loss clearly hadn't worked. 'Maybe good deeds are rewarded,' he thought, as he hurried to catch up to his two companions.

The captured assassin was taken to a secret location and interrogated. When that failed to make him talk, he was tortured. Physical torture that would have made any normal human talk. Acid dropped on to bare skin. Fingernails extracted slowly with pliers. Waterboarding. And electric shocks to the genitals. Still he remained silent. Not only was he fearless and brave, he was bloody tough and resilient too.

But no matter how tough he was physically, mentally his brain had no answer to the latest truth drugs, the successors to Sodium Pentothal. The interpreter listened intently as he told them of the planned attack on the Cryonics Facility. An attack that could now be prevented.

His information gave them time to respond. To assemble a team of the best SAS soldiers, together with the best of the Spartan-dog hybrid soldiers they'd recently cloned, to attack the twelve strong cell of assassins before they launched their murderous attack.

A ferocious firefight left ten assassins dead and two wounded. But victory came at a cost. Two SAS soldiers and two Spartan-dog hybrids were killed, and another four wounded. But the pre-emptive strike had thwarted China's plans. The Cryonics Facility, and its scientists, were safe.

Similar scenarios were enacted in the USA, with similar outcomes. China's assassination attempts had been foiled.

54

REPRISALS

Britain and America were incensed by the actions of China and North Korea. Incensed by their brazen attempt to assassinate leading political, military and scientific personnel on home soil. Their response was swift. The Chinese and North Korean ambassadors and their staff in London and Washington were ordered to leave the country within 48 hours, and the British and American ambassadors in Beijing and Pyongyang were recalled. As a further measure, all trade links with both countries were severed and all Britons and Americans were advised to leave China and North Korea.

In a further response to the assassination attempts, the governments of both Britain and America put their countries on red alert, the highest threat level. Increased security was provided for leading public figures such as senior politicians and military leaders, as well as for the top scientists. Security at key installations, such as nuclear power stations and major airports, was also ramped up, as it was at iconic institutions like the Palace of Westminster, Downing Street, Buckingham Palace, the Tower of London and the London Eye. And the border agency was told in no uncertain terms to tighten up the borders, especially for any Chinese or North Koreans wishing to enter the country. In addition, MI5 in Britain and the FBI (Federal Bureau of Investigation) in America invested vast amounts of time and effort in scouring their respective countries to either round up or disrupt any remaining Chinese or North Korean sleeper cells.

Repeated interrogation – torture would be a better word – of the captured assassins failed to unearth any new information. They knew only of their mission. Both Britain and America contemplated informing the United Nations about the attacks, but decided against it. They'd have to admit they'd tortured the assassins, something they weren't prepared to do. Anyway, China and North Korea would deny any involvement, saying the attacks were the work of terrorists.

Britain and America had to decide their next move. They couldn't afford to dally. The fate of the world was at stake. A top level meeting was convened. An old fashioned face-to-face meeting that included the highest ranking officials of both countries. A meeting chaired jointly by the President of the United States and the British Prime Minister. A meeting that would be held in the White House.

55

JIGSAW

The sun shone down from a clear blue sky. The early May air was crisp and clear. It was a fine spring morning in Washington DC, the capital of the world's most powerful nation. It was the morning of one of the most important meetings in the history of the human race. The Cobra teams of both countries had already held pre-meeting meetings to decide how to present their findings and, more importantly, how to try and fit together the pieces of information they had.

'Good morning, ladies and gentlemen,' the President of the United States said. 'Welcome to the White House.' Sat in the Oval Office were some of the most powerful and influential people in the world. The President of the United States, the Prime Minister of Britain, their senior ministers, top military and intelligence chiefs and, last but by no means least, the top scientists of both countries. 'I think you all know why we're here,' continued the President. 'We're here to work out what the Chinese and North Koreans are up to. Their intentions. Their plans. Their aspirations. Their timescales. And to decide what our response will be. From what I've been told, they're evil. Evil beyond comprehension. We must do everything in our power to stop them.' He looked at the man sat beside him. 'Have you anything to add?' Prime Minister.

The British Prime Minister arose from his chair. 'I think you've summarised it succinctly,' he said. 'All that I wish to add is this. It's imperative, absolutely crucial, that we figure out exactly what China and North Korea intend to do. And when they intend to do it. Then, having done that, we need to decide how to respond.' He sat down.

'Right,' said the President, 'the Cobra teams of both our countries, facilitated by the British Home Secretary, have been at the heart of these, er, developments, so I'd like to invite the Home Secretary to bring the rest of us up to speed. Is that okay?'

The Home Secretary stood up and gave a brief overview of the events thus far. In conclusion, she said, 'Charles has been at the forefront of our cloning research and of the events in China so I think it's best if he leads the meeting.' She sat down and handed the floor to Charles.

Charles began by saying they needed to piece together the two separate sources of information, facts and rumours, into one coherent whole. To link the pieces together like a jigsaw to obtain the complete picture. He started with the facts. 'We have four facts. One, we know from the Russians that the notorious TRIAD gangs have infiltrated all the key positions in China and North Korea: the government, the military and the upper echelons of academia. Indeed, both countries are now run by the TRIADs. Two, we know from our spy at the Central Research Laboratories that they're cloning 10,000 ultimate soldiers and three, that they are developing a super weapon, an ethnic genetic virus based on a synthetic ebola virus targeted at Caucasians, a virus that would wipe out 90 per cent of the white populations of the United States, Canada, Britain, Europe and Russia. And finally, thanks to Jim and his team at the CIA, we have two dates that are very important for the Chinese. Two dates that both occur in 2019.

The 100th anniversary of their hallowed 4 May Movement and the 70th anniversary of the founding of the Peoples' Republic of China.'

'What date is that?' asked the President.

'The first of October, Mr President,' replied the Head of the CIA, Jim Greer.

'Those are the facts,' continued Charles, 'now we'll move on to the rumours. Whilst at the Central Research Laboratories our spy, Chang Lee, heard rumours that China intends to invade its old enemy, Japan and, at the same time, North Korea will invade South Korea. He also heard rumours that China and North Korea intend to launch their EGV against Caucasians sometime in 2019. If successful, it would leave China and its ally North Korea as the undisputed rulers of the world.

'Those are the facts and the rumours, ladies and gentlemen. It's up to us to provide the speculation and piece together the jigsaw.' Following his final remark, Charles sat down.

After a hesitant start, the room hummed with ideas and suggestions. There was unanimous agreement that both attacks would take place in 2019 to coincide with the two anniversaries, but disagreement as to the order. Would they be launched simultaneously on one of the anniversaries, or separately on both anniversaries? And, if separately, in which order?

It was agreed that China and North Korea would have to subjugate Japan and South Korea by military means. Both countries were part of the same Mongolian race as the Chinese and North Koreans so, unless the Chinese had developed an EGV for an ethnic sub-group, which was highly unlikely, Japan and South Korea would have to be defeated militarily.

The most logical, and therefore most likely, scenario was for China to launch their EGV on the first of the two anniversaries, the 4 May 2019 because, if the EGV strike was successful, it would remove the threat from the West. The threat of retaliation from the USA, Britain and Europe, as well as Russia. With the threat of retaliation eliminated, it would leave them free to invade Japan and South Korea on the second anniversary. On the 1 October 2019, they could execute the invasions with impunity, using either conventional or even nuclear weapons.

'Well,' said the President, 'I think we've achieved our first objective. We know of their plans, their aspirations and their timescales. If I've understood it correctly, the conclusion is that the Chinese and North Koreans will launch an EGV strike against Caucasians on 4 May 2019, and that they will invade Japan and South Korea on 1 October in the same year. Is that correct?'

'It is,' replied Charles. 'The question is: what do we do about it?'

56

OPTIONS

Day two of the meeting was opened by the President of the United States of America. He welcomed back all the participants, saying he hoped that everyone was refreshed and ready to go after the previous nights lavish dinner. 'Anyone nursing a sore head or a hangover may leave the room now,' he joked. No one left, even though some did indeed have sore heads. And hangovers. 'We need to consider all the options available to us in this grave matter,' he continued, 'decisive options that we can implement.'

After several hours of discussion, the options were narrowed down to three. The first option was to confront China and North Korea directly. To tell them in no uncertain terms that America and Britain knew all about their plans, and to tell them to back down. Back down or face the consequences, although what the consequences would be had yet to be decided. The second option was to go through the United Nations. To inform the member countries of China and North Korea's plans and to get the United Nations Security Council to pass a resolution to send inspection teams to look for Weapons of Mass Destruction (WMDs). The third and final option was for Britain and America to go it alone.

All three options were discussed, often with heated exchanges, before a decision was reached. If Britain and America acted on their own, it would seem as if they were ignoring international protocols and acting in a gung-ho way. It was not the favoured option at this stage but a fall-back position if other approaches failed. Confronting China and North Korea directly was also dismissed. They'd simply deny the accusations and the rest of the world would be unaware of what they were planning. The favoured option was to proceed through the United Nations, but there were some misgivings. Not only could the process be tedious and protracted but also, as an organisation the United Nations had often shown itself to be ineffective and toothless. Furthermore, it was all too easy for a country to veto a resolution. On the plus side, it was the correct, legal way to proceed and all of the countries would be made aware of China and North Korea's intentions. It was agreed that Britain and America would present all their findings to the United Nations assembly and press for the Security Council to approve a resolution to send inspection teams to China and North Korea to look for WMDs. China and North Korea would probably object in the strongest possible terms and it was likely that other countries might use their veto, but it was something they had to try. Crucially, Russia might, just might, support the resolution given it was they who informed the West about the TRIAD gangs. Although it was far from unanimous, it was agreed that the United Nations card would be the one they played first.

The other decision taken was to approve the synthesis of a Caucasian EGV, a Caucasian EGV they hoped would be similar to that the Chinese were developing. An EGV against which they could test the antidote. A decision that was forwarded to Debbie and her team at the Cryonics Facility.

57

INSPECTION

The United Nations assembly fell silent as first the US delegate and then the British delegate presented their findings about China and North Korea. About their biowarfare research. About their cloning of 10,000 ultimate soldiers. About their planned invasion of Japan and South Korea. And, most terrifying of all, about their plan to unleash an ethnic genetic virus targeted at Caucasians. An evil super weapon that would wipe out 90 per cent of Caucasians, 90 per cent of the white populations of Britain, the USA, Canada, Europe and Russia. The delegates were also told of the likely dates of the attacks and, to complete the picture, of the recent assassination attempts in Britain and America. The assembly listened in stunned silence, their incredulity and disbelief mounting by the minute. They just couldn't believe what they were hearing. It was like a horror story. A work of fiction. Something out of a book. A nightmare dreamt up by a mad scientist.

The British and Americans were dismayed. At the end of the presentation, the delegates asked for proof. For evidence to back up their outlandish claims. Proof they didn't have. It was obvious that most of them didn't believe what they'd just heard. And who could blame them? On the face of it, it did seem like a fantasy. A fairy tale. An evil fairy tale dreamt up by Britain and America to discredit China and North Korea. Just as they were beginning to despair, something unexpected happened. The Russians, who normally vetoed any actions by Britain or America, actually supported them. Russia, the close ally of both China and North Korea, told the assembly how the TRIAD gangs had indeed infiltrated the key positions of both countries and how they posed a threat to the rest of the world. This new revelation changed everything. If China and North Korea's staunchest ally was speaking out against them, then perhaps there might be some credence to what Britain and America were saying.

Of course, China and North Korea denied everything. Yes, they said, like many other countries they were doing cloning research, but cloning research that was for the benefit of mankind. And yes, they were doing some work on viruses too, but only to benefit the human race. We have nothing to hide, they said. And then, to everyone's complete surprise, especially that of Britain and America, the delegates of both countries said they had no objection to the United Nations sending specialist teams to inspect their activities.

A few weeks later, teams of highly skilled specialists were despatched to China and North Korea to inspect their research. Teams of international biowarfare experts to search for WMDs. But the Chinese and North Koreans were ready. They willingly showed them all the 'legitimate' research centres, such as the Shandong Stem Cell Research Centre. Centres doing therapeutic cloning of human organs such as kidneys, livers, hearts and lungs to replace diseased or defective ones. Research to benefit the human race. The inspection teams were even shown around the top secret Central Research Laboratories, the laboratories where the most advanced cloning research was done. Cloning of human brains to replace those damaged as a result of accidents or strokes. Brains to replace those that condemned their owners to be vegetables for the rest of their lives.

The teams were also shown the pioneering work on Parkinson's disease, and even the preliminary work on human cloning, such as the cloning of a child killed in tragic circumstances. To the astonishment of the British and American scientists, the teams even had access to the work on viruses, including the ethnic specific viruses, but with the facts distorted. The work was, they were told, aimed at rendering the world's most potent pathogens harmless, pathogens like the ebola virus. Indeed, they said, they'd even gone to great lengths to synthesise their own virus since neither the USA nor Russia would supply them with the natural ebola virus. Their scientists had discovered that attaching specific nucleotide sequences to the virus rendered it harmless, a significant finding in the quest to eradicate ebola from the face of the Earth. All of this was true, but it wasn't the whole truth. There was no mention that the nucleotide sequences were designed to attack Caucasian genes, and that they planned to launch the ethnic genetic virus in 2019. No mention of that at all.

The inspection teams weren't stupid. They requested samples of the viruses for analysis. To check if the nucleotide sequences that rendered the ebola virus harmless were also designed to attack Caucasian genes. Once again, the Chinese granted their request. Indeed, during the entire inspection visit, the Chinese and North Koreans were obliging in the extreme. They were portrayed as countries doing cutting edge research for the benefit of mankind. The inspectors had no inkling that inside a vast cavern concealed in the bowels of the mountain, 10,000 ultimate soldiers were being cloned.

In short, the inspectors found nothing untoward. On the contrary, they were impressed by China and North Korea's efforts to benefit the human race by performing cutting edge biological research. The analyses of the ebola virus confirmed their view. The attached nucleotide sequence was just a random array of DNA. There was no evidence whatsoever that it was designed to attack Caucasian genes. Not surprisingly, the inspection teams concluded there was no evidence for any WMDs.

To Britain and America, it was the Iraq scenario all over again, except this time there *were* WMDs, but WMDs that had been cleverly concealed.

The inspection teams report to the UN Security Council meant there was no chance of any sanctions being imposed on either China or North Korea. Britain and America would have to go it alone.

Back in China, the President, his senior officials and the scientists involved in the visit congratulated themselves on a job well done. The scientists plan to show the inspection teams their early attempts at a Caucasian EGV, attempts that rendered the virus harmless but had no specificity for Caucasian genes, proved a masterstroke. Their subterfuge had worked a treat. Now, they could forge ahead with Project DARIT. There was no one to stop them.

58

GUINEA PIGS

In May the teams at the Cryonics Facility received a directive from the summit meeting in Washington. A high priority directive to develop a Caucasian EGV. An EGV as similar as possible to the one being developed by China and North Korea. An EGV based on the ebola virus with an attached DNA sequence targeted at Caucasians. An EGV that was required urgently to test the antidote.

The decision to develop a Caucasian EGV pleased everyone at the Cryonics Facility, particularly Debbie and her team. Even though it meant diverting precious effort, and time, away from the Mongolian EGV, the work was given top priority. Research on both the Caucasian EGV and the antidote was accelerated. Everyone redoubled their efforts. It was vital to finish the work on time. The fate of the world depended upon it.

The teams at the Cryonics Facility and Porton Down had made excellent progress on the Mongolian EGV. They'd already developed a prototype that would be similar, very similar, to the final version, but not identical. The final version wouldn't be ready until the end of December, just four months before the Chinese planned to launch their own EGV. Having successfully identified the techniques and procedures for producing an EGV, it shouldn't take them more than a few months to design one that was targeted at Caucasians.

Over the following weeks Debbie and her team focused solely on developing an antidote for Caucasians. An antidote to protect them against any hostile EGVs. This focus, allied to the unwavering commitment from her team, paid handsome dividends. Research on the Caucasian antidote was completed successfully just seven weeks later, on 30 June 2018. Research done in parallel on the Caucasian EGV was also continuing apace and it too would be completed soon. The time had come to make a decision on the testing.

Although it was highly likely the antidote would work, for something with such Draconian consequences if it didn't, Debbie, Steve and Ruth knew that it had to be tested. Tested on Caucasians. Caucasians like themselves. After all, they were the ones who'd designed it so, they argued, they were the ones it should be tested on. The guinea pigs.

'I don't know,' said a grim faced Charles. 'I'm not comfortable about using three of my best scientists as guinea pigs. Three scientists from the same team. Suppose something goes wrong. I'll have lost a complete team. No, there must be another way.'

Debbie was disappointed. Herself, Steve and Ruth really wanted to be the guinea pigs. They were confident, really confident, that the antidote would work. And she'd put forward a good argument. But she could also see Charles' point of view too. She thought quickly. Testing had to be carried out on a minimum of three people. One male, one female and one other to cover both the gender and the age profile. She was a 55-year-old female and Steve a 29-year-old male. Ruth was also 29. She needed someone in-between 29 and 55.

'What if we replace Ruth with Adam?' said Debbie. 'At 38, he gives us the right age profile and he's from a different team. Surely that's acceptable.'

'But I want to be…' protested Ruth.

'I know you do,' replied Debbie, 'but Charles is right. We can't afford to lose a whole team and anyway, you've got a three-year-old boy to look after. A boy who needs his mother. No, Ruth, we can't let you do it.'

'She's right,' said Steve. 'I'm sorry, Ruth.'

'But what if Adam refuses,' said Ruth, clutching desperately at straws.

'He won't,' said Charles. 'There's no way he'll let you do it, Ruth. You know he won't.'

Ruth knew that Charles was right. Adam would never agree to her putting herself in a situation that could leave Dylan an orphan. Never.

'Anyway,' continued Charles, 'it's all academic at the moment. It's up to the Cobra team as to whether we test the antidote on humans. I'll keep you informed.'

The Home Secretary seemed troubled. 'I'd like to make the decision,' she said to her Cobra team members, 'but I haven't got the knowledge to do so.'

'No one has,' said the Chief of the Defence Staff, 'but it's a decision we have to make.'

'There's only one decision we can make,' said Charles. 'We have to test the antidote on humans. I know it's putting three lives at risk but we have to be sure, absolutely sure, that it works. If it doesn't, we're putting billions of lives at risk.'

'That's perfectly true,' said the new Chief Scientific Advisor, 'but it's still putting three peoples' lives in danger. Real people. People who have families and friends.'

'I'm not happy with it either,' replied Charles. 'Debbie, Adam and Steve are not just colleagues, they're my friends. Friends I've known for some time. But I can't think of any other way.'

'Are there any further suggestions?' asked the Home Secretary.

She scanned the faces in the room, searching for someone to suggest a better way. A way that didn't involve human sacrifice. A way where people didn't have to suffer an agonising, painful death. But all she found was silence. Deafening silence. Her shoulders slumped. Reluctantly, she said, 'No suggestions. In that case, we'll go along with Charles' view and test the antidote on three of his scientists. I hope for everyone's sake that it works.'

'If the antidote works,' said Charles, 'we'll mass produce it and begin the inoculation programme.'

'And if it fails?' asked the Home Secretary.

'If it fails,' replied Charles, 'I'll have lost three top scientists and the world will lose billions of people.'

59

IMMUNITY

Charles looked concerned as he peered through the glass window into the small isolation room. Debbie was coughing again. Six days had passed since she'd been infected with the Caucasian EGV. The first five days had passed without incident but now, on the sixth day, Debbie had developed a dry hacking cough, one of the symptoms of ebola.

The EGV teams had worked wonders. Instead of taking the expected three months to synthesise the Caucasian EGV, they'd developed it in just six weeks. And so, in July 2018, Debbie, Steve and Adam had been inoculated with the antidote, placed in separate, small isolation rooms, and infected with the EGV. An EGV that mimicked the one being developed by the Chinese.

The other two 'guinea pigs' appeared fine. So far. Debbie was the worry. 'Do you think her cough is a symptom of ebola?' a worried looking Charles asked the doctor from the medical centre.

'It's too soon to tell,' replied the doctor. 'It could just be a normal cough that's been lying dormant, but it could also be…' He turned his attention to the woman in the room without completing the sentence. The 55-year-old woman who was coughing violently.

'When will we know?' asked Charles.

'Within the next few days. Once the incubation period of 4-6 days is over, the symptoms begin abruptly. A sore throat, headaches, diarrhoea and vomiting, as well as the dry hacking cough. If she develops those, then I'm afraid she's got ebola.'

It was something Charles didn't want to think about. To watch one of his top scientists die a painful, horrible death in front of his eyes. And, more likely than not, Adam and Steve would suffer the same fate. If the antidote hadn't worked for Debbie, it was unlikely to have worked for them. If that happened, the rooms would be flooded with high intensity ultraviolet radiation to destroy every last trace of the EGV, and the bodies incinerated. That was bad enough, but he didn't dare think about the billions of innocent men, women and children who could suffer the same fate if the Chinese ever launched their EGV. It was too terrible to contemplate.

60

DEADLINE

After further deliberations at the highest level, Britain and America decided to inform China and North Korea about their own super weapon. A super weapon of mass destruction that was more deadly than theirs. An EGV targeted specifically at the Chinese and Koreans based on a genetically altered ebola virus with a mortality rate of 99.9 per cent. An EGV that killed within one week. An EGV they'd have no hesitation in using. An EGV that would wipe out over 1.3 billion Chinese and 23 million North Koreans. Men, women and children. Rich or poor. The ebola virus didn't discriminate. Also, they'd tell them about the antidote. The antidote that would be administered to all Caucasians in a mass inoculation programme. The antidote that rendered their own EGV useless. And then they'd tell them to back down. To abandon their grandiose plans for world domination. If they didn't, well, they'd have to suffer the consequences.

China and North Korea were given a deadline. They had until the end of the year, 31 December 2018, to respond. If they refused or didn't respond, Britain and America would unleash a massive propaganda campaign on China and North Korea. The general population would be told how the notorious TRIAD gangs had infiltrated the upper echelons of government, industry and academia and taken over their countries. And they'd tell them about Project DARIT, a project that was evil beyond description. A project that, if implemented, could signal the end of the human race.

The information would be conveyed to the Chinese and North Korean people using a mixture of old and new technology. Billions of leaflets would be dropped on the major population centres such as towns and cities. Their TV stations would be jammed using high energy radiation beamed down from orbiting satellites, and the programmes replaced with information about Project DARIT. And the Internet would be flooded with information. Also, thousands of *agent provocateurs* would infiltrate the key towns and cities in an attempt to incite the people to rebel and remove the hard line rulers.

It was a tense time, a time reminiscent of the Cuban missile crisis in the early 1960s when the world was on the brink of nuclear war as the two superpowers confronted each other. The world waited with bated breath. On that occasion, the Soviet Union backed down at the eleventh hour. Would China and North Korea do the same?

61

RELIEF

'Thank God,' muttered a relieved Charles. 'Thank God it's just a normal cough and not ebola.' Three more days had passed without Debbie developing any further symptoms. And Steve and Adam had remained fine and healthy too.

The doctor nodded his head. 'Yes, if it had been ebola, she'd definitely have developed other symptoms by now. I think we can safely say that the antidote works.'

The bodily excretions from all three volunteers were collected and subjected to high intensity ultraviolet radiation to kill any surviving EGVs, as were the three isolation rooms. It was imperative that every single virus was destroyed.

The positive result heralded a period of frenetic activity. Teams of scientists in both Britain and America began the urgent task of producing enough of the antidote to inoculate two billion people before the 4 May 2019, just ten short months away. It was a race against time.

62

TESTING

Work on the Mongolian EGV was progressing well. The teams at the Cryonics Facility and Porton Down, in collaboration with their American colleagues, had successfully designed and attached the ethnic DNA sequences for the Mongolian race to the genetically modified ebola virus. In addition, they were close to finalising the trigger mechanism that would release the ebola virus. They already had a prototype and were confident that, after some fine-tuning, the finished EGV would be available by December. Importantly, the teams had been able to mass produce the prototype EGV without it mutating, and were confident the finished EGV would behave the same. They hadn't had time to design an EGV specifically for the Chinese – that would come later. Everything was on track.

Delivery of the EGV had also been finalised. It would be delivered by rocket and dispersed at various altitudes depending on the terrain and prevailing weather conditions at the target cities and towns, towns and cities whose coordinates had already been programmed into the rockets.

Everything was almost ready. The only outstanding issue was the testing. The EGV would have to be tested on humans to verify its effectiveness before production could begin. The results would also tell them how much they'd have to produce. They hoped it wouldn't be a lot.

Christmas Day, 2018. What a time to test the Mongolian EGV, the EGV that, if unleashed on China, could wipe out 99.9 per cent of the population. Over 1.3 billion men, women and children. However repugnant that might be, they had to be certain, absolutely certain, that the EGV worked, and for that, it had to be tested on humans. There was no alternative. And so, on Christmas Day, the most important day in the Christian calendar, a day of joy and celebration, three captured Chinese assassins were about to suffer a horrible, painful death. Adam couldn't help thinking that Good Friday would have been a more appropriate day, the day that Jesus was crucified.

None of the prisoners knew what was happening. They'd been placed in three separate, sealed, isolation rooms 'as part of an experiment' and told there was nothing to worry about. Then, six days ago, the Mongolian EGV, the final, finished EGV, had been introduced into each room through the air vents to mimic an airborne attack. Different concentrations were used to determine the minimum lethal dose. A high concentration in Room 1, a medium concentration in Room 2 and a low concentration in Room 3. The results would enable them to calculate how much EGV was required to kill 1.3 billion Chinese and 23 million North Koreans. The less they had to produce, the better, and so they hoped the low concentration in Room 3 would prove fatal.

The virus acted quickly. Symptoms of ebola appeared after just two days. A sore throat, headaches and diarrhoea, followed two days later by vomiting and a dry, hacking cough. By the fifth day, all three prisoners had developed a high fever and become delirious. They'd also become aggressive, smashing crockery, throwing furniture around and banging on the windows with their fists. By the sixth day, Christmas Day, they'd developed rashes and were beginning to bleed.

'Oh my God,' exclaimed Ruth, peering into Room 3. 'Is there nothing we can do for the poor creatures? It's obvious the EGV works. Can't we give them a vaccine or an antidote?'

The doctor stood beside her shook his head. 'I'm afraid not. There's no effective treatment for ebola.'

'What on earth's happening to them? It's horrible.'

And it was. As the the ebola virus spreads through the bloodstream, it multiplies rapidly, preventing the body from mounting an effective immune response. It produces proteins which increase the permeability of blood vessel membranes, leading to haemorrhaging (internal bleeding) within the body. Death follows from pulmonary haemorrhaging, gastrointestinal haemorrhaging, hepatitis and encephalitis (swelling of the brain).

As her gaze returned to the window, Ruth screamed and recoiled in horror at the face pressed against the glass. A face with a rash that had started to peel. A face with blood seeping from every pore. A face with red, bulging eyes imploring, pleading, begging to be released from their terrible torment. A face begging for mercy. For death.

Ruth wept.

By the end of Christmas Day, all three prisoners were dead. The EGV had killed in six days with a 100 per cent mortality rate, even at the lowest concentration. This time, humans had been sacrificed.

Although it was an excellent result, there was no rejoicing. No celebrations. Just a mixture of relief tinged with sorrow and sadness at the loss of three human lives. But the result meant that mass production of the EGV could begin in earnest. It definitely worked and, furthermore, they now knew how much to produce.

The deaths of the three assassins, particularly the manner of their deaths, caused unrest amongst the scientists at the Cryonics

Facility. Unrest that millions, even billions, of innocent men, women, children and babies could suffer the same horrible death because of the actions and aspirations of a handful of deluded and fanatical men. They demanded to know if there was another way. A better way, like assassinating the people responsible; the politicians, the top military personnel and even the key scientists, and returning control of both countries back to the Chinese and North Korean people.

Charles assured them that every possible avenue, every single option, would be explored. No one wanted Armageddon.

63

CHINESE TORTURE

In China, a similar scenario was being enacted. Scientists at the Central Research Laboratories had successfully completed the work on the Caucasian EGV, an EGV based on a synthetic ebola virus. They'd resolved the outstanding issues and overcome the mass production problems. The moment of truth had arrived. Did it work?

It was early December 2018, the year of the dog. If the tests were successful, it left just four short months in which to manufacture enough EGV to wipe out the Caucasian race. And to load it on to the rockets, the rockets whose targets were already pre-programmed in their guidance systems; large cities and towns in Britain, Europe, the USA, Russia, Canada, Australia and New Zealand. Two for each destination to allow for any losses. In reality, they had less than four months. The rumour was that the launch date would have to be brought forward to pre-empt what Britain and America might do.

The EGV had to be tested on Caucasians, preferably Britons and Americans. They had the ideal candidates. Not only was Chang Lee's last message traced to Britain and America, it was also traced to a residence in Shandong. The residence of Skip Meyers.

Since that message, they'd monitored his every movement, every meeting, and every call he'd made to his network of spies. British, American and Chinese spies. Most had been rounded up and imprisoned. The Chinese spies, the traitors, were tortured and executed, but the British and Americans had been kept alive. A different fate awaited them.

The President smiled as he watched Skip Meyers draw his last tortured breath. A futile attempt to draw breath into his lungs. His lungs that were flooded with blood. Skip Meyers had, quite literally, drowned in his own blood.

'Was he the last one?' the President asked Xiong Kang.

'No, Mr President. He's the ninth person to die, but one has survived.'

'Was he the one given the lowest dose?'

'No,' replied Xiong Kang, 'he was given one of the highest doses.'

'I don't understand,' said the President. 'Why isn't he dead?'

'Because,' interjected the Chief Scientist, 'the mortality rate for the EGV is 90 per cent. Nine out of ten. He's the one in ten survivor.'

'So the EGV works fine,' said the President.

'Yes, it does,' replied the Chief Scientist. 'It works perfectly.'

'Then begin mass production immediately,' said the President. 'The sooner it's ready, the better. Soon, the world will be a different place.'

'What shall we do with the survivor?' asked the Chief Scientist. 'We'd like to keep him alive for research purposes, to see why he didn't die.'

'Kill him,' came the curt reply. 'Kill him now.'

Part 3

. . .

ARMAGEDDON

64

THEY'RE BLUFFING

'It's impossible!' shouted the Chief Scientist thumping the table with his fist. 'There's no way they can have developed an antidote against our EGV *and* an extremely deadly EGV targeted at Mongolians. At us. No way at all. They're bluffing.' The Chief Scientist sat down, his face red with indignation. He was adamant, completely, utterly and totally adamant that Britain and America were bluffing.

'Is that the opinion of everyone?' asked the President, looking around the room of twenty-odd people. A room containing the top scientists, politicians and military leaders. The dozen or so Team Leaders, and Xiong Kang, nodded their heads in agreement.

'I can't see how they could have developed either one so quickly,' said Xiong Kang. 'They're years behind us in their research. Ewan told us that.'

'I agree,' one of the Team Leaders chipped in. 'We're so far ahead it's inconceivable that Britain and America could have overtaken us.'

'And how,' said Professor Hui Wang, 'can they have developed an antidote against our EGV without having access to it?'

'Good point,' said the Chief Scientist. 'It reaffirms our belief that they're bluffing. Trying to scare us off. Trying to make us back down.'

After further discussions, the overwhelming consensus was that Britain and America were indeed bluffing, and a decision was taken to ignore the deadline and proceed as planned with Project DARIT. They were concerned about the effects the propaganda might have on the general population. It could make them uneasy or, in the worst case scenario, incite an uprising, but they'd worry about that later. In four months time, they'd have wiped out the Caucasian race and be masters of the new world.

65

THE FINAL COUNTDOWN

The first few months of 2019 saw frantic efforts by the West to avert Armageddon. Summit after summit was held with the leaders of all the major countries to try and resolve the crisis. The Prime Ministers and Presidents of the UK, the USA, Canada, Russia, France, Germany, Japan, South Korea, India and Australia trying everything in their power to formulate a solution.

At the same time, the mass inoculation programme was ramped up. Strenuous efforts were made to inoculate the bulk of the Caucasian populations in the UK, Europe, Russia and North America. The aim was to have inoculated 90 per cent by 1 October, with the focus on the future: the young and middle-aged. The elderly would be left until last.

The Cobra team in the UK and its counterpart in the USA had been expanded. Both were now led by the Prime Minister and the President respectively. They worked overtime, exploring every avenue. No stone was left unturned. Heated exchanges were commonplace. Conflicts between the hawks and the doves were rife. Tempers flared. Everyone was edgy. Eventually, after almost three months of intense arguments and discussions, the options were narrowed down to a manageable number.

Option one, to intensify the propaganda war and plant more insurgents, more CIA agents and MI6 operatives, to incite the Chinese and North Korean people to rebel against the TRIADs, was agreed unanimously. It was the option favoured by the doves. Although they voted in favour, the hawks argued that it wouldn't deliver results in time to stop the attacks.

The second option, of using covert Special Forces to 'eliminate' the key TRIAD leaders and return control of the two countries back to the people, was seen as too risky. It could provoke a retaliation from China and North Korea, precipitating both the invasion of Japan and South Korea and an early launch of their EGV.

Option three, favoured strongly by the hawks, was to launch a pre-emptive nuclear strike on their rocket bases. Their locations were all known from years of detailed satellite surveillance. In the end, like option two, it was deemed too risky. The Chinese and North Koreans would detect the incoming missiles before they reached their targets, giving them time to launch their rockets before they could be destroyed. Also, it might provoke a retaliatory response with nuclear weapons.

The fourth option involved demonstrating the awesome power of the West's own super weapon by carrying out a single EGV strike on a remote town. At the same time, a massive propaganda campaign would be unleashed explaining to both the Chinese and North Korean people why such drastic action had to be taken. Hopefully, it would provoke a backlash, a rebellion, that would topple the TRIAD regimes. In deference to the doves, China and North Korea would be given a final warning *before* the strike was launched. A last chance to back down. If it was ignored, it would leave them with no other option but to proceed with the strike.

The fifth and final option was to launch a pre-emptive EGV strike on two densely populated cities. Tens of millions would die but it would demonstrate both the awesome power and the devastating effect of the West's super weapon, and their resolve to use it. It would be similar to the dropping of the atomic bombs on Hiroshima and Nagasaki in World War II, a decisive action that ended the war. Hopefully, dropping the EGV would produce the same result.

The discussions continued day and night, 24/7, on both sides of the Atlantic. No one wanted to inflict mass genocide, not even the hawks. But they had to do whatever it took to stop the Chinese and North Koreans. After all, inflicting mass genocide didn't seem to bother them.

Conflict was rife on both sides of the Atlantic. Exhausted people were at breaking point as they wrestled to reach the correct decision. The doves favoured options one and two and, if pushed, option four. In contrast, the hawks favoured options three and five, with option four a fall-back position. They argued that the anti-rocket missiles, coupled with their Star Wars technology, extremely powerful and accurate lasers located on orbiting satellites, would destroy any rockets that China and North Korea managed to launch. And, they argued, they'd already have massive forces in the South China Sea to protect Japan and South Korea from invasion: all their aircraft carriers and nuclear submarines armed with the latest anti-missile weapons.

The discussions continued for weeks. No consensus was reached but a decision was taken. It had to be. Time was running out.

The month of March was crammed with last ditch talks between the West on one hand and China and North Korea on the other, but to no avail. No agreement was forthcoming. The West issued a final ultimatum. Give up your plans by 31 March or face the terrible consequences.

The world held its breath.

66

ARMAGEDDON

The 31 March deadline passed without any response from China or North Korea.

The massed forces of the West and Russia, both on the seas and on the ground in Japan and South Korea, were put on red alert. The inoculation programme was running at full speed. Approximately 85 per cent of Caucasians had been inoculated with the antidote. Even so, hundreds of millions would still die if the Chinese launched their EGV.

In the war rooms of the Pentagon and London, the USA COBRA team and the UK Cobra team were ready to implement the decision taken at the summit meeting. The rocket was armed and ready to launch. Precise coordinates for the target were programmed into its guidance system. All that was needed was the order from the President and the Prime Minister. It came at midnight.

Just before dawn, on 1 April 2019, just 66 days before the 75th anniversary of D-Day, a solitary stealth six rocket unleashed its deadly cargo of Mongolian EGV into the atmosphere above the town of Urumqi in the remote Province of Xinjiang. One point six million inhabitants would arise and breathe in the deadly EGV. Innocent men, women, children and babies. Breathe it in before the sun's rays reached their full power and destroyed it. Breathe it in and die a horrible death within one week. 99.9 per cent of them. Virtually everyone.

The two teams of four men watched as the rocket unleashed its deadly payload. Watched through powerful binoculars from safe vantage points well away from the trillions of EGVs descending on the inhabitants of Urumqi. Watched in silence as the first rays of sunlight, weak early morning rays, appeared over the distant horizon. Dressed in camouflaged biowarfare protection suits, the covert teams of MI6 and CIA field operatives were invisible to any prying eyes.

As the watery dawn light crept over the rooftops of the sleeping town, isolated specks of light began to appear. Flickering spots of light dotted around the town like stars in the sky. First, just a few, then more and more as the sun continued its relentless rise above the horizon. People switching on their bedroom lights at the start of a new day. Before long, they began to leave their houses. Soon, the initial trickle of people became a torrent. A torrent of workers making their hurried way to work. The streets were alive with pedestrians, cars, buses and especially cyclists. Thousands upon thousands of people pedalling their way along the crowded streets. In no time at all, the once deserted streets were alive with a jabbering, jostling throng of humanity.

Although the orbiting spy satellites provided excellent images, there was nothing quite like a first-hand view from operatives on the ground. Operatives who would relay real time images to the 'War Cabinets', one buried deep in the innards of the Pentagon and one in the bowels of Downing Street. Real time images for them to monitor the effects of the EGV on the inhabitants of Urumqi. To watch first-hand as events unfolded.

For the first two days life went on as normal. People went about their business as they'd always done. Workers going to work. Children going to school. Mothers staying at home to look after their babies. Everything seemed normal. Not a single person realised they'd breathed in the deadliest virus on the planet. The virus that would kill 99.9 per cent of them in the next six days. Kill them without any warning. Kill them in a horrible, painful way.

On the third day, the first symptoms began to appear. A mild fever, headaches, diarrhoea and vomiting. The whole town was afflicted. Doctor's surgeries, pharmacies and the single hospital were overwhelmed as people flocked to obtain medicines to cure their sudden afflictions. It was utter chaos. Pandemonium. The town simply couldn't cope.

Those fortunate enough to obtain medicines found they had no effect. The symptoms just got worse. By day four, people developed a rash and a dry, hacking cough. No one went to work. The town became paralysed. Panic set in.

The fifth day saw the first deaths. Deaths of the weak and vulnerable. Young babies, the old and infirm, and people with existing illnesses. They all suffered the same agonising, painful deaths. Blood seeped from their pores, their lungs filled with blood and their brains swelled. They drowned in their own blood.

Fear and hysteria gripped the town. People panicked. They couldn't understand what was happening. Couldn't understand the pestilence that was engulfing them. Those who could tried to flee in whatever transport they could find: cars, buses, trains, bicycles. Many walked. It was futile. They'd all been infected and they'd all die the same horrible death. There was no escape.

The streets and outlying roads that were once filled with thousands of people were littered with abandoned vehicles, bicycles and bodies. Tens of thousands of bodies. Bodies that lay in pools of blood. Blood was everywhere. It was as if the streets of the city had been painted red.

Realising there was no escape from the terrible pestilence, by the sixth day most people accepted their fate. If they were going to die, they wanted to die beside their loved ones. Families gathered together for one last time, usually in the family home, huddled together to await their fate. Mothers cradled their babies in a final deathly embrace. Fathers hugged their sons. Some died on their knees praying to their God to be spared from the terrible pestilence. Many died in the hospital. In just six days, the thriving, bustling, provincial town of Urumqi had been reduced to a ghost town.

Almost 1.6 million people had died but, to the watching observers, it didn't look like a war zone. None of the buildings, or indeed any of the infrastructure, had been damaged. There were no soldiers, tanks or planes. No bombs had been dropped and no shots fired. There was none of those, just 1.6 million dead bodies.

To the operatives on the ground it was an eerie, spooky scene. The silence was deafening. No sounds of human civilisation. No human voices. No sound of conversations. No sound of laughter. Of children's excited shrieks and screams. No traffic noise. And, worst of all, no sound of birds, or animals. Nothing. Just complete and utter silence. Silence permeated with a gruesome stench. The stench of death.

The dead bodies and blood, especially the blood, attracted millions of flies. Flies that were gorging themselves on the biggest banquet they'd ever known. The operatives wondered if the flies too would die of ebola. They didn't know.

But flies weren't the only living creatures in Urumqi. On the sixth day and beyond, solitary people began wandering the streets. At first, just tens, then hundreds and finally a few thousand. They looked utterly confused. Like people in a dream. Or sleepwalkers. And distraught. Distraught at the catastrophe that had enveloped their town and its people. Their families. Their loved ones. They wandered the streets like zombies. Like the living dead. Their whole world had been snatched away. Destroyed. They were the one-in-a-thousand survivors. The few survivors who were either naturally immune to the ebola virus or, more likely, hadn't inhaled the EGV. The 'lucky' ones. Most of them wished they were dead.

Deep within the bowels of the Pentagon and Downing Street the 'War Cabinets' of the United States of America and Great Britain watched in stunned silence as the carnage unfolded before their eyes. The observers were dumbfounded. Even the most aggressive hawks were shocked. Men who had seen many atrocities committed in the name of war, hardened men, had tears in their eyes. Formulating and approving the EGV strike was one thing; witnessing its devastating effect was another thing entirely. Everyone in the room was shocked and saddened by what they were seeing. Even the hardest of people have consciences.

The carnage caused by the pre-emptive strike prompted heated discussions. Angry exchanges. Fierce arguments. And much soul-searching. Soul-searching to try and justify their actions. Had it really been necessary to drop the EGV? Couldn't they have found some other way? Would a ramped up propaganda campaign have worked eventually? At the end of it all, it was the British Home Secretary who summed it up. 'What's done is done,' she said, repeating her famous phrase. 'All we can do now is decide what to do next.'

When the news of what the West had done reached the Chinese leaders, they were furious. Furious that the entire population of one of their towns had been wiped out. Obliterated. Furious that the West had executed their threat. And furious with the massive propaganda campaign which accompanied the EGV strike. The West had implemented option four.

Rubbing salt into already raw wounds, the West issued another ultimatum. Abandon Project DARIT or else they'd launch similar strikes on China's largest cities. Cities like Shanghai, with a population of 15.8 million, Guangzhou, with its population of 9.5 million, Hong Kong with a population of nearly 7 million and even the capital, Beijing, with 11 million. Tens of millions of Chinese would suffer the same terrible fate as the inhabitants of Urumqi.

Infuriated by the West's actions and demands, the Chinese President called an emergency meeting of his top aides and military leaders. An emergency meeting to decide their response to the unprovoked attack on one of their towns. An emergency meeting to decide what type of retaliatory action should be taken. He knew what action he favoured and he was sure that most of the others would have exactly the same view.

Not only was the President furious with the West, he was also furious with his scientists for getting it wrong. Completely wrong. The West hadn't been bluffing. They had developed a deadly EGV and almost certainly an effective antidote too. He'd been made to look foolish and he wanted revenge. Revenge on the people who'd failed him. Let him down. He ordered Xiong Kang to gather all the scientists who were present on that fateful day, the day when the Chief Scientist and all the Team Leaders assured him that the West were bluffing. He was coming to meet them with his top aides and military leaders. He wanted to know why they got it so wrong. Got it so very, very wrong.

The news of the 'Urumqi genocide' spread around the world like wildfire. It was headline news in every country. It wasn't clear if it was a natural outbreak of ebola or a man-made one. China was adamant it was the latter and accused Britain and the USA of launching an unprovoked biological attack on one of its sovereign towns, a biological attack using a deadly ethnic genetic virus, an accusation that Britain and America refuted. However, as the reports came in it became increasingly obvious that a natural ebola virus wouldn't have killed 99.9 per cent of the population in just six days, and speculation mounted that it must have been a man-made strain. The pressure on Britain and America intensified.

As discussions raged in the Pentagon and Downing Street about the best course of action, a code red phone call interrupted proceedings. It was the Commander-in-Chief of the massed forces in the South China Sea. China and North Korea, he said, had just launched their rockets. All of them. Over a thousand. Rockets carrying a deadly payload. Rockets headed for Britain, America, Europe and Russia.

His forces had acted immediately. Some of the rockets were destroyed before they left the ground but most were destroyed in the air by anti-missile weapons from the aircraft carriers and nuclear submarines, and by the satellite lasers, the Star Wars technology initiated by Ronald Reagan. But even the best technologies in the world couldn't destroy over one thousand rockets launched within minutes of each other from different locations. A few got through. One or two to Europe, one or two to Russia and one or two to the USA. He was awaiting instructions. Did they want him to retaliate and launch their own rockets? The rockets that carried the same deadly EGV that had killed the 1.6 million inhabitants of Urumqi. He needed to know. Urgently.

The President of the United States of America and the Prime Minister of Great Britain chaired an emergency meeting of their top aides, military leaders and scientists. Chaired the most important meeting in the short history of the human race. A meeting that had to deliver a quick but correct decision. Should they retaliate? If so, on what scale?

An urgent discussion began. Should the USA and Britain launch their own rockets, the rockets that were primed and ready to go? The rockets that would unleash the deadly EGV that would wipe out 1.3 billion Chinese and 23 million North Koreans. Or should they just target a few cities and spare the rest? The other option, of course, was not to launch any of their rockets. Whichever option they chose, they had to decide quickly.

Given the gravity of the situation, the discussions were surprisingly rational and objective. Several factors influenced their decision. The terrible effects of Urumqi were still fresh in their minds and no one, not even the hawks, wanted to inflict the same horrific suffering on almost 1,000 times that number of people. Also, they argued, even if a handful of rockets the Chinese had launched did get through the anti-missile defences, they might not reach their intended targets. Even if they did and unleashed their deadly payload, the effect would be minimal because of the antidote administered to 85 per cent of Caucasians in the mass inoculation programme. At best, no one would die. At worst, just a few elderly people who hadn't been inoculated would perish.

Much to the relief of almost everyone, a decision was taken NOT to launch a retaliatory strike. Instead, they would wait and see what unfolded in China and North Korea.

67

RETRIBUTION

Professor Hui Wang and the other Team Leaders were angry. Angry at being blamed for the catastrophe that was engulfing their country. And the world. On the evidence available, they'd made an informed decision. A decision that, under normal circumstances, would have been correct. They hadn't known about the genius of Albert Einstein, Isaac Newton and Charles Darwin, three of the finest scientists the world had produced, providing the inspiration to move the Mongolian EGV work forward. They hadn't known any of that but they knew they'd be the ones to pay. The ones to suffer. The President was ruthless. They knew he'd kill all of them.

'HOW THE FUCKING HELL DID YOU GET IT SO WRONG!' shouted the President, thumping the table with his fist. His face was red with anger. 'Unless you have a fucking good explanation, I'll personally shoot each fucking one of you.' Furious and shaking with rage, he waited for an answer.

'We gave you our considered opinion,' the Chief Scientist replied calmly. 'We still don't understand how Britain and America managed to do what they did.'

'Is that the best you can fucking do?' snorted the President, spittle flying from his mouth. 'A whole fucking town of 1.6 million Chinese completely wiped off the face of the earth and all you can come up with is, "we gave you our considered opinion",' repeating the Chief Scientist's answer in a mocking, derisory tone. 'It's just not fucking good enough!' he bellowed, banging the table with his fist to emphasise each word. 'It's just not fucking good enough,' he repeated, this time more quietly.

A silence fell over the room. Everyone sensed what was coming next.

The President wiped his face with his hands, then scanned the faces of the scientists sat in silence around the large oval table before asking his next question. 'Is that the opinion of all of you?'

'It is,' replied the Team Leaders in unison.

'In that case,' continued the President, 'you're all finished. I'll get people who are better.' He turned to the top military figure beside him. 'Give me your fucking gun!' Surprised by the unexpected 'request' – order would be a better word – the general withdrew his automatic pistol from its holster and handed it to the President. Taking the gun, the President got up from his chair, walked to where the Chief Scientist was sitting and placed the barrel of the gun to his temple. 'Have you any last words before I blow your fucking brains out,' snarled the President.

'Only that you're a misguided, arrogant fool,' replied the Chief Scientist, knowing that he had nothing more to lose. 'A deluded megalomaniac.'

In the small room the sound of the gunshot was deafening. Blood and gore flew everywhere. The Chief Scientist slumped forward on to the table. Dead. Half his head had been blown away.

The President walked calmly around the table, executing the twelve Team Leaders in the same manner. It was a ritual he was accustomed to. A ritual he'd had to perform many times as Dragon Head of China's largest TRIAD gang. A ritual that didn't bother him in the slightest. What did bother him however, was the demeanour of the victims. He couldn't understand why none of them tried to flee or beg for mercy. And he certainly didn't understand why some of them smiled.

Xiong Kang was aghast. Never before had he questioned the actions of his trusted boss. His boss as Dragon Head of the *Sun Yee On* TRIAD and now his boss as President of China. Almost without thinking he said, 'Mr President, you've just killed all our top scientists. Don't you think you've made a mistake.' They were the last words he ever spoke. The President nodded, smiled and then shot him between the eyes.

About a week later, the President, his aides and all the military leaders present at the meeting developed similar symptoms. A sore throat, headaches, diarrhoea, vomiting and a dry hacking cough. At first, they put it down to a severe bout of flu, but when the fever, the rash and the bleeding began, they knew it was something more serious. Within two weeks, everyone who'd been at the meeting was dead.

Before the meeting with the President, Hui Wang and the other Team Leaders knew what their fate would be and, rather than die in vain, they'd agreed to use the only weapon at their disposal to kill the men responsible. The pure, unadulterated, synthetic ebola virus. The deadly virus that would kill within two weeks. The tasteless, odourless, undetectable virus they'd introduce into the meeting room through the air vents prior to the meeting to kill the President, his senior politicians and the military leaders.

In formulating their plan, the scientists hoped for a quick execution. It was preferable to a painful, lingering death from ebola. By eliminating the key TRIAD leaders, Hui Wang and the other Team Leaders hoped the destiny of both countries would return to the Chinese and North Korean people. If that happened, their sacrifice wouldn't have been in vain.

Part 4

. . .

∧ NEW BEGINNING

68

RECOVERY

The death of the President and his senior aides from ebola, along with the deaths of the military leaders and most of the country's top scientists, effectively ended the influence of the TRIAD gangs and allowed the Chinese people to regain control of their country. Within weeks, both China and North Korea surrendered and the world returned to some semblance of normality. Armageddon had been averted.

The unprecedented devastation and destruction caused by the awesome power of the atomic bombs dropped on Hiroshima and Nagasaki in World War II, and the deaths of tens of thousands of innocent civilians, ensured that such weapons would never be used again. The world hoped the same would apply to biological weapons. The terrible suffering and deaths of 1.6 million innocent people inflicted by the EGV dropped on Urumqi was a stark reminder of what would happen if ever a biological world war broke out. It would be the end of the human race.

Those EGVs that didn't find a human host were destroyed rapidly by sunlight. Mother Nature worked her magic yet again in cleansing the earth from a man-made disaster. But sunlight couldn't destroy what it couldn't reach. Around the world a few, a tiny, tiny fraction of the trillions of EGVs launched in the darkness of the night, avoided the lethal ultraviolet rays of the sun. One of nature's smallest creatures, the humble earthworm, inadvertently carried one of the EGVs that had fell on the land down into the soil. Down into the domain of the earthworm. A domain it shared with billions of bacteria. And that's where it remained, entombed in the cold, dark voids of the soil, protected from the sun's fierce glare. Waiting. Waiting for a suitable host.

Five years had passed since the surrender of China and North Korea. Priorities had changed at the Cryonics Facility. The focus of the work had switched from human cloning to therapeutic cloning. The original experiment, on nature versus nurture, was still ongoing. It was still too early to tell if the twins being reared in The Nursery were different to those being fostered. They were still only 10-12 years old.

The ultimate soldiers had acquitted themselves well in preparing to defend Japan and South Korea against the invaders. And Alan Standish had been told the background of Johnnie Standish, C47SO. They became firm friends.

Adam and Ruth had married and produced a bouncing baby boy, a little brother for Dylan. Everything was rosy. The world had recovered. It was time for a new beginning.

69

A TWIST IN THE TAIL

Soil bacteria are hungry little creatures forever foraging for food. A strand of organic matter lying dormant in the soil, a tasty morsel, was too good to spurn. The EGV was devoured eagerly. For most of the bacteria, that's all it was – a tasty snack. But for one bacterium, it proved to be the last supper.

By a cruel twist of fate, a chance in a million, *pseudomonas aeruginosa* secreted an enzyme which cleaved the chemical bond binding the ethnic DNA sequence to the virus, releasing the pure, unadulterated virus into the unfortunate bacterium. The deadly ebola virus for which there was no effective treatment. In effect, the enzyme had activated the trigger mechanism. The virus replicated rapidly, one ebola virus becoming millions, before bursting out of its dead host. And waiting. Waiting in the safety of the soil for its next victim.

The summer of 2024 was one of the finest for years and Adam and Ruth had decided to take advantage of the splendid weather by having a week's camping holiday in Snowdonia. A week of peace and quiet with Dylan and their young baby. A week where they could get back to nature and enjoy the simple things in life. The magnificent scenery, the clean, crisp air of the Welsh mountains, and the stunning sunsets and sunrises.

Last night, the final night of their holiday, the sky was so clear that the heavens seemed within touching distance. The stars sparkled like diamonds against a black velvet sky. And there were so many. So many nuclear infernos twinkling in the night sky. They sat for hours gazing at the wonder of the universe, a universe created 13.7 billion years ago in the Big Bang. It was so beautiful they agreed to rise with the lark on their last morning to watch the sun rise over the mountains. It should be a spectacular sight.

Although the clear night sky afforded a spectacular view of the stars, it was a view that came at a price. With no clouds to trap the sun's warmth, the heat of the day evaporated rapidly into space, causing the temperature to plummet. And the cold caused the moisture in the air to condense into fine droplets. Droplets of mist.

In the dim dawn light, Adam awoke to a valley shrouded in mist. A cold, amorphous grey mist that caressed his face like a clammy hand. A hand searching for something within, something invisible. A cold, icy hand. He raised his hand to his face half expecting it to be seized by something wet and foggy, but all he encountered was... droplets of water. Cold droplets that he wiped away. He grabbed the *Aquaroll* and began the short walk to the stream to collect some water. As he walked, his foot dislodged a virus in the soil, propelling it into the air. It was a small step for Adam but a catastrophic leap for mankind.

'Daddy, wait for me,' shouted an excited young boy running after his stepdad. Running towards the virus floating in the fog. The deadly synthetic ebola virus developed by the Chinese that was so close to finding what it had waited for. A home. A home in the body of the young boy running after his stepdad. Dylan. This time, the fog was definitely alive.

Isolated cases of ebola had been springing up around the world. In Europe. In Russia. In Canada. In the USA. And soon, in Britain. Springing up in the places where the handful of rockets that had avoided destruction by the missiles and lasers had unleashed their deadly cargos.

Cases of ebola were reported in China too, especially in the Province of Xinjiang.

Armageddon hadn't been averted at all. Just postponed

ACKNOWLEDGEMENTS

I would like to thank all the people who gave so generously of their time to read the entire manuscript of this book. Their invaluable comments, insights and observations have undoubtedly made *DARIT* a better book. People like my two sisters-in-law, June Gent and Elaine Johnson, my two nieces, Michelle Johnson and Natalie Johnson, and my cousin, Brian Gregory. And to my friends, Neville and Phyllis Jackson, and Ian and Sharon Taylor. To all of you I offer my sincere thanks.

Special thanks go to my two sons, Andrew and Michael, not only for their comments concerning the manuscript, and for proof reading it, but also for their help in resolving issues with both my computer and printer, and to my nephew Stuart Gent, for helping design the front cover.

Last, but by no means least, I thank my wife, Vera, for reading the manuscript and proof reading it, and for being so patient and understanding during the writing of this book. Writing a book takes up a huge amount of time, time that could have been spent with my family.

To every one of you I offer my heartfelt thanks.

ABOUT THE AUTHOR

Professor Peter Gregory spent his entire career in chemical research, first with ICI, then AstraZeneca and lastly Avecia. His hi-tech colours group were the world leaders in inventing and supplying ink jet dyes and inks to the major ink jet printer manufacturers such as HP, Canon, and Seiko Epson. During his time at work Peter was in constant demand as a speaker at prestigious international scientific conferences, published numerous literature papers and has over 100 patents to his name. He co-authored a best selling text book *Organic Chemistry in Colour* and is the author of *High Technology Applications of Organic Colorants*. He retired in 2002.

Whilst at work, Peter always had a dessert with custard at lunchtimes. During his 37 years, he calculated that he had consumed 3.5 tonnes of the stuff, and that's without the jam roly polys, spotted dicks, etc.

In his retirement Peter has used his scientific background to write two sci-fi novels and a crime thriller, as well as his autobiography entitled, unsurprisingly, *Professor Custard. DARIT* is the second of his sci-fi novels to be published. (*The Dark Freeze* was the first.)

In addition to writing, Peter is an avid fan of Wigan Warriors Rugby League Football Club, a keen gardener, and a walker, his favourite area being the Lake District. He lives in West Bolton with his wife Vera. They celebrated their Golden Wedding in 2019 and have two grown-up married sons, Andrew and Michael, and a grandson Joshua.